Sisters of Wind & Wood

Nia Bansal

Printed in India

IndiePress

ISBN: 978-93-6045-146-2

First Printing, 2025

IndiePress

A division of Nasadiya Technologies Private Ltd.

Koramangala, Bengaluru

Karnataka-560029

http://indiepress.in/

Edited by Literary Connect

Typeset by MAP Systems, Bengaluru

Book Cover designed by Keerthipriya PH

Publishing Consultant: Bulbul Brahma

For Gargee & Zahin,

If I had a flower for every time I thought of you, I'd be walking in my garden forever. And no matter what happens, we will always be walking hand in hand.

&

For Mihika Salunkhe,

You never abandoned me.

Table Of Contents

Prologue

Abandoned Haeems, Frances

The pine trees were lonely and immensely dark, as though midnight ink had been smeared on each leaf. How could one not feel sorry for the leaves? The once diligent workers, who borne the sun for our contentment, were now but mere sorrowful shadows of the blissful shade they once cast on us. The night sky, too, depicted sadness and despair. The gloomy clouds obstructed moonlight like black drapes blocking out sunlight. The stars, however, did not give up on the Merrycks. They showered streams of ashen white light for the witches despite all the darkness. Somewhere, waiting in the shadows was a boy with wild raven hair, whistling a sombre, melancholy tune. Was this rhythm to entice new recruits of the Merrycks into the darkness? No one could ever know his grotesque ways. He walked the serpentine path, going deeper and deeper into the woods of the Merrycks with every step. As he reached the courtyard where the festivities were taking place, he grinned widely.

Jack Fynn was with his people, rejoicing in the peace and intimacy the forest provided.

The tell-tale celebratory music rang in his ears. The chilly breeze played with his tousled locks. The Merrycks were performing the Charling, the ancient dance inspired by will-o'-the-wisps and spirits of life. Part of the forest was darkness and sorrow. Part of the forest was brilliance and joy. Jack Fynn loved his home.

He walked the path again, skipping away from the celebrations. The last sounds Jack heard when he reached the moorland were his very own: his melancholy, petrifying, mysterious whistles.

Chapter 1

Marilyn, the Capital of Frances

I've been having some strange experiences over the past few days. Whenever I enter a brightly lit room, the candles go out, the temperature drops and the curtains move thunderously, even though the windows are shut tight. My fingers twitch constantly, and I have throbbing headaches. Whenever I stroll in the gardens, the withered leaves and dried petals twirl as though they're dancing to a sad melody. It's as though I have stepped out of the cosiness of Marilyn and into the dusky pines of Abandoned Haeems. I've never been to the forest before, but something about it is so peculiar, familiar even.

But I must forget about all these strange things, as Esther's birthday ball and succession are around the corner. She is going to assume the title of Marchioness of Frances, as Father is stepping down in favour of someone younger. It is a position requiring a responsible, diligent woman, all of Esther's abiding qualities.

After dinner, I retire to my bedroom earlier than usual, dark circles forming beneath my eyes. I tried to spend time with my sister today, but she seemed so utterly busy with the succession preparations. I blow out the scented candles that light the corridors of my confused, tired, and doubtful heart. My lady's maid withdraws the drapes. She briskly steps out of my room after wishing me good night and settling me under the duvet. Heather, my lady's maid, is like a second mother to me. When Esther and Father are at the House of Lords, and I have something on my mind that I wish to share with them, Heather listens to me. Really, really listens to me. She's like a warm hearth, jasmine tea, and sprigs of lavender. Calming, soothing, and comforting.

I stretch my legs under the green, feathery duvet, as dark as the damp lands of a forest. Sleep hits me hard, like a harsh, raging wave washing over my face, drowning me in the depths of dreams.

The trees looked daunting and threatening; they towered over me like intimidating monarchs in polished black shoes and bejewelled cloaks. I gulped and took two steps further into the forest, the balmy breeze brushing against my face. The winds picked up the withered leaves, and the grass swayed back and forth like exploited labourers being whipped by ruthless capitalists. And then, I heard whistles.

Petrifying, mysterious whistles. A discordant melody that would evoke pathos in the listener.

Waiting in the shadows, I saw a boy. Dressed in a black and white striped shirt and a sleeveless overcoat, he showed me his dashing yet hair-raising smile. I couldn't hold back all the zooming thoughts in my head and asked the boy, 'Who are you?' with a rather fearful expression. My voice echoed and bounded off the dark trees. Something resembling a magical spark flickered in his eyes like the figure before me was magic himself. He took a step towards me and grinned widely, 'What are you?' He asked. He stepped back and turned around, facing a path leading deeper into the forest. He stretched out a hand and beckoned me to follow him, but I stood still on the damp forest floor and just stared as he slowly ebbed away and away and away.

Numerous thoughts raced through my mind as the dream shifted, and I drifted into deeper, darker oblivion.

I wake up at dawn. The sky is a perfect mixture of coral pink and saffron. The clouds drift by in the sky at a leisurely pace, tentatively, as though they are waiting for me to notice them. It's as though they're trying to tell me something. *When we cry, you get rain; when it's summer, the fields dry, and you're in pain. We're sorrowful, unremarkable, cold and teary. Are you?* No, I'm not any of those things. All these peculiar experiences are making me have second thoughts about myself—who I am and if I actually belong. Who am I, actually?

I glance at the grandfather clock in the far corner of my suite. 6:30 am. Esther's birthday ball gown fittings are just after breakfast, so I can easily take a stroll in the misty Manor Gardens. Heather arrives with a cup of hot, steaming chamomile tea to soothe my headaches. The fragrance is ever so lovely. After sipping the aromatic tea, I slip into a decent dress and a green loden cape and walk through the dusky corridors of Marilyn Manor. As I pass through the hallways, the ancient portraits of past marquesses stare at me with their beady eyes as though I am an inconvenience. The intricate, textured wallpaper is tattered at the edges. I wonder when was the last time Father had the walls redone. If Mother were here, I'm sure she wouldn't be too happy with the old walls.

My mother died when I was five. Yes, died. Why call it anything else? She didn't pass away like a blissful wind; she was shot in the head by a malicious outsider, and that was it. I don't remember much from the fleeting time Esther and I had with her, but I know she was beautiful. Like, really, really beautiful. And I have a grand portrait right in front of me to prove it. Hers is the only painting that stares at me in a compassionate way. Hers is the only painting carefully preserved, unlike the other bygone ones. Hers is the only one for which I would go to the ends of the world if ever lost. And if I didn't find it, I'd keep on looking.

I miss her. I miss her too much.

I slink through the serpentine, winding halls and nondescript staircases until I reach the front door of the Manor. I am reaching for the rusted door handle when a voice calls out to me. 'Jessi?' I jump, but I'm instantly relieved when I turn around to find a very familiar girl sitting on a couch, quite casually, nose buried in a mystery novel.

'Ah, Esther, you scared me,' I say, looking down at the maroon carpet.

'Up so early?' she says, as though she isn't reading a bloody book on murder at seven in the morning.

'Thought I'd take a walk. Care to join me?'

'Let's!' Esther sets her book down on the nearest table, flattens the creases of her night cloak, and skips towards me. As soon as I unlock the main door, she dashes out like a gust of wind.

'Hey, wait for me!' I laugh as I, too, find myself running into the gardens, which are extremely damp from last night's torrential rain.

'Father's going to kill us if we get mud on the carpet!'

'That's the whole fun of it all!' shouts Esther as she zooms into the meadow, grinning, the vivid red faces of the poppies smiling right back at her.

Decades ago, a Lord had a willow tree planted in this very meadow, and that tree has now grown so tall and grand. Esther drops down under that tree and stretches her legs, her boots caked with fresh dirt and withered grass. Her hair is undone, as always, and her collar isn't buttoned up properly, again, as always. That's the Esther I know and love—remarkable, carefree, lively. As a child, she loved to run around the moorlands of Haeems and the bustling towns of Frances. I really don't think this quality has ever left her, nor ever will. Esther has always been so keen and curious, the first one to spot a tiger on hunting trips, the first one to question the moral code of society. She might be carefree and slightly reckless, but she will still make the best Marchioness of Frances with all her steadfastness.

We relax under the willow tree and listen to the birdsong, wishing a new sparrow arrives to entertain us with his merry tunes. About an hour passes, and I can hear Heather ringing the bells, indicating that breakfast is being served. I pull Esther by the arm and drag her inside the Manor, hoping to take a quick bath and not get mud everywhere. We run up the stairs, chuckling because of our enjoyable *walk* in the gardens.

I sit down at my vanity and remove the sticks and stones from my brunette hair. I take a quick bath, wash my face, and dress in a violet tea gown. As I cross the room, I catch a glimpse of myself in the jade-panelled mirror. I stare at the reflection of my ebony-coloured eyes. They look especially dark this morning, like ink stains on pages of writing.

All thoughts aside, I stride down the nondescript staircase and meet Father and Esther in the dining hall. The pastries look even more lavish than usual, the glowing honey causing the special appearance. The tea is so fragrant that I could probably smell it miles away. I take a seat next to Esther, who is already picking at her eggs in her usual carefree manner yet trying to remain as graceful as possible.

Comfortable, familial silence prevails in the dining room, the only sounds being forks scraping plates clean of any leftover breakfast.

Once we finish breakfast, Esther and I go to the fitting room to try on the newly made gowns for Esther's birthday ball. Mine is teal, heavily embellished with pearls and lace. I'm truly taken with Esther's gown, lightly embroidered with diamonds and diaphanous tulle. Her dress is midnight blue, as dark as the world during an untimely death.

As I make my way towards my suite, I suddenly recall one of my mother's sayings: *Light a candle in a dimly lit hallway, and all sorrow will go away.* Years ago, I had no idea what it meant, but I'm starting to comprehend its meaning.

When there's darkness, find the light.

But the real peculiarity is…where is the darkness?

Chapter 2

March the 23rd. Esther's birthday. She turns 20 today. I zoom into her suite at 7 AM, only to find her still tossing and turning around on her bed.

'Let me sleep!' groans Esther.

I ladle ice-cold water from the washbasin into a glass and splash it on her. She is never one to wake up early on important occasions, even if that occasion is her own birthday. Esther shrieks instantaneously, followed by a smirk forming on my lips.

'Congratulations! You survived another year!' I laugh and immediately earn a feather pillow striking my face.

'At least you used your brains instead of those old "happy birthdays!"' She rolls her eyes, then chuckles.

'Thanks. Now get dressed, we have a long day ahead of us.'

'You're sounding like Gwendolyn.'

'Oh please, I'm nothing like that governess. The long day includes getting dressed at this instant, a ride through the moorlands and forests, shopping, and then back home in time to prepare for the Ball.' I do sound like Gwendolyn.

'Glad I get to spend my birthday with you.'

'You have no idea how much I begged Father to free you from all those meetings with the Lords.'

'Silasbury I can bear, but I personally think Leigh and Duxubury have meetings outside the House of Lords and are... y'know... engaging in matters other than - well - lordly.'

'Isn't Lord Duxubury 50? And Mary turned 36 last year. And they both have conflicting opinions on all bills proposed.'

'You never know, darling,' she smirks with slight soberness.

I admire Esther's forthrightness.

'Come on, up with you; I promised Father we'd be in the carriage by—'

'That man can go to hell for all I care.' She interrupts.

'Esther!' I chide her for cursing at her own father. Maybe I don't admire her forthrightness so much. Father isn't a bad man at all, though he doesn't really spend any time with us anymore. He's always in his chambers, going over documents and reform bills. I hope giving his title to Esther will cause him to become the loving paternal figure he once was.

Esther gets off her bed, folds the creases in her nightgown, and calls for Keira, her lady's maid. Keira enters the room immediately and says to Esther,

'May you have a brilliant day, Your Grace.'

My sister smiles and replies, 'Thank you ever so much, Keira.'

'Shall I have your bath drawn?' says Keira. Esther nods. I step out of the room to allow Esther some privacy while she bathes and head to my suite to dress myself.

The serpentine hallways are decked with teal blue and sea green sashes, with sunny yellow chrysanthemums tied around them. Fresh gerberas are planted in the gardens, and even the trees are adorned with golden ribbons to celebrate the new Marchioness of Frances. Esther is going to be the youngest Lady that Frances has had in decades. The youngest Lord is Charles Silasbury, 19. When we were younger, Charles was great friends with Esther and me. We'd play together in the moors and run around all day long until our legs couldn't carry us anymore. We were quite the trio.

I remember one day when we were playing 'hide-and-seek,' and Esther decided she wanted to be impertinent and make me the seeker. I was never the strongest seeker; I'd always look in the most obvious places, even when Esther and Charles were camouflaging in plain sight. I'd never notice them as they were always so still while hiding. Stillness is all it takes to be invisible, right?

When I was made the seeker, Esther forced me to count to a hundred and hid with Charles behind the big boulder near the river. The sun's bright saffron rays bathed the boulder, and the massive rock literally looked like a tiger. As I approached their hiding place, I shrieked. My loud scream caused Charles to jump, and he fell right into the river. I recall jumping in as well to save him, as neither Charles nor Esther could swim properly. They began to laugh so hard when I bounded into the river like a fish who'd been taken out of the water for a bit too long. Esther sniggered at the sight of Charles and me in the water. She jumped in to join us, and we splashed water at each other for hours. Father, Lord and Lady of Merlin rebuked us for much longer than our time in the moors.

I do hope Charles is present at Esther's ball. It would be nice to reconnect with an old friend.

I enter my suite and get dressed as swiftly as I'm able. I wear a simple white shirt-waist and a moss green travelling cloak.

I then stride to the Dining Hall for breakfast, where I meet Esther and Father. Father is going over the final preparations for the Ball, and Esther is eating her breakfast as casually as one pleases.

'Morning, Jessica, dear,' Father greets, not unkindly.

'Good morning, Father.'

'I assume you and our birthday girl have a good plan for today?' he says indifferently, not bothering to look at us, skimming through the documents sprawled out on the table. A fountain pen leaks undisturbed on the pages.

He chuckles at Esther, who is about to take a bite of her cherry tart. She gives him a smile that certainly tells me she would do anything to have a chance to kick him under the table.

'Yes, we'll get into the carriage by 9 AM, a ride through Walsh Vale, and then we'll go to Madame Wilson's Boutique for some shopping,' I say with as much enthusiasm as I can muster. My fingers are twitching again; they feel warm and fiery. The curtains move vigorously. Suddenly, the morning sun is covered by thick, dark rain clouds.

What the hell is happening? Oh, of course, those 'peculiar experiences.' A strong gust of wind causes the blinds to whip thunderously and hit Father's head.

'Goodness gracious!' he lets out a small scream. I stifle a chuckle and instantly run to assist him. Esther springs up from her seat too, spooked by the instantaneous drop in temperature and darkening sky. My legs feel numb. My shoulders feel slouched no matter how much I roll them back. My fingers are moving so swiftly now I have to bury them in my skirts to hide their movement. As fast as this peculiarity invaded my peace, the odd sensation subsides. The sun emerges from behind the clouds, the curtains return to their original tranquil position, and my fingers finally decide to stop twitching. My hand aches terribly, but there's nothing I can do.

'Oh, look! The weather's better now. Oh, Father, could we please leave for the ride now?' says Esther.

'Well prepared, are you?' asks Father.

'Definitely!'

'Off you go then.'

Esther is wearing her blue brocade coat, which I assume is a birthday present from Father, as I've not seen it before. The embroidered patterns depict numerous hooded figures skipping around a bonfire. If I peer closely, a face in the flames is remarkably visible, with light blue sparks dancing around the other figures. Looks like a witch hunt. But it's too brutal an embroidery for a woman's coat, especially one about to become a member of Parliament.

Esther and I stride out of the Manor and step into the carriage. The door of the carriage locks with a 'click' as soon as we sit down on the crimson leather seats. I wonder how the door locked by itself; it could be because of the wind. My sister sits right next to me, our knees pressed together, and I can feel her presence. Comfortable and familial.

I rest my head on her shoulder as the driver pulls the reins of the horses, urging them to move forward. Numerous thoughts race through my mind, each getting louder and louder with every trot of the horses. I try not to think about my fit in the Dining Hall, but the silence in my mind kills me more. I wrap my arms around Esther's waist. I can give myself this, this content, sisterly affection. She turns to me, her blonde hair glowing in the sunlight, and jokes,

'My, my, Jessi, what a beautiful portrayal of a perfect bond between loving sisters.'

I punch her in the shoulder playfully and respond,

'Be happy it's only for your birthday. I'm back to cursing at you by midnight today, as the day will be officially over.'

'I'm just too wonderful, aren't I? Oh, look, the townsfolk have put out turquoise bunting!' Esther points to the triangular flags hanging from washing lines and jute ropes draped over windows and lampposts.

'Oh, they've even got an embroidery of you!' I say.

'Ah, my eyesight's far too bad to see the intricacy. All I can see are blue-coloured triangles hanging from invisible strings.'

The look of horror on my face is genuine. 'You— you're joking, right?' I say meekly.

'I genuinely don't know...' Esther laughs. It's typical of her to fool around and make me completely horrified at a simple joke.

We've crossed the town now and are riding through the fields. The grass is short, and I can see bright yellow chrysanthemums blooming from the green patches. It's a bit more than a three-hour drive from Marilyn to Walsh Vale, which is on the outskirts of Haeems. Haeems and Marilyn used to be a joint estate, but there was some bygone political rivalry that caused the splitting of the two. Thus, they are neighbouring cities, only an hour apart.

Walsh Vale is part of a chain of Irish villages comprising O'Sullivan and Fin'Olinn as well. Most of the Vale consists of plains and fields that support agriculture and the cultivation of flowering plants, which is the sole reason why it's more prosperous than the other villages. It's mesmerising to walk along the dandelion paths at night, but certain 'witch rumours' about the abandoned, forested part of Haeems don't encourage people to stroll in the vicinity after dark. So, we take carriage rides through the fields on special occasions, like Esther's birthday.

About an hour later, we enter the golden grounds of the wonderful Vale, relishing the fresh breeze that brushes against our faces. How I wish I could get out of the carriage, lie down on the spiky grass, and feel each blade pierce me harder than a fencing sword. There's a certain satisfaction I get; the pain brings me the feeling of being alive, helping me understand I haven't lost all my emotions to the peculiarities around me.

But a wild boar was spotted hiding in the grass last night, so it's probably safer to stay in the carriage at all times.

While the carriage makes its way through the clusters of elm trees, Esther pulls out two flasks of steaming hot peppermint tea and hands one to me. I shake my head 'no', but she laughs and says, 'Shut up and drink.' I open my flask and take a big swig, hoping it's not as warm as the container. *How stupid of me, of course, it's extremely hot.* I survive, thankfully, with a burnt tongue, though.

'Don't you just love the fallen leaves? They remind me of autumn,' says Esther, while pointing to the fresh leaves on the forest floor. They must have fallen because of harsh winds, merciless winds. I almost feel sorry for the leaves.

I'm admiring the elm trees when I see a shadow right next to the tree on my far right. At first, it is something so fleeting, but then it starts moving with the pace of the carriage. Then I realise it is not a shadow at all, but a person.

A boy.

Part of me hopes that he's the one I saw in my dreams a while ago, but that'd be too much of a coincidence. He is so far away I can only catch sight of the curls of his hair. I'm not sure if it's a boy at all or if I'm even seeing things.

And then, I hear sounds. Melancholy and sombre. Exactly like the whistles in my dreams. But these are more prominent now.

I think I recognise this tune, an old Irish folk song, one about people who knew each other in another life.

I am deeply surprised at how swiftly the boy is running, not breaking a single twig on the forest floor. Suddenly, the carriage takes a sharp turn, and we're moving back towards Marilyn for Esther and my shopping outing. I've lost sight of him now, the mysterious, shadowy forest boy.

Chapter 3

'The crimson one suits you more,' compliments Esther while we're looking through an array of differently styled hats in *Alicia's Boutique*. Esther is holding out a blood-red bowler hat with a brown ribbon tied around the trim. It reminds me of the fancy hats detectives wear in mystery novels, how every single one looks different like each hat has its own story to tell—how it got on the detective's head and the crime scenes it witnessed.

I try the bowler on and admire myself in the shop mirror. Esther stands near me, wrapped in an intricate emerald shawl she picked from the clothing section. The shop owner walks up to us, and with a smile, she says, 'Good afternoon, Your Graces. Have you both finalised what to buy? I'm sure you'd look stunning in whatever you choose.' Madame A. Wilson, who's been embroidering dresses and clothing items for decades now, smiles warmly. No one knows how old she is, and it's quite impolite to ask. She may be at least 65 if my calculations are correct, but the wrinkles on her forehead and the dark circles under her eyes suggest that she is far older. Still, there's some beauty in Madame's blue eyes, the colour of an azure ocean wave.

Esther breaks the seconds of silence by saying, 'Thank you, Madame Wilson, lovely store, stunning indeed! We'd like to purchase this shawl, the red bowler hat, and the two gowns that I've laid out on the counter table. Do come to today's evening Ball. I understand you're incredibly busy, but I'd really appreciate it.'

'Many thanks for the invitation, Lady Harrington. I'll bring my son Henry as well if he returns home on time... the dresses and accessories will be couriered to Marilyn Manor as soon as I am able.'

'Delightful!'

Esther and I walk out of the shop, hand in hand, giggling about our fetching looks in the shop mirror. We hop into the waiting carriage, and the driver pulls the reins of the stark brown horses, urging them to start trotting forward.

It's a quiet ride back to Marilyn Manor, as I'm supposing my sister is as tired as I am. But I can sense a spark of fear and angst in her. Well, she is going to take her seat in the House of Lords in a week's time. That is a mighty big responsibility. But Esther is so astute that this obligation should weigh nothing on her shoulders; she'll be such a visionary, eligible for Duchess, even though we're not royal.

I take her hand in mine and give her an affectionate squeeze. That just about does it because she gives me a weak smile and says, 'Thanks. For everything.'

We enter through the colossal, cast-iron gates of our home, and Esther's worried, pale facial expression returns. Oh. She's genuinely scared.

She doesn't speak at all until we're inside the walls of her chambers, and the door is locked. My back rests against the cedar wood door, and I fold my arms across my chest. Esther lies down on her bed and stares up at the ceiling.

I sigh and say in a tender voice, 'You know Keira is going to come soon to get you dressed for the Ball. Then there's the arduous job of smiling and keeping polite conversation with the Lords. The next time we speak could very well be tomorrow afternoon, lest the Ball ends post-midnight and you wake up late in the morning.' I chuckle a bit to create some liveliness in Esther, as I think all the happiness in her has died like a snuffed-out candle.

'Tell me, Eshy, are you scared of not making a good impression today or adjusting to the idea of being Marchioness?' I'm surprised by how forthright I am. Before I can apologise for triggering her feelings, she responds, her voice breaking like overly stretched twine, 'The latter. You think I care about what those earls think of me? I care about I—what I think of me—myself.'

It's only when a single tear trickles down her cheek that I realise she's not as carefree, formidable, and outgoing as I've known her all my life. Even the greats have off nights, I suppose. I'm about to go over to her bedside and comfort her when Keira strides into the room, her cupboard-like chest filled with dress materials, creams, scented soaps, silk ribbons, and whatnot.

I give Esther a final, sisterly hug before we go back to being distant because of the bloody, consuming politics she'll have to deal with now. I hope the Lords don't trouble her with their part-drunk, unbearable forms. I hope they let Esther introduce reform bills in peace and give her a chance to express her opinions on matters, just like she does in meetings with Father in Aurelia.

I walk to my own suite, where I find Heather arranging my turquoise gown.

'Ready?' she asks, placing a motherly arm around my shoulders.

'As I'll ever be.' I sound like I'm ascending my seat at the House of Lords, which I certainly am not. Hopefully, I'll never have to.

I take a bath, wear a robe, and settle at my vanity table so Heather can do my hair. She smooths my dark hair out and makes a bun, leaving a few strands out and tucking them behind my ears. She ties a thin silk blue ribbon around the bun, matching the teal of my dress. Heather gently helps me into my definitely uncomfortable ball gown, but Esther's is likely to be ten times more horrendous than mine. I admire the lacework and paper-white pearls embroidered into the masterpiece of a dress, starting from the hem. The amount of skirts underneath the outermost layer is unimaginable.

Hours pass while Heather highlights my face with powders of gold and pink and applies a slightly reddish French pink colour on my lips. I get slightly agitated by how slow her movements are. A sort of electric jolt zaps in my fingers. They half shake, half twitch. To hide it from Heather's concern, I bury my hand in the folds of my dress. Will I be hiding this unnaturalness forever?

Her final touch is a necklace, one with a crescent moon charm. I'm immediately struck with a memory—Mother, Father, Esther, and I relaxing on a mattress in the Manor gardens, admiring the moon in its waning crescent phase. It had secrets of its own I was longing to know. That moment was so long ago, but it hangs there in my mind like a broken picture frame, unwilling to fall from the single nail embedded in the wall. If the picture frame falls, I'll lose whatever few evanescent memories I still have left of my deceased mother.

Snapping me back to reality is a knock on the door.

'It's time!' says Esther, in such a joyful way, I wonder how the spark of effusiveness ignited in her after her sombre breakdown. I tuck the necklace charm under my corset so that a simple silver chain is visible. I smile too, and together we walk out of my room, down the decorated and candle-lit hallways, and into the grand room, where Esther's 20th birthday ball celebrations await us.

'His Highness, Lord Harrington, the Marquess of Frances!' the announcer booms, trying to attract the attention of those in the hall. Esther and I are standing right behind the double doors, waiting for our turn to be introduced to the guests. It's not that they don't know us; it's just formal to announce the names of the distinguished members of the Ball.

Next is me.

'Presenting, Her Grace, Lady Jessica Harrington!' I hear a round of thunderous applause the second I enter the balcony overlooking the Ballroom. I try to put on my best, dashing smile and wave at the crowd. Thankfully, I spot Heather in the sea of men and women and draw my focus towards her, a support pillar keeping me upright and sane. I wish Mother were here to witness this glorious event. She would have loved seeing Esther and me transform into respected, wonderful ladies—if we have. I'm contemplating about my late mother again when I miss the announcement for Esther. At least the guests are clapping like their lives depend on it, so I know the world already loves her for the bright Marchioness she's going to be. Now, the other Lords and Ladies are going to enter; all my sister and I need to do is force a smile courtesy and wait until the actual Ball part begins.

I barely pay attention to any of the announcements. *Highness Leigh, Lord Aurelia, James that, why is the speaker going so agonisingly slow? Or is it just my impatience? I'm not that impatient.* I smile when Lady Mary Leigh steps onto the balcony. I've had a few chats with her—not about politics—she seems nice.

There's only one smile and courtesy of mine that is genuine.

'With pride, I address His Grace, Lord Silasbury of Merlin!'

He strides in happily, and the crowd bursts into applause. The people love him, really. A visionary, he is, the youngest Lord, a man with revolutionary ideas that certainly have brought about economic and cultural change in not only Merlin but in the entirety of Frances. My old best friend, I really don't know what happened with our trio of Esther, him, and me. I suppose we grew up, grew distant. He became an Earl, and Esther started her studies for Marchioness. Politics consumed them.

He crosses me, looks my way, and smiles brightly, the kind of friendly smile I have missed. I'm overpowered with happiness and simply put on a facial expression that hopefully portrays, *Hiya, Charles.*

All the Earls, Father, Esther, Charles, and I walk down the staircase, decorated with gold ribbons and pink gerberas, and join the partygoers in the hall. The Ball commences, and I see gentlemen marking their names on the ladies' dance cards. I receive a tap on my right shoulder and jump instantly.

It's Charles.

'Jess, long time no see,' he says, clasping his hands.

'Hi, Charles.' I pray he doesn't notice my completely frozen form. 'So, how's life being an exceptionally annoyingly perfect Lord?' I joke.

'Well and good, how're you?' he asks.

'Good, as well. Enjoying the Ball?'

'Thoroughly. Well, since we haven't spoken to each other in a fairly long time… would you like to dance?' The nervousness on his face screams out to me. How can Charles Silasbury, the most natural, perfect person in all of Frances, be nervous?

Without hesitation or even the slightest form of reluctance, I agree. I pull out my dance card, and Charles marks his name next to the first waltz in neat penmanship.

'Ladies and gentlemen, the first waltz of this Ball shall commence in two minutes. Please take your places with your partners at the centre of the hall,' the conductor of the orchestra announces in a loud voice.

Charles extends a welcome hand to me, and I place my palm over his. F*inally, some time with my best friend.* I remember dance lessons with Sir Antonio when I was 10 and Charles had just turned 12. We stepped on each other's feet the entire time and laughed our lungs out. Sir Antonio—known to us as 'The Dancing Ant'—gave a disappointed sigh and stormed out of the ballroom, raging that we were two kids who certainly could not be mentored in dance.

That made us laugh more.

The dance begins, and the orchestra starts to play Waltz in A minor. Charles leads me in a beautiful waltz, and I can see the eyes of the audience trained on us, on me. The last ball I went to was the Senators' Ball in Aurelia, the business capital. That was months ago, and I haven't really danced since then. Still, I try not to step on Charles' toes as much as possible. I'm too tired to worry about the fine leather of his loafers getting damaged by the hard soles of my sandals. I'm so deep in thought about the thing *or boy* or whatever I saw in the woods today that I almost trip on Charles and go careening to the ground. He catches me at the right moment before anyone can let out vexing gasps.

In a kind, soft voice, he asks, 'Jess, you're fine, right? You seem a bit drained.'

Continuing orderly, graceful steps, I answer, 'Yes, uh, thanks, I am fine, just a headache from the sunlight during the carriage ride—'

The last notes of the piece, a sharp A minor arpeggio, end the first dance of Esther's Ball. Charles bows to me, and I courtesy. We both give each other warm smiles and head off in opposite directions. He strides towards Esther, who has just danced with Madame Alicia's son. I walk to the side of the ballroom to allow guests swift movement in the hall while they sign dance cards or laugh uproariously at petty wives' tales.

While admiring the ruby chandelier, merely hanging from the high ceiling, I see a familiar person standing on the side of the hall opposite to me. Tall, with a head of wild raven hair and a curious, secretive expression on his face.

The look of horror on my face is genuinely genuine.

It's him. The boy.

Chapter 4

My legs refuse to move; they are positioned permanently on the blood-red carpet. A knot of fear and anticipation twists inside me. What is he doing here?

You fool, that's not the question. Who the hell is he? This certainly can't be a coincidence. There has to be a logical explanation. I don't want to be here; anywhere but here will do. I want to run away from this—this perplexing, vexing, hair-raising, horror-stricken, aching moment.

I don't even know why I'm panicking at this point. This *boy* is not some kind of threat. But, he appeared in my dreams, put on a show in the forests of Walsh Vale, and now is present at my sister's Ball. Is this what the universe fated for me? Confusion and utter annoyance?

I turn around and receive a surprise that doesn't even surprise me.

Even a commoner could guess the person I've seen. His eyes are black, like ink. He is definitely 18 years of age; otherwise, he wouldn't be admitted into the Ball. The freckles on his fair skin are arranged in the shape of gibbous moons.

I immediately feel the presence of the crescent moon necklace, its delicate charm weighing on my skin.

'Good evening, Mr—' I begin, with a forced smile. I have no interest in knowing the secrets of this mysterious boy who's been playing with my thoughts for quite a few days now. It could be fun.

'Fynn, Jack Fynn. May I have the pleasure of knowing your good name?'

'Lady Harrington, daughter of the Marquess of Frances. Call me Jessica.' I chuckle and try to remove the tension I'm feeling in this conversation.

'Ah, Lady Jessica! I'd be delighted to sign your dance card for the Grand March. May I?'

I hold my dance card out for Jack to sign, albeit quickly, as the March will start any moment now. He writes his name in impressive cursive, making a little design on the tail of the letters J and Y.

'Ladies and gentlemen, please assemble with your dance partners for the Grand March!' the announcer booms.

Jack extends a hand out, and I take it. He smiles at me like he's known me forever. Well, that would be likely since I've been seeing him everywhere lately. The musicians start playing *Hungarian Dance No.5*, a piece that I, too, know how to play. I remember my piano teacher made me write the entire piece on sheets with the treble clefs, note values, key signatures, and everything. I don't think he was in a good mood that day. Drifting my thoughts back to the March, we position ourselves for the dance and move along with the rhythm of the music.

The minor chords in the piece are what make this moment so tense, overwhelming, and eerie. I need to get answers from Jack Fynn and find out more about who he is. Maybe I can connect the dots and understand why the world has thrust this mysterious man into my life.

'You know, I could have sworn I've seen you somewhere. Have we met before?' I ask, not unkindly.

'Nah, I don't think so. Though, since you think you remember me, have I threatened you before?' I hope he is joking. Jack laughs, and I do, too, then rack my brains, trying to think of a humorous response that matches his.

'Where're you from, Mr Fynn? I certainly haven't seen you around Marilyn.'

'My mother's from Haeems, dad's from Fin'Olinn. I'm a representative of Merrycks Home for Mentally Challenged Children.' Father has mentioned this organisation before when he came back from the House of Lords. It's doing respectable work, helping children in need, and giving shelter to orphans and the mentally challenged. Merrycks Home has also raised funds from businessmen in Aurelia to keep the firm going. I don't know the firm's exact location, somewhere near the forested area of Abandoned Haeems, I guess.

We cease our conversation as I feel the weight of odd glances in my direction from Lord Duxubury. My focus is drawn to the dance and the wide grin on Jack's face. A loud *G minor* chord indicates that the Grand March is over. A short interval starts, and I relax my muscles after the two consecutive dances I've done.

'Farewell, Lady Jessica. May we meet again soon,' says Jack Fynn, looking at me in such a peculiar way that I fear he might eat me up. That's cannibalism. He could verily be executed for that. Jack strides off, and I swear I hear him whistle. It's such a soft and low sound that the whistle could just be the wind outside being playful. No, but it really is a whistle.

Whistles.

Melancholy.

Petrifying.

Mysterious.

'Let me tell you a story about how grot and picture are exactly alike!' I say to Esther, in my half-drunkenness. I may have downed a glass of champagne when Father wasn't looking, as I'm underage. My darling sister and I are in her chambers, sprawled across her bed, our minds clouded, and thoughts obscured from all the wine at the Ball.

'Grotesque and picturesque both end with the damned suffix, 'esque', which means 'alike'. So it only makes sense that grot and picture are alike!' *I'm going to die of laughter tonight.*

'Okay, okay, stop!' Esther manages to speak a few sensible words before dissolving into a fit of giggles. We both laugh a bit more, then take deep breaths to stop ourselves from genuinely getting a heart attack.

'Enough chatter, I need to know, who was that handsome stranger you were dancing with tonight?' Esther smirks and edges closer to me.

Memories of the ball stir through my mind: the blinding, bright ruby chandelier, the eerie notes of the Grand March, the freckles on Jack's achingly perfect face, and his wild, tousled hair.

'He wasn't that handsome… well.' My cheeks turn strawberry-red.

'Ah ah, I sense something, darling.'

'Shut up.'

'No!'

'Wait, how don't you know who Jack was? It was your birthday ball; you're supposed to know who's on the guest list, right?'

'Name's Jack? Anyway, Father invited "distinguished members of society", and those from organisations to find a suitable groom for me. I never cared much for the announcements.'

'Mr Fynn is a representative of Merrycks Home.'

'Ah, that place. Rumour has it that the Home isn't exactly a shelter for children. At the House of Lords, I've heard people talk weird things about it. Something fishy is going on there, best to stay away from it at this age.'

'As you say, Your Diligent, Oversmart, Wonderful Grace.'

Esther throws a pillow at me, chuckles, and pulls me into an encompassing hug. I cherish this moment, one of hope and relaxation amidst all the peculiarities of the world.

'Thanks.' She whispers.

'What for?' I ask.

'Believing in me. I wouldn't have had the courage to even enter that ballroom today if you weren't with me.'

'That's what I'm for, Eshy. Being there.'

'Always?'

'Always.'

I'm cold. Ice-cold wind pierces my skin. The hair-raising breeze carries this unfamiliar chill that I can't even explain. I feel scared as I walk into the pines of this tell-tale forest. I'm barefoot, and wet dirt finds its way between my toes. I look in one direction only—that is, in front. I'm not ready to see the darkness all around me. The clouds obstruct the moonlight, and faint rays of white light fall on the pines, making them look even more ghostly. I take a step forward and scream.

It's because there's a hand moving agonisingly slow down my neck, sending chills down my spine. I want to shriek again and call out for help. Who knows what this *hand* may do to me if I react? My own screech drives the life out of me. My pale night dress turns wet due to my profuse sweating.

From afar, I see a creature hiding in the dark, cackling loudly, its eyes full of fire and rage. It's a woman. One with straight black hair and an even blacker dress. Silver rings adorn her fingers, and a belt of daggers encircles her thin waist. Before I know it, my fingers are twitching again, this time non-stop. I don't understand what's happening, but it seems like the heat and energy from my fingers seems to be attracting something.

Your goddamn fingers are trying to pull the dagger out of her belt.

Realisation dawns on me when a sharp, bloodstained knife floats inches away from me. It gently fits into my hand, and some arcane, hidden power causes the light grip I have on it to tighten. The blood-curdling hand on my neck has disappeared now, but no wave can wash away the horror I'm feeling. Blood from the dagger seeps into my skin, staining it deep red.

It's only when I wake up from this absolute nightmare that I realise I'm sitting on the floor of Esther's room, sweating profusely, watching something very unexpected and horrifying take place.

A white, smoke-like, will-o'-the-wisp-shaped creature is hovering over my sister with an unlit candle in its hand. *Sradagan a' bhàis*, the creature whispers, though I'm not sure it has a mouth. The candle comes to life. A bright orange flame burns on the wick, and it's urged closer and closer to Esther's body. *Oh, wait, what?*

As a reflex to what I just saw, I scream, and my hand stretches out, fingers twitching faster than ever. I find the courage to stand up and run towards the bed, where Esther sleeps soundly, unaware of the impossibilities taking place. Golden sparks arise from my fingertips as I push the creature away from Esther. Not by physical touch but by some invisible force emitted from my fingers. I turn towards the creature, which is recoiling from the unexpected blow, and ball my fists, ready to fight. The smoke twists and turns in a spiral shape and transforms into a monster.

A literal, real, monstrous monster. It's still made out of the white vapour, but the creature is larger and scarier now—grey fur, bloodied talons, and pointed teeth.

I've changed, too. I don't have control over my body anymore. My hands are making funny gestures involuntarily, and golden sparks are zooming out from my fingertips, striking the creature. It takes me a moment to understand what is happening.

It's probably magic. Or so I've read in stories.

The creature makes the first move. It lunges towards me, grabbing my wrist with its vapour-like hand. It's confounding and blood-curdling how mere mist is grasping onto me. I try to kick the monster away to loosen its iron grip, but my leg only passes through the creature. A feeling made of bewilderment and pure fear weighs down my heart. So, this smoke-like will-o'-the-wisp can touch me, and I am powerless?

Suddenly, I feel a sort of flame flickering in my heart. A gentle fire, a warning. That I might not survive tonight—if I don't fight.

I extend my hand out, and a gust of wind thrusts the monster into the back wall. The curtains billow around it like fire engulfing a house. It gets entangled in the blinds and struggles to release itself. Hastily, I scamper in front of Esther so my body can form a wall, an obstacle between the demon and my sister.

And then the walls come crashing down as the creature throws me away. My hand bangs against the dresser. A ghastly wound tears open the soft skin. Rivers of blood flow, both warm and chilling at the same time.

I hear a squelching sound. And it's not from the gurgling of blood that pools around my wound.

I know what has happened.

The creature has won.

I feel the Devil dancing on my chest, gripping my heart and bruising it with his talons.

I don't want to see my sister die.

The door swings open, and I don't bother to look at who's just entered.

I'm knocked unconscious by a blow to the head.

I'm sorry, a familiar deep voice in my head says, though not the guard before I drift into oblivion.

Chapter 5

Each blade of grass is ever so yellow because of the generous rays of the sun. The long, withered grass sways in the wind, dancing like gentle ballerinas. The bare trees toss their branches high, joining in with the rhythm of the grass. Each twig of the scattered elms in these fields attempts to receive as much sunlight as possible.

The dead leaves on the heath, however, are still lifeless and don't possess the slightest flame of hope. Nature stomped those sparks out a long time ago; there's nothing I can do to rekindle them.

From afar, I see a girl a bit older than me. She wears her silvery blonde hair tied up in a French braid, her skin ghostly white, and her dress the perfect shade of pale blue. I wave out to her aimlessly. There's a chance that the girl is not looking at me, looking at someplace like a haven to her—peaceful, familial, and *good.* Those are emotions I certainly did not feel last night.

This sunny afternoon is intensifying in heat. Instantaneously, the temperature rises so swiftly that the collar of my dress chokes me. Beads of sweat trickle down my forehead like crawling spiders. The girl disappears, and the white clouds turn grey. The sun gets hidden by the rain clouds, and all flames of generosity, tranquillity, and merriment get extinguished.

Now, the temperature drops to something definitely lower than 'very cold.' I'm standing in a field of dandelions, wondering how those blissful flowers are surviving, wishing for some warmth before I freeze to death.

The world containing my screams turns black. My vision is blurry, but I think I see pillars of rusted black and brown in front of me. The dead leaves from the dream-like fields have returned, covering the damp, cold ground. Then, everything becomes clear.

I awake, my hand pressing my head, throbbing with pain. Memories from last night's dreadful incident rush back with an uneasiness I am not ready to deal with.

I couldn't protect her. I *looked* like a murderer last night.

That's why I'm sitting in this prison cell, fighting with my sanity. I'll be executed for sure, though I won't be joining my sister in heaven. I deserve hell after last night. It's what I need, what I—

Oh my.

My thoughts are disturbed by an ear-splitting noise coming from probably the side of the prison building. I'm in the middlemost cell, surrounded by chambers containing several ghastly-looking men with bloodied faces and yellowing teeth, so I don't know what's happening at the far corners of the structure. The noise sounded like a crash of sorts; maybe the guards were bringing the noose on a wheeled cart, and the cart just struck the prison building, caked with grime, blood, and death.

The noose is obviously for me. I'm headed for the gallows, laddies.

Wonder what Esther would think of me? Performing grotesque trickery and seeing unpleasant things in the middle of the night.

Oh, goodness gracious, glory me.

The silence in my tranquil hell of a prison cell is shattered by a thunderous blow right at the wall my back is resting against.

I let out a hair-raising shriek and recoil to the corner, as far from the damage done to the wall. I realise impenetrable chains are clawed to my ankles, forbidding me from crawling more than a few metres away. The red bricks of the broken wall are scattered like helpless remains of dead bodies after a mine explosion. I'm panting heavily and grasping the rusted iron grid, deeply mortified by the crash.

A small automobile had burst straight into the prison cell wall. One adorned with violet fabric and mahogany wheels so ornate that you could see pixies and olive branches carved into them. The back of this breathtaking vehicle is towards me, and I hear groans coming from the front.

'Why ain't this woman just hurrying up?' moans the voice.

The engine of the automobile starts running, and the vehicle is pushed further into the chamber, crashing more bricks and ruining all structures.

There's a humongous hole in the wall or whatever is left of it. Other prisoners would have used this to their advantage, escaped, and celebrated the moment with rum, only to eventually return to their abode in the prison building. But I, oh, I just simply stare, scream, and wish to be back in bed with my sister, who died a few wretched, soul-sucking hours ago. *Yes. Died. There's really no other way to put it. What about murdered? That's actually factually accurate as well.*

A woman emerges from the opening. Early 40s. She wears a purple travelling dress matching the colour of the pristine automobile, a golden belt across her mid-sized waist. Her brown hair is in a messy bun, her eyes sharp and searching, and her facial expression tired and sick of nonsense.

It's Heather.

My mouth is agape, but before I can close it, Heather says roughly, 'Don't worry, darling. We're here to help.'

I'm petrified, sorrow-stricken, angry. My lady's maid just crashed into a prison cell in a fancy automobile the morning after Esther's death. And she expects me not to worry. Her rough, careless accent worries me more.

'Firstly, I'm tied to chains. Secondly, HEATHER, WHAT THE HELL?' I cry. It's not every day that you see a person who is like a mother to you break down the walls of a prison to let you out. I'm relieved that Heather is here, looking audacious and gallant. Though, there is a parade of questions looming in my head.

'Shush now, Jessica, no one has noticed yet. You got your magic last night; you have to trust me now. Alright?'

No one has noticed yet? Certainly, that's a joke. I want to laugh, but that wouldn't be appropriate as of now.

She snaps thrice, and the painful, tight chains unlock, and I free my ankles from their grasp. I stand up, stretch my legs, and relish the sunlight that I would have enjoyed with Esther on any other beautifully ordinary day.

'Come along now, hop in the carriage, I'll explain along the way. Don't worry. You're safe now; you didn't do anything wrong last night. Nature took its own course. The world doesn't mean harm to us. Sometimes things happen, but we need to stay strong throughout,' reassures Heather in her usual tender and kind manner. But how does she know about last night? I assume it has become the latest gossip, the kind whispered within the walls of every house, in every stairwell.

Heather beckons me towards her and places a familial arm over my shoulder, assisting me to climb into the automobile. As soon as she starts the engine, I hear shouts and yells from Manor guards and townsfolk.

'Hope you're ready.'

'As ready as I'll ever be?'

'There's one thing I've never mentioned to you, Your Grace. You're too doubtful. Merrycks will increase your confidence. Here we go!'

The automobile begins to move at top speed. Guards try to follow us but are thrust away by an invisible shield around us, conjured when Heather mutters something in Gaelic before starting to drive.

I say goodbye to Marilyn, to the shadows of my sister, who I'll always keep in my heart, and Charles. He's likely in his sitting room, sweat beading down his face, head in his palms, and mind filled with frustration. I feel I should apologise for all the confusion, distress, and horror I've brought to not only him but Father and all the Lords and Ladies.

'I state with pride that in a few short hours, we will reach Abandoned Haeems, the woods of the Merrycks, where you will witness amazing sights, practise otherworldly arts, and figure out who you are in this world,' announces Heather, exuberantly.

It's only when she reveals the reason for my kidnap of sorts that I realise I can't really comprehend what is happening. Pure bewilderment is all I'm feeling at this moment. All I know is that I'm entering Abandoned Haeems, the feared woods of pines. I turn around and find out that we have already crossed the bridge over the creek. No one is coming for me. I'm sitting, hands on my lap, fingers trembling terribly, next to my motherly lady's maid, riding an elegant automobile and pondering over impossible things.

Heather's words ring constantly in my head. *You got your magic last night; you have to trust me now.* I can trust her with all my willpower, but the former part of her words can only mean one thing.

I'm a witch. Witch. Witch.

A magical, fantastical, paranormal, literal witch.

Chapter 6

I recall the last time Esther and I played near Haeems as children. We travelled through the meadows with Father and halted the carriage for a picnic beside the clusters of pines. That was the first time Father took a break from politics and joined us sisters on our monthly trips outside of cosy Marilyn. I stretched my legs on the red and blue chequered mattress, and Esther discoursed with Father about how Leigh wasn't looking after the villages of Haeems and leaving all the work to the Secretary-General. Connecting the pieces of their perplexing puzzle of a discussion seemed like a deathtrap. So, I diverted my attention to the pine trees, their merry movement in the light wind.

Standing in a thicket of trees was a figure wearing the same purple and gold robes that Heather is now. Violet loden cape, classical yellow threads of king's garments, and embroidery of a crimson bird etched on the collar. An undoubtedly fierce, impressive design for a woman's coat. Society would think otherwise.

She looked at me, not unkindly, but her stare was achingly long and knife-edged as if she were searching for the most vulnerable, broken parts of me, waiting to burn them.

I turned my chin up, stared at her back, and showed her that I was not a little weakling who could be looked down upon.

The woman had the audacity to laugh and shake her head. I didn't hear the sounds of her cackle, but one could make out that it was pessimistic and sinister. Before I could stand up and investigate this headache of a woman, she was gone.

'Oh my!' I exclaim as the automobile rides over gravel, making me jump up and down on my seat. I fold the creases of my cloak and realise I haven't changed from my nightgown since last night. I was dragged to a prison cell by my hair, probably. There was no time.

Last night. Memories hit me like pebbles thrown at a window on a late rainy night.

Esther. My darling, sweet older sister. Heir to Father's estate. The girl I've spent all my life with. My best friend. Is she really no more? Or was the entire ordeal an illusion?

The wretched, monstrous, wisp-shaped creature killed her. And I did nothing to stop it. My toes begin to wriggle vigorously out of the stress of this situation. So do my fingers. Red sparks emit from my fingertips, and my whole body enters a state of twitching, irregular movement. Tears stream down my eyes, remembering Esther's eyes when she was murdered. Closed, cold, and unseeing.

I can't control myself. I want to flee out of the automobile, but Heather has bolted it shut, forbidding my escape. I'm in a forest, travelling to the asylum for the mentally ill. Maybe I deserve it. Collapsing on the velvet seat, I wail. Who wouldn't if their sibling were dead? If their life took a sharp turn into the darkness? My vision goes blurry, and I feel nauseous. My damned mind starts imagining impractical things and such nonsense. Though, there's a chance it may all be true.

Remnants of bones. Human ashes. Severed limbs. Handless arms. Silver, spine-chilling eyes scattered over the automobile floorboards. And blood. So much shiny blood that I can see my reflection in it.

I hyperventilate and try to upright myself. It's not working; it's like I'm physically tied to the seat by the elongated, deadly fingers of the monster. I scream out loud, hoping someone will hear my pleas and come to my rescue. Esther would always be the one to come. Now she's not here. Oh God, take care of her, please. More and more grotesque visions flood my brain: disfigured creatures lurking in the dark, a younger, gullible me tiptoeing on thin ice. Jack Fynn's secretive smile.

Grasping me from these brutal chains of thoughts is Heather's loud, exuberant voice announcing, 'We're here!'

She says this as though literally nothing has happened to me in the past few minutes. The blood and bones disappear. The opulence of the velvet returns. The sinful visions get suppressed for the time being. The only thing on my mind is his grin, his hand pressed on my waist, his heedful, particular steps leading us into a march. Jack will be at the Home. One familiar face in these waves of peculiarity and horror. Heather hops from the driver's seat and approaches the door of the passenger compartment. She doesn't unlock it with a physical touch, of course. By snapping twice, the door is opened swiftly, like it was never locked at all. Heather extends out a warm arm, which I take out of habit. My trust in her has been gradually decreasing throughout the whole ride, and I wonder who she is and if everything she ever did for me was all true. Still, there is keenness in her grass-green eyes, an eagerness just waiting for me to know her secrets.

I step out of the automobile and pat the resplendent, breathtaking, ravishing vehicle. When I look around, the scenery in front of me is absolutely captivating. Pines rustling in the breeze, wintry, carefree wind playing with my hair, the ground damp, and a sky so achingly, wonderfully blue. I look up at the clouds, drifting by and acknowledging my intrusion in these tranquil woods of Abandoned Haeems. If I pay attention, I think I can hear gurgling streams not far from here. I breathe in and fill my lungs with moist air, something I'm not able to do in the city of Marilyn.

Then, I gaze back at the automobile, unmoved. It's staring back at me with an opulence I could never match. The hills of this forest are quite high and carpeted with deposits of gravel. It's a wonder how Heather's automobile made the journey uphill.

'What do you think?' Heather's polished voice cuts through the thick atmosphere of silence and peace that I've been feeling for the last few moments. I hate her for reminding me of my purpose here. Do I know why? That's for me to know and for you to discover.

'What do I think? Of this hiding place or the possible untruths you've told me?' I try to be as confident as I can, but the words come out small and unconvincing.

'Listen, Jessica, I'm aware you may think all this is a practical joke, but you have to trust me. We'll be meeting the Head of the Home, so mentally prepare yourself for the outcome. Don't worry; I'll be sitting with you the entire time.' Her answer doesn't calm me. It aggravates my angst and impatience further. She expects me to not worry while my mind constantly dwells over the thought of me being a witch. My old lady's maid gently takes my hand and walks with me across the gravel path. Her entire motherly façade and caring countenance have disappeared now. I can't trust her anymore. I don't want to. I want Esther now; she'd undoubtedly help me in this mess. But she's dead, and I'm alone in my mind. *Isn't it lovely? All alone?*

Heather and I approach a homely, rustic cabin enclosed in a thicket of pines and firs. Vines run across the dirt-encrusted, obscure windows, and wilting black roses adorn the footsteps. Heather leaves my arm, pats me on the shoulder, and gives me a comforting glance. I take a wary step on the archaic, rickety staircase of the cabin, and a droughty, bleak breeze almost pushes me behind. Another gust of wind, damp and icy this time, flings open the jagged, time-worn door with a screeching, ear-pinning voice.

The first thing I see is the trim, well-groomed black bun of a woman who's in her 60s. Next, the wrinkles running across her tired forehead, then her azure eyes, wide and searching. Lastly, I take a glimpse of her violet robes with the royal golden lining. Colours similar to the automobile. Cloak is exactly like Heather's. Face precisely like the woman I recalled during my journey here. She looks up from whatever she is writing and looks at me. It takes her a second to realise that I am as bewildered as she is. Her life-questioning facial expression shifts to a more effusive, imposing disposition.

'Oh, Jessica, what a wonder, we've been waiting for you for a mighty long time! Come sit, dear! Tea or coffee? Oh, how grandly we'll exercise your magical powers! Just you wait!' chirps the woman with a level of excitement I have never witnessed before.

One, she knows my name. Two, she has been waiting for me. Three, she is using the word 'we' a bit too much. Four, she said magical powers, which is something not as gruesome as the past events, so I'd believe anything right now. Five, the goddamn woman didn't care to mention her name.

Six, 'I prefer water.'

Chapter 7

The woman in the purple coat eyes me up and down with severity as I take a seat in front of her oak desk. I sink into the safety and warmth of the leather chair, which reminds me of home, Esther, and of nights by the fireplace. We'd gaze at the flickering flames until they died down, ashes dancing like fairies and fireflies on a balmy evening.

She takes a sip of her tea, which smells so strongly of herbs that I have to hold my breath for a moment. She places her cup on the desk, right above several concentric rings of dried, crusted tea. It's clear she's a heavy drinker and doesn't clean daily. The scattered papers, outworn clothes, broken piano keys, and soiled teacups all prove it. It's funny how not a single hair on her head is out of place, yet her cabin is the complete opposite.

I think this careless woman notices my eyes wandering around the room as she breaks the silence between us. 'I wonder what you're contemplating, Jessica dear… your dead sister, perhaps? I never liked her reforms, but her death is quite commendable, hmm?'

The humph at the end of her belligerent statement gets on my nerves. How dare she have the audacity to speak of Esther like this, using my sister's name to provoke me? I hold back all the tears that want to break away from my control. This *shameless, abandoned, worm-eaten* woman will now face the consequences. Blood rushes to my muscles, hot and fiery. My chest heaves, filled to the brim with anger and unwavering rage. Then, the tell-tale twitching of my fingers starts. First painstakingly slow, then utterly unstoppable, emitting sparks with eerie intensity.

Without warning, my right-hand shoots up and magically produces a powerful, instantaneous gust of dry wind, carrying dust and light objects like hairpins straight at the woman who spoke ill of Esther.

Hairpins killing her? Wonderful. But my hand launching wind? It's either more wonderful or terrifying.

With the slight, feeble raise of her pointer finger, the woman instantly stops the wind and hairpins from reaching her. I sit down, dumbfounded, yearning for the warmth of the leather chair.

Her stare could break through even the most secure prison building.

Oh wait, that's already broken.

At first, she glares at me, probably furious that I've stripped her of her fake dignity. I glare back at her with a potency she doesn't match as she laughs, claps, and effusively, annoyingly exclaims, 'Marvellous, that's exactly what I wanted! I didn't know Winnie's daughter could be so powerful! Commendable indeed! Astounding, by Hecate!'

'Hecate?' I'm tired of being introduced to new mysteries all the time.

'Goddess. Of magic.' The woman replies casually while skim-reading through what are probably important documents, tossing them about as if she couldn't care less.

'We'll get to that later. First, I need to know your name.'

'Aren't you the impatient one? My name should be the last thing on your mind. What you should focus on now is what we will make possible—the reality of you being a witch.'

'Please, just tell me who you are! I—I'll listen to you patiently then. I've dealt with a lot in the past few hours!' I whimper, and tears stream down my cheeks. I can't believe I'm crying in front of her. I want to go home; I want Esther next to me, I want to murder that monster who killed her. The woman signals to Heather, whose presence in the room I hadn't acknowledged, to calm me. I don't crave Heather's motherly touch anymore. I rise from the chair like a shot from a gun and scream, 'HOW CAN SHE BE A PART OF THIS!' I shoot a finger toward my once kindred spirit, Heather. 'I'M TIRED AND BAFFLED. MY SISTER DIED, AND YOU HAVE NO IDEA HOW GRAVELY THAT HAS IMPACTED ME. I CAN'T SIT AROUND HERE WAITING FOR ANSWERS. I WANT THEM NOW!' I collapse on the floor, a whining, wailing mess, and bang my fists against the cool wooden floorboards. The sound of my punches echoes beneath me, but there's nothing under the floorboards. It's like crying next to someone cold and heartless. Hollow and broken from the inside, too. Like me.

Heather and the woman are not even the slightest bit concerned about my outburst and continue looking elsewhere or whistling folk music.

'Ailis Millerwood,' the woman sighs.

'What?' I muster a faint reply.

'My name, as you wanted. Now, answers are what you seek. Get up, dear, and I'll explain everything. Good truths, this time.'

Heather bends down to help me, and I allow her. It's pointless to keep hating her now. She's the one who's been with me all my life; one petty misunderstanding shouldn't change the deeply rooted-bond we share.

It's the good truths that Ailis has promised that thrust my heart into my throat.

I settle myself on the leather chair, legs crossed, and Heather fixes a cup of tea into my hand. 'Drink. For the headaches, remember?' I grin at this act of kindness. Her smile and the tea remind me of days at the Manor—waking up to Heather drawing my bath, listening closely to her extinguishing the candles while I slept, dozing off in front of the mirror as she gently tied my hair in neat braids or elaborate buns. Ailis Millerwood and I both take cautious, deep breaths before she begins her tale.

'This is the Merrycks Home of Magic. Disguised as Merrycks Home for Mentally Challenged Children, as we all know, magic is an absurd concept. But for the witches and magicians who live here, it's their life. I'm not lying. What you did just seconds ago, what you did that night, what you've probably been doing for a very long time but never noticed… is magic. You're a sister of magic. We prefer using the term "sisters" instead of witches and "brothers" in place of magicians. We are united in our coven and live in peace. The main goal of this organisation is to rekindle the flame of unity and friendship between the sisters and the brothers.

As old wives' tales go, there's been bloodshed and wars between the women and men who possess power. Misuse of magic, utter madness, and disunity all lead to horrifying consequences, like witch hunts and burning witches alive. Who wins at the end of the war? Sisters or brothers? Neither. The ordinary men win—the men who have another kind of power of their own, like monarchy or papacy. They can't stand the fact that there are women out there being so independent and powerful and men using their magic to get into filthy politics. We need the sisters and brothers to unite. We can't wage wars any longer, neither between the magical and townspeople nor between sisters and brothers. And that's the sole purpose of Merrycks. We live here, in the tranquil, safe forests of Abandoned Haeems, and we live in peace. Any questions?'

Well, that was a surprisingly short tale. Crisp and clear, though.

'Why am I *magical?*' This question sticks in my throat, like candle wax, unwilling to be scraped off the candelabra. *Am I really a witch? One who can conjure otherworldly, unspeakable things and be different? One who is eventually burned at the end for God knows what reason?*

'If there was an answer to that, I certainly would have given it to you. Magic is like your own hidden power, the expansion of your soul, your body doing things the average human being would never even think of attempting. It means you're special. You're an elemental witch. You belong here, whether you know it or not.'

'Elemental witch? Like fire, earth, wind, and water?' I almost whisper. The fact that I possess magic is truly petrifying, but elemental magic is something I could try. I've always been a stickler for nature.

'Eh, your water's a bit weak, but earth, wind, and fire are quite strong. Fascinating, right?' Ailis says, almost rolling her eyes.

'Oh, you have no idea.' My back falls against the backrest of the chair, and I'm grinning. I'm grinning, and I'm happy.

Today, I found out I have powers. Preternatural and unbelievable. Magic—a truly absurd but breathtaking concept. I laugh and stare up at the ceiling, hoping it will open up and I can gaze at the sky, watching the stratus clouds pass by, welcoming me to the Merrycks—Home of Magic.

'Here at Merrycks, we will teach you how to harness your powers and fully control them to prevent imbalances in the future. I know you might be scared of giving up your past life to train here, but it'll be worth it. You'll be a new Jessica Harrington. An elemental witch. And Heather, I, and all the other children here will help you achieve that, alright?' Ailis's facial expression changes from casual and enthusiastic to kind, tender, and genuinely sweet.

A new Jessica Harrington. I marvel at the thought, but is it what I really want? I'm casting away my life as a Lady and succumbing to a forest for magic. Even if I went back to Marilyn, I'd be chained up and left to die on the cold, leaf-covered ground of the crumbling prison building. And there's no use crying about Esther's demise now. I love her, and she loves me. We'll be together forever in my memories. The gratifying silence of my thoughts fades as Ailis speaks.

'You'll be assigned a cabin, which you'll share with two other girls of similar powers. Training begins at seven every second day. Other days are for you to exercise your own powers freely and find out who you are in this world by yourself. We encourage self-discovery, skill-based education, free thinking, and safe but creative use of magic. Now, let us delve into your questions, shall we?'

I have a mind bursting with questions and worries. She can't possibly think that her monologue solves them all. Or is it me who is addressing this matter more seriously than it should be? Nevertheless, I remark with assertive optimism.

'None, actually.'

In answer to my confidence, Ailis says, 'Good, good, very good. Also, Jessica, you need not worry at all. We are all here for you. You just need to trust us.'

I'm intrigued by this. 'Who said I was worrying?'

'It's all written on your face.' Is it?

After a few seconds of staying silent, I ask another question that has been scorching inside me, like a hot, blazing sun on an already unbearable summer afternoon.

'Would you— is it possible for you to explain what happened that night, the night that creature attacked my sister?'

Ailis sighs and smiles at me. I can sense the massive ocean of pity she feels for me, drowning me whole. She replies, 'According to my knowledge, I suspect a witch or magician transformed themselves into that thing and went after her. Lady Esther had been introducing several bills in the House to complement her reign before she would assume the title of marchioness. These reforms could very well have been resented by others, especially those far from Marilyn, who haven't spent enough time with the Lords there.'

'So, you're saying that someone in Abandoned Haeems did it?' That really narrows down the options for the murderer.

'I'm not saying anything. All I want to say is that this could be the reason your magic unlocked and how you were able to fight the magical creature and cast it away.' Ailis assumes a serious expression, different from her usual nonchalant countenance.

I'm dissatisfied with this response. It answers none of my doubts. But I know she is not going to help me further unless it's about magic lessons. I thank her and gesture for Heather to lead me out of the cabin. She takes me along a pine-needle-filled path, which I think leads to the place I'll be staying—another prison cell. The only difference is that I hopefully won't be executed in this one. My new roommates can't condemn me for anything yet.

Memories of slow walks with Esther strike me. Leisurely strolls in the gardens of Marilyn Manor, Keira, and Heather right behind us. How we'd traverse through the snow, breathing in deeply, filling our lungs to the very top with the wintry air. How we'd sit in the gardens, and she'd create the most breathtaking flower crowns out of chrysanthemums and carnations. How I'd share every single scrap of gossip, each pain of growing up, and every lesson with unbearable, vexatious Gwendolyn with Esther. Heather would listen too, keenly.

Esther wasn't around much, so I made the most of my time with Heather. She's more than just a maid to me. She fills all the empty spaces where I feel a motherly figure is imperative.

We were closer when I was younger. We played games that involved me running around the entire Manor, hiding in the most shadowy nooks. I'd frighten her with a surprising yelp when she came near me, trying to find me. We'd laugh it out in the end, giggling at the silliness of it. Though the cords binding Heather and me have frayed quite a bit, I'll try my best to tie us together once again.

We reach a clearing in the forest. The pines are more scattered, and sunlight penetrates through spaces between the tree leaves. Large, almond-coloured cabins are scattered everywhere, each with dried rose petals on the steps leading to the oak doors. Heather slows her pace and stops at a smaller cabin, enfolded by trees casting shadows on the dewy forest floor. It looks so homey, like the hunting sheds Father would have built. The winds blowing are chilly and carry a taste of rain, but they calm me further. The cobalt blue sky is adorned with stars, blinking their eyes at me, accepting my presence in the Merrycks.

With relaxed breaths, I calm the indignant fire steaming in my soul, craving explanations and longing to uncover the secrets the world is hiding from me.

'Do a pulling sort of action, like you're pulling the doorknob,' advises Heather as we ascend the steps to my cabin. I obey, awkwardly moving my fingers next to the doorknob as if I'm balling my fists for a fight. The door opens, surprisingly. I realise this is a spell and that I have performed magic. That's... thrilling.

Inside the room, three feathery beds are arranged in a line, covered in crimson velvet. Opposite the beds are three chests of drawers. Moving closer, I observe that the drawers are carved with intricate, albeit chapped, designs of fire and leaves. The suite I have back home could easily fit five replications of this detailed but inconsequential cabin. Yet, I'm bewitched by the peacefulness this little home exudes. Esther would have loved this and considered it more spacious than the mind-boggling, overwhelming, and maddening hustle and bustle of the rest of Frances.

There's no one else here apart from Heather and me. I guess the other girls are off gallivanting, discovering new things about themselves and their lively powers. I turn around to see if Heather is content with the pleasant, reposeful environment as well, but she's disappeared. The ordinary being I was a day ago has disappeared along with her.

I step warily towards the bed in the far corner of the room, where a Merrycks uniform is laid out for me. An untouched grape-coloured Victorian cape with lemon-yellow lining and beige boots. Thank God, no stockings. I can't bear the norms of society anymore.

I sink into the bed, wrapping myself in the satin blankets and stretching my legs under the duvet. I think I'll start classes tomorrow morning. Hopefully, my roommates will be kind enough to guide me. A gust of parched wind shuts the door, and the birds tunefully sing a melancholy rhythm.

Melancholy.

His whispers are melancholy.

I doze off, luckily no nightmares, and dream of his dashing, elated smile, the richness of the automobile that brought me here, and the unseeing eyes of my sister, her skin icy cold and her body lifeless. I was wrong; I'm not immune to nightmares. I jolt awake at a sound. It's not birdsong. The suspense and sadness the tune conveys equips me with enough knowledge about what—or who—I am about to deal with.

I climb out of the soft, heaven-like bed, and when my feet brush the surface of the wooden floorboards, piercing chills rush up my body. His whistles are so petrifying I want to cry, but I'll try not to be timid and face whatever is in these woods.

When I walk out of the cabin, I spot a trail of footsteps, presumably guiding me deeper into the forest. The pine trees rustle, and twigs point toward the destination that the mysterious footsteps lead to. The sun has set, and the sky is partially dark now, with faded constellations gazing down at me.

His affable expression is all I need to relax. It's a wonder how his whistles are filled with depression, yet he is so cheerful otherwise. He smiles at me like he's really known me forever.

I gather the courage to meet his eyes and accept him as a companion who will help me find out who I am in this world, especially now that I have this newfound magical power.

With a convivial show of my teeth, I say, 'Hiya, Jack.'

Chapter 8

'Good evening, Lady Harrington,' says Jack, happy to see me—or so I hope. Jack's raven hair is more unkempt than ever, and dark circles hang under his eyes, suggesting that he hasn't rested for quite a while now. He's wearing a white shirt with a ruffled front, an aged overcoat with loose threads, dark trousers from an old suit, and he's barefoot. Here is Jack Fynn, looking all dignified even in his time-worn clothing, and me, in a pristine, embroidered cream-coloured nightgown, still giving the impression of a tired, burnt-from-the-inside, timid little girl. I envy his ability to appear attractive even in an ungroomed state. Who said he was attractive? A playful voice inside me whispers.

'You call me "Lady" once again, and I'll address you as Mr. Fynn forever.' I laugh, and Jack chuckles, too.

'So, what brings you here, Jess?' Charles calls me that. I beg myself not to remember him now that I am miles away from home. He and Father have probably already sent out search parties for me, either to have me killed or to have me paraphrase my side of this ordeal.

'Magic, I suppose? Ailis told me I have elemental magic. What kind do you have?' Just then, another thought pops into my head. I haven't even considered whether Jack has magic too! How mindless of me! I've been thinking about him for so long and haven't even thought about the fact that Jack Fynn is a magician. *Why have I been thinking about him?* He's just too annoyingly secretive, that's all—or is that the reason?

'Ah, that's something we really don't need to know.' Jack looks down at his feet and toys with the mud between his toes.

'And why is that?' I hate myself for prying, but I'm curious about why he doesn't want to tell me what powers he has. Maybe it's because they don't work that well, but I'm not an expert on magic, so he could very well be hiding something more alluring from me.

Jack sighs and replies, rather unwillingly, 'I'm like a wild card. All sorts of magic. Elemental, creation, clairvoyance, divination, casting, entering minds or dreams—you name it, I have it. I don't like talking much about them, as people always have a cluster of questions I don't want to inspect.'

'Oh, I'm terribly sorry—'

'Don't be.' He gives one of his reassuring, simple smiles, and that's all we need to remove any form of discomfort or tension from this conversation. But the fellow feeling doesn't last long. As horribly awkward silence overshadows us, Jack does something immensely spellbinding. He closes his fists lightly, brushes his fingers with his thumb, and then opens his hand. A lily gently hovers above his palm, untouched by the horrors and cruelty of this world. He extends it out to me and chirps, in a faint voice, 'For you,' while his cheeks turn red. I swear I see him smirk. I take the lily and spin the stem, and the innocent, minuscule flower merrily twirls as well. I bite my lip to suppress my blush, with no luck, but I feel the urge to reply.

'Thank you, it's... it's lovely,' I stutter.

Jack resumes his confident, always-grinning countenance and puts his hands in his pockets. The cold wind plays with his inky locks of hair and brushes his eyelashes, making him look a bit scary, but I know he's kind. Utterly, painstakingly kind.

I tilt my head upwards and relish the night breeze, appreciating the stars showering streams of light on me and Jack, trapping us in this beautiful, cordial, friendly—yes, friendly—moment. A high-pitched, clamorous chime sounds, making me jump, and the hairs on the back of my neck stand on end.

'Don't worry, that's the dinner bell. I'll take you to the cottage where we all settle for mealtimes. They're serving roast chicken tonight. You're going to love it!' Jack assures me. *I think he notices my nightgown and realises my underdressed state. If he does, he doesn't say a thing. I'm still a Lady. I have a power he surely does not possess.*

We walk along a gravel path bordered by spindly pine trees, leading to a cottage covered in rose vines, with lanterns hanging from rusted hooks attached to the roof. We're only a few meters away, but I can still hear the ear-pinning din of the children's laughter as they thoroughly enjoy themselves. Magic must be exceedingly delightful indeed. Not only magic but also the freedom the children must experience here. While more than half of Frances assumes Merrycks to be an asylum for mentally challenged youngsters, it simply houses exceptional individuals, saving them from the rotten minds of the backward people and emboldening them to be who they truly are. They practise magic, live together, and live in peace.

As soon as Jack approaches the doorstep, the rickety door flings open, even though no wind or external force has grazed it.

'After you.' says Jack, courteously, like a gentleman. Well, he did attend Esther's birthday ball; he's expected to be genial and modest. I hitch up my nightgown a bit, sodden from the damp forest floor, and step over the threshold. Luckily, I'm wearing a warm, concealing cloak that makes me look appropriately dressed. It doesn't matter anyway—a few girls are in nightdresses as well, some are in the Merrycks' uniforms, and the boys are mostly clothed in white and black or purple jackets with sunny embroidery. They barely notice me, like I'm simply a pawn in the games some teenagers are playing in a corner, huddled up and muttering confidential words that I may never know.

Jack strides over to a group of chuckling boys seated at a table farthest from the one where Ailis Millerwood, Heather, and a few other adults are sitting. I'm a bit disappointed that he left me alone in this dining cabin, feeling out of place, like a fish out of water. I peer at an empty spot between two girls—one with tanned skin and ill-kept short hair, tall, achingly familiar. The other, smaller in height, has a nasty gash down her left arm, masked with a single piece of shredded cloth, though she doesn't care. The second I take a seat between them, a plate of clean-cut pieces of lip-smacking lemon chicken appears before me, along with a glass of water. Magic, of course.

I'm about to plunge my fork into the succulent food when the injured girl to my left speaks up. 'You're the new girl, aren't you?'

New girl. They already know me. They're judging the latest recruit either based on her attire or the way she comprehended the conjuring of chicken in front of her.

I force a flat smile and reply, 'Yes. Jessica. Jessica Harrington.'

'Honour Blackbell. A pleasure to meet you. Ailis informed us we'd be having a new roommate. This is Caitlyn." Honour beckons to the girl on my right, who is wolfing down her dinner, murdering the potatoes and tearing apart the chicken with her fork.

I look at her, and she looks at me. Realisation washes over me like a salty sea wave.

This girl is Caitlyn Howell-Davies. Caitlyn was a crew-hand on the Harrington Business Craft before she absconded from the docks one day, never to be seen or heard from again. A good friend of mine tutored me on how to throw a punch in secret lessons below the deck. Fierce and a force of nature, she was better at sailing than any of the experienced male captains. Always wore men's clothing—a flannel shirt with trousers, wide-brimmed hat with swan feathers. She's wearing the same outfit right now, a sleeveless violet overcoat hanging over her shoulders. Esther fancied her, and I would catch them together on the quarterdeck, stargazing or just having a stolen moment. Her disappearance affected us all, even Father, who didn't even bother to learn the female crew-hands' names, though they were limited in number.

I never dreamed she could have magic.

Caitlyn is so startled right now; I can sense the fear in her eyes. Maybe she thinks I'll chain her up and drag her by her hair back to Marilyn, or perhaps she fears I'll simply despise her for fading away from our family ship.

She puts her utensils down, wipes her hands on a towel, and nervously says, 'Lady Harrington.' The guilt in her brown eyes is clear.

'Miss Howell-Davies.' I hold my head high and confidently respond.

'Lady? Miss? The formality is annoying!' Honour interjects, slapping her knee and bursting into a fit of giggles.

'Jessica, listen to me, please. We'll sort this out later.' With her plea, she gets up, hands basking in the warmth of her pockets, and walks the path to the children's cabins.

'What was all that about?' asks Honour, eyes narrowed.

'I don't know,' I say, ashamed that I couldn't rekindle my friendship with Caitlyn and just scared her off. The truth is, I genuinely don't know.

People I know and love are turning out to be witches. A mysterious boy in the woods, who's been perplexing me for all eternity, is a master of magic. If the world keeps hiding secrets from me, how can I find out who I am?

After an hour of picking at my chicken, having completely lost my appetite, Honour airily waves her hands, and both of our hands are unstained from the food. She trots away from the cottage merrily, and I hitch up my nightgown skirts to keep pace with her. While Honour skips zealously towards our cabin, she waves her hands again. This time, she magicks creatures behind her: wisps, pixies with wings as diminutive as specks of dust, and dragonflies with colours so vivid that I want to reach out and take one. However, I'm unable to, as these breathtaking, peculiar creatures are just illusions. There one second, gone the next. This must be Honour's power—creation. I shudder to think what Caitlyn's might be, given she's always so untamed, dauntless, and radiant. Shouldn't magic be a reflection of one's being? Isn't that what Ailis implied during our conversation?

As I reach the door, I repeat the 'pulling action' Heather instructed me to do the first time I approached this cabin. A few tries later, the door unlocks, and upon entering the room, I find a meek Caitlyn, looking all forlorn, sitting cross-legged on her feather bed, profusely sweating with her head in her palms. I step across the room and sit heedfully beside her. I've never seen her like this before, even when we lost the mizzenmast of the Craft during an unforeseen thunderstorm. I remember her words then, still undisturbed and steadfast despite the unforgiving, monumental ocean waves. 'It's thunderstorms like these that let buds of sailors bloom into flowers.' But now, she's totally different. I think she senses the weight of my dark eyes resting on her as she whimpers in a rough accent.

'Jessica, I'm sorry, I really bloody mean it. One night, I was sailing Dying, my raggedy ship, when lightning struck the foremast, and it came careening downwards, almost crashing me. Just then, my hands shot up and produced some waves of water that uprighted the mast. I was shocked to death then, but I kept going. The other day, I experienced similar things. I could spin the wheel without physical contact and even control the waves during storms, allowing Dying to move seamlessly. I thought it was just the wind being funny. Then, one unnatural, godforsaken day, I was brought here and told I'd been given water magic. No chance had I to hand in my resignation from the Craft and no time to tell you or Esther. I'm so sorry, please—'

I sigh at her story and embrace her. 'You don't need to explain a thing.' I try to reassure her, but the words come out faint and unpersuasive.

'What a beautiful portrayal of a friendship I was unaware of,' Honour taunts, hands on her waist. Even with her short stature, Honour really does look threatening. I kiss Caitlyn on the cheek and stride to the drawer opposite my bed, pulling out an unblemished, woollen nightdress—so much softer and warmer than the ones back at the Manor or the heavily embellished one I'm wearing right now. It's probably because I have a high social status in Frances, and I'm expected to be modestly, decently, and elegantly dressed even when I'm sound asleep, and my suite door is bolted shut.

I go behind a changing screen and slip into the dreamlike, warm dress, undo my hair, and stockpile the various pins and clips in a small box placed in the centre of the drawer. I retire to my crimson velvet-adorned bed and collapse on it, face down. I've had quite a day, and I couldn't care less if Honour or Caitlyn decided to judge me. Abandoned Haeems is the one place where I don't think I will be reduced to the title of daughter of a Marquess. I want to be something more than that. Something powerful, like a witch—carefree and high-spirited like the wind or unrelenting like blazing fire.

As Honour puts out the candles illuminating our shared bedroom, she exuberantly says, 'First training day tomorrow. Excited?'

'Maybe?'

'They warned us you'd be too doubtful.'

Doubtful. Another ash, the flames of my soul are forced to dwindle too.

Chapter 9

I awaken to the sonorous notes of a sparrow perched on a pine tree just behind the frosted window that separates me from the woods. The time is 6 AM, as shown by a grandfather clock in an unsightly corner of our room, dirtied by soot from the adjacent fireplace. The sun has just started to rise, its light masking everything in its midst.

Usually, around this time, Heather would arrive at my suite, throw aside the drapes, and serve me a cup of steaming fragrant tea. The rest of the day would be spent being doted upon by servants, occasionally by Father, piano lessons, and hour-long rides into the city.

I have to remind myself I'm not in Marilyn anymore, and this cottage is not my Manor.

I'm going to train for my magic today! A cheerful voice in my head exclaims.

I move over to the washbasin and splash ice-cold water on my face. The droplets crawl down my forehead like blood trickling from a wound. That's when I notice Honour tending to her own injury. She removes the temporary bandage from her arm, revealing a filthy, creviced scab, which she picks at and doesn't stop until the blood flows in streams. I consider telling her to stop, but I think

Honour knows what she's doing as she wraps another cloth over her small arm and stops meddling with the injury.

I withdraw the pale white curtains, letting more morning light penetrate through the windows. I prop my elbows up on the windowsill and relish the sunlight, unlike Caitlyn and Honour, who are scurrying around the room, getting dressed. Caitlyn dons her men's clothing, and Honour wears a frock the colour of olives. Their hurried movements make me recall the busy environment in Frances that prevailed during Esther's birthday ball. Servants rushing around, clutching varieties of linen and tablecloths, cooks banging crockery in the kitchen, ladies-in-waiting touching up Esther's ball gown with ribbons and tulle.

What would she think of me now that I am a witch? Preposterous or extraordinary?

The tranquillity of my thoughts is disrupted by Caitlyn when she throws a dress at me. When I turn towards her, determined to catch it, the dress stops moving and simply levitates below my chest.

'Wow. You're so powerful that things start floating with mere head movement,' marvels Caitlyn, surely with a hint of sarcasm in her voice.

I'm a bit confused. 'What—how? I didn't even summon a spell or something like that. I thought you stopped it.'

Caitlyn sighs and shakes her head disappointedly. 'Dear Jessi, when will you understand?'

'When will I understand what?'

I deadpan, gazing at the pines, which are moving calmly, savouring the sunlight as I was just a few minutes ago. I envy them for always being so still and sure. The trees never hither-thither; they just *stay there,* poised and focused, knowing fully well that their life's goal is to thrive and help others thrive. Here I am, the idiot who doesn't know what to do half the time, let alone know her life's goals.

'Nothing. Just get dressed, we have to be at the training ground soon.'

I heed her words and grab the dress from its floating position in mid-air. I soften the creases in the fabric. It is a nondescript outdoor dress, dark grey, with a lace collar. An indigo-blue silk ribbon runs along the waistline. I slip behind the changing screen and put it on. It's ethereal and light on my slender frame. I step into the beige boots and pull on the Merrycks cape, left out for me on my bed yesterday. I walk across the bedroom to meet with a restless Honour and a patiently waiting Caitlyn, who are already standing next to the doorway. The door has long since been opened.

I know this because of the leaves and dust carried by the wind that collect near the threshold. I wonder if they will clean it up or leave it there.

The girls lead me along the millionth path I've seen during my time in this forest. This particular road is caked with withered leaves and occasional stones, not the usual gravel or pine needles. So many paths, but none of them lead back to the person I used to be.

Soon, we reach an expansive forest clearing, and I think this is the training ground, as there are three more girls and six boys, either stretching their arms and legs or gossiping about something frivolous someone even more frivolous did last night.

'Why are they stretching?'

My question is answered when a firm, grave-looking woman steps onto the ground, immediately instructing the kids to line up in a semicircle and start running.

God, I hate running. And we're supposed to do that under a flaming sun, in oven-like uniforms. Though the dusky outdoor dress is dainty and comfortable, the cloak will definitely have me baked and burned by the end of today—or possibly midway through the run.

I sigh and begin running, following Caitlyn, who's right in front of me. She's moving her arms energetically, and her elbows dig into my ribcage when I move slightly off course. I've earned three jabs so far. 'Caitlyn! Must you dig your elbows—' I hiss but am instantly cut off by the instructor, who glares at me even if I make the slightest whimper. She has a club in her hand, and a glance at that wretched, forbidden object has me running faster, relentlessly.

My aching body feels like nearly an hour has passed when the instructor orders us to stop and huddle up in the centre of the forest clearing. My heart is beating at a speed I have never witnessed before. My hands are about to fall on my knees when our instructor says, 'Averil, Caitlyn, Jessica, Ezra, and Theodore, I want you there.' She points to a spot I don't bother taking a mental note of because I'll just follow Caitlyn. 'Honour, Adrian, Ebony, Cadell, you'll practise flowers from scratch today.'

'But Priscilla! We did flowers last week! Can't we move on to wisps now? I'm fully capable of conjuring a lily,' Honour wails. I understand that Priscilla is the instructor's name and that here at Merrycks, we do not formally address the teachers, which makes me feel at peace. *I'm fed up with calling my governess, Gwendolyn, 'Miss' all the time, though she doesn't deserve it.*

Priscilla cocks her head to the side and sternly responds, 'You can verily produce a lily, but can you make a rose that doesn't wilt seconds after being created? Because that is what happened with you last week if I'm right.' Well, that was... rude. I'll settle on rude for now.

Honour just groans, rolls her eyes, laughs with Priscilla for a while, and then joins her group to create roses. Most of their roses stop at buds, a few burst open, and the petals begin to fall off. Other students get pricked by the thorns. They use similar hand motions to the one Jack used to make me that lily. Was that lily just a symbol of our newfound friendship, or was it something more? I don't have time to contemplate this question as Caitlyn grabs me by the arm so we can start practising our elemental magic.

Theodore, a boy still in his nightclothes, disgustingly meretricious and aggressive, introduces himself and says that he, too, has wind magic, like me. He shows simple finger movements that cause the wind to change its course and follow the commands he gives it. Apparently, if I move the index and middle fingers of my right hand in a circular motion above my left palm, the wind picks up shrivelled leaves from the ground and swirls for a bit, like a trivial version of a cyclone. Surprisingly, the magic works on the first try, and Theodore gives his 'nod-of-approval' and tells me that I am a natural at wind manipulation. I smile, and he demonstrates more elaborate spells that either stop all wind from blowing, leaving the rest of us choking for air, or make the wind play with the flowers that Honour and her group are creating. I picture myself producing a gust of wind, keeping a fresh rose afloat, drifting through the various trees, and landing on Jack's hand, open to receive my gift.

He would definitely grin at this gesture, and I would simply watch as he displays more of his flawless, ineffable, boundless magic. Then we would laugh, only to be interrupted by the boisterous, ear-splitting sounds of Honour's wails when I make her late for training or when Priscilla won't let her conjure anything more than a petal. Then I would chuckle alone, like I am now when Caitlyn nudges me and snaps me from my daydream about a dream-like boy.

She says we have to move on to water magic, and her face beams with delight. Water is the power she's well-trained in. I'm slightly on edge, as Ailis did say that my water magic is weak and needs work. But if I could control the wind on my first try, there's a chance water may be merciful towards me, too.

Caitlyn clasps her hands together, and when she pulls them apart, an ocean-blue, ample blob of water hovers between her palms. While my mouth remains agape, she says, 'Spread the water above the ground. First, concentrate on the water droplets, and then conduct your hands like you're throwing away papers from a desk out of anger.' I do as Caitlyn instructs, only to completely drench Theodore and the girl beside me. I almost cry as a surly Theodore shrieks and blurts out numerous horrible curses at me. I look down at my feet, ashamed for doing the spell wrong, and muster a timid 'sorry', but Theodore doesn't seem to hear me as Caitlyn begins her own list of horrible curses at him. 'You demented, tyrannical, embittered bastard, she's just learning! Don't you see how committed she is?'

Theodore just scoffs, probably because he's lost for words and can't think of a comeback to Caitlyn. And now I hate myself even more for showing weakness. Oh, I pray for the day when I won't feel so frail and spineless anymore. As I try not to snivel, Priscilla insipidly commands, 'Aight, kids, I want five rounds up and down the hill slope, till the first banner and back. Jogging, no running.' I don't know where the first banner is, but all I need to do is encourage my legs and follow Caitlyn's swift movements.

As we jog down the slope, sweat beads down my forehead like a flowing river. It's unfair that some of the girls are wearing trousers, and I am being baked in this ankle-length tea gown and thick cape. This is what Esther would call 'a test of a lady's character.' She can flee from trouble in a restrictive ball gown, or she can't.

you for when I abandon you again.'

full of sarcasm and smiles in that one statement he means as a joke to soothe me after my first .

here are more training sessions, please, I beg you,'

the break we have now. 30 minutes.'

ll I get to meet Jack and prepare myself mentally for the next class. It's a generous amount of time, as it was 7 o'clock when we were ordered to run. Caitlyn, and I walk out of the dining lodge, I bring meeting Jack in the library. The two look at each ment, bewildered, then look back at me and smirk.

Jessi gotten herself into, eh?' snickers Honour.

y would you say that?' I can vouch for Jack's

The guy isn't even that handsome!'

clap my hand over my mouth. *You fool, you had to*

...but not surprised,' says Caitlyn, who continues to e me to my left, a warm hand over my right shoulder. r course and shift to a path leading to a cottage made od and incredibly sooty windows, so much so that sure if there are any windows at all. If that's the der how people read. Upon opening the door, a bell vhen I look up, I see the bell is attached just above the ones in shops.

for?' I ask. This is clearly not a shop. Shelves and ooks and smudged, antique leather armchairs are

I bite my lips to stifle the pain my entire body feels, only to make my chapped lip bleed profusely. I can't stop and tend to my cut, as Theodore is right behind me, and who knows the consequences of not letting him complete his training in peace? He's at least cooled down by the water, so if he curses at me again, I will throw candles at his face and mar his pulchritude. Then Caitlyn can deal with him physically.

After five rounds, we assemble at our old spots on the training ground, but this time, Theodore heads to another group, replaced by Averil, a girl who claims to help me with my fire magic. I instantly like her, even though the spells she demonstrates are abstruse and confounding because she isn't rude and prickly like Theodore.

'To make a small fire without rubbing two sticks together, breathing is of paramount importance,' says Averil, and this baffles me. *I'm breathing right now; shouldn't flames surround me?* I almost laugh at this. 'You need to summon your fire magic, as this kind of magic is literally like a fireball resting inside your soul, craving for you to unlock it. Watch this.'

Averil closes her eyes and mutters something that I think is '*Sradag*'. I successfully finished a Scottish Gaelic course with Gwendolyn a month ago, and I know all the basics. *Sradag* means a spark, and that's exactly what Averil has created on the ground. It crackles and sizzles for only a few seconds before dwindling to a minuscule pile of ashes.

She eagerly looks at me, wide-eyed like a puppy dog, and says, 'Your turn. Be as creative as you can. The more unique, the better the fire.'

I take a deep breath, and my mind is desultory for a while, trying to think of something that could conjure a fire. At once, I remember my wind magic. It comes when I call it, and by waving my fingers towards twigs on the floor, they float on the wind and fall a short distance from my toes. Then, I imagine the twigs rubbing themselves against each other, and they do so. I am pleased and bewildered at the same time. Saffron sparks arise from the point the twigs intersect, and soon, that spark catches fire. The flames are small, but they burn persistently. I heave a sigh of relief as Averil is awestruck and congratulates my ingenious display of fire magic.

'That was prodigiously executed, Jessica.'

'Thanks very much.' *Maybe I do have a place here with the Merrycks. A future of being a witch.*

A distant bell rings, indicating breakfast. I'm sweating profusely, so I unbutton my cape and tie the sleeves around my waist. I feel lightheaded, but I don't want to make myself the focal point of anything here, so I wiggle my toes under my boots to prevent myself from fainting. Caitlyn and I start walking down the gravel path that leads to the dining cottage, and Honour joins us after quarrelling with Priscilla about the bouquet of roses she created, debating that she should be moved to a more advanced batch for magical creation. I wonder how powerful Honour must be to contradict a Merrycks instructor and demand more reckless, bombastic lessons in magic.

The three of us take our seats at a table in the packed lodge. I guess the others had to run, too, as they are devouring their food like animals. A plate of two baked tomatoes with smoked mozzarella, hard-boiled eggs, a hunk of bread dipped in honey, and strawberries appear before me. It's simple food but appetising.

I'm thrusting my fork into the tomatoes, inspecting the roasted film over the delectable layer of cheese, when I receive a cold

tap on my shoulder that se
When I turn my head to th
just Jack. For a moment, I t
grotesque monster who kill
blood-curdling, repugnant
glinting talons. He pushes a
makes me feel nauseous aga
ear and whispers, 'Meet me
the girls along.'

There's a library? Though I s
to meet me, I pray he doesn'
the strawberries on my plate.

'They'll show you the way,' r
and a disappointed look cross
table, and continue nibbling n

I pick at the remnants of the j
when I've finished. This is be
on with their breakfast, and i
cabin alone after what happe
show I put on for Averil. I just
cupped in my palms and stare
get bored easily, so I try to ma
that Honour is having with
about how she earned the gash
stammering little five-year-old
and flung herself over the child,
unoriginal and definitely fake t
rest of her group claps and chee
selflessness. Either they're blin

Caitlyn clears our plates, and
doesn't let me.

'Save that than

There's a rive
that I'm sure
training sessio

'Don't tell me
I cry.

'Just two afte

30 minutes is
and physicall
actually, seei
While Honou
up the topic o
other for a m

'What has de

'Nothing, w
goodness.

'I mean, Jack

'Yes, he is!'
say that?

'Disappointe
walk alongsi
We change o
of archaic w
you can't be
library, I wo
chimes, and
the door, lik

'What's that
shelves of

scattered around the disorderly room. Distinctly coloured candle wax stains the floorboards, and dust obscures every surface.

'To mark who goes in and out. The sound awakens the sparrow that nests in a pine near the library cottage, which keeps watch over the new arrivals and informs Ailis. It's rather silly, but a few months ago, some kids were caught here doing interesting things. You're too innocent, you wouldn't understand,' replies Honour nonchalantly. Oh, when the day comes that I am the one doing *interesting things* in the library, Honour will be very mistaken.

Caitlyn heads to an armchair, plops down with a loud thud, and then props her legs on a table, knocking down a stack of books. Since she looks blithe about picking them up, I stride across the room, the floorboards creaking under my feet, and return the dusty books to their stacked state of perfection. A black book, smeared with dry blood and detailed with golden patterns of swirls on the edges, catches my eye. I sweep my hand over the book, brushing off the dust that has caked itself over the dull surface. No title. Eyebrows furrowed, I sit down on the armchair next to Caitlyn and open it. No words run across the ochre pages, only splotches of blood that have browned over the years.

'Girls, take a look at this,' I say to an impassive Honour, who is leaning against the window, and an indolent Caitlyn, who is snoring in a library of all places. After flipping through the crusty pages with no luck, Honour groans and stands next to me, determined to put an end to my meek, useless research as I scour through nothing but blank pages. She takes the book in her lap, sits down on the floor, cracks her knuckles, and flips to the first page. She runs a finger from the left corner to the right as though crossing it out. But writing bubbles through the surface of the page.

Stunned, I ask, 'How'd you do that?'

'Witch', replies Honour, thoroughly pleased with herself.

'Aren't I one too?' I ask a question to no one in particular. It is more of a question to myself, one I don't want to answer. Let's leave all the work to Ailis, who can peacefully confuse herself while working out whether I am worthy enough to have magic or not.

'A terribly diffident and unamusing one, I'm afraid.'

Honour repeats the same action with other pages of the black book, revealing more and more mysterious texts. Incantations, drawings of ingredients for spells, places for prayer to mythological gods—all adorn the pages of this peculiar finding.

One particular, familiar name has me breaking Honour's swift and assured movement.

'Hecate!' I gasp and snatch the book from Honour. She shoots me an unnerving stare, clearly infuriated that I've stopped her from showing off her magic. I wonder what she will do to me, I think sarcastically. I flip back to the page where I saw Hecate's name. Ah, there it is. A poem titled 'Hecate's Vengeance.'

Despite my not calling Caitlyn, she rises from her armchair and joins Honour and me on the cold floor of the library. Her heroic figure has shrunk to a passive one. The colour drains from her face.

'I, um, what does this mean? The revenge of Hecate, the goddess herself? Why?' she manages to stutter.

'Well, it's a poem. Let's read it and find out.'

The text, in bold handwriting so red it reminds me of the blood splattered on the rest of the book, reads:

Who dares to be mightier than Her,

Shall meet the end of their path.

She'll kill, control, protect Her own,

Lest ye incur Her wrath.

Moons ago, there was one,

Who neglected Her superiority.

They were killed, controlled, defeated by Her own,

Their Child shall now suffer this destiny.

She swears her vengeance, cold and sharp,

Like the penetration of her eyes.

The Child of Frances shall breathe their last,

The Son of Hecate shall rise.

'The son of Hecate,' Caitlyn murmurs under her breath. The bell rings, signalling the end of our break.

It's then that I realise that Jack failed to meet me here today, even though he was the one who'd planned it and cajoled me with the graze of his finger behind my ear. How dare he have the temerity to entice me into meeting him for God knows what and not show up at all? He is exactly the kind of man Esther warned me to stay clear of. I will know better next time than to fall for the ploys of boys with playful, wide grins and mysterious whistles that really can pull you like ropes.

The three of us march out of the library in a straight line. I hope we aren't suspected of the baffling knowledge we unearthed. The poem hangs in my mind like a broken picture frame precariously balancing on a single, rusted nail. Even if I put the pieces of the picture together, it still won't make any sense. Lost in thought, I trip over the gravel path, and the last words of the text resonate in my mind:

She swears her vengeance, cold and sharp,

Like the penetration of her eyes.

The Child of Frances shall breathe their last,

The Son of Hecate shall rise.

Two things. One, half of the population of Frances is children, myself included; there is no specification as to who the Child of Frances is. Two, who is the son of Hecate, and what or who is he after?

I dust off the dirt on my tea gown and examine my limbs for any injury. None. Honour breaks away from Caitlyn and me as we near the forest clearing for the second training session.

'You're not coming with us?' I inquire.

'Different powers, remember?' replies Honour, and she conjures a chrysanthemum while walking away, which bursts into multitudinous, diminutive bougainvilleas. I feel slightly intimidated by her power and turn to the students, huddled in a cluster. An instructor steps onto the ground, looking so different and yet the same. Heather. Her alarmed eyes search for mine, but she relaxes her tense muscles once she finds me. I promise myself to train my best under her watchful gaze.

Heather comes with a crate of candles, levitating behind her. She whispers an incantation, and a candle flies to each of us. She then commands,

'Good day, loves. Today, I'll divide you into pairs. I want you to practise the breathing spell and rekindle and extinguish the candle flames.'

Heather starts allotting pairs, and I am so engrossed in my ghostly white, jasmine-scented candle that I miss who my partner is. After seconds of picking at my nails out of worry, as people have already begun their spells, a boy walks towards me, hands in his pockets. I don't need his familiar grin to tell me who he is.

Of course. Both Heather and the universe want me to partner up with Jack Fynn and practise magic with the boy who ghosted me today.

Something resembling a crackling, small, otherworldly fire glints in his eyes.

Should I stomp the sparks out?

Or should I let the flames engulf me whole?

Chapter 10

I don't know the breathing spell that Heather has instructed us to practise, so for now; I have to swallow my self-pride so that Jack can help me with the spell. I still haven't forgiven him for the library meeting, and I want him to feel ashamed. But I refuse to give him the satisfaction of a melodramatic reaction out of me, so I'll play nice for the sake of my magic.

Jack pulls out his candle from his pocket, with his cold hands and holds it out in front of me. I hold my candle at the same height as his and tilt my chin up slightly to show my boldness. It doesn't work as Jack doesn't acknowledge it and says, 'So, the breathing spell. Breathe in, the candle flame extinguishes; breathe out, the flame rekindles. Understood?'

I despise him even more for not greeting me or anything, but I know I wouldn't have returned his salutation anyway.

'You know the spark spell? *Sradag?*' he asks.

'Yes', I reply confidently and begin to demonstrate the spell that should produce a simple but unrelenting spark of fire.

'Sradag', I mutter, and a bright orange flame glows and sizzles on the wick. I follow Jack's earlier instructions and breathe in. This mere action temporarily puts out my candle. Without warning,

Jack takes a gentle grip on my hand, almost frightening me and making me drop my candle. He breathes out, causing the candle wick to catch fire again. The fire grows bigger now, stubborn and resistant to the whipping wind.

'How did that happen? I didn't do anything,' I ask, a grin forming on my lips.

'Touch is a way to connect magic without any regretful consequences. I touched your hand and created a passage for both our magic to travel through and meet. That resulted in a greater fire,' reveals Jack, who then proceeds to light and extinguish his own candle. The light of the flame dances across his face, making him look a bit daunting, but I know he isn't.

He's just a boy who's perhaps magic himself. I don't know much about Jack Fynn, but my purpose is not to unravel the knots of the mystery of his existence in my life. My purpose is to find answers about myself and myself only. Answers about my own powers and why I possess them. Let this sound as solipsistic as it is.

Sometimes, I feel like my life is like a play—scripted, directed, and criticised just to please the audience. Sometimes I'm right. Other times, I'm definitely right. I am not just a girl with a fancy title, a grand manor, and thousands of servants trailing like insects behind me. I don't want anybody here to think of me like that, even though it's a common expression, 'It doesn't matter what others think.'

I want to be like my magic or something more. I want to set the world on fire but not let a single flame touch anything. I want the winds to be headstrong and blow thunderously yet still follow my plain commands. I want to be carried aloft on the wings of the breeze and go up, up, and up until I tower over everyone who ever thought of me as weak. I want to be frozen in time and relish the moment when I step on the earth, feel the woods envelop me, and make a home in them. A safe one—one I can come back to, should I have to run from all that haunts me and all the haunting ordeals yet to come. A heart filled to the brim with desires and a soul courageous enough to fulfil each one.

I stare down at my candle, still burning with the unabating flame. *If I could be like this fire, I would be content. Not happy, but content.*

All the emotions inside of me waned when I saw Esther die. I can't evade the grief for so long. Someday, I'll have to face it. And Esther will be watching from above, watching me crumble to bits and then to nothingness.

There are so many things I wish I could tell her, starting with Heather. It is remarkable how she turned from a maid in Marilyn to a witch in Abandoned Haeems. For how long has she known the Merrycks for? Has she secretly been slipping off to the woods at night, like how neophytes do in books, only for them to meet their doom later on? She kept this big of a secret from me, but it doesn't matter now anyway. What would she have told me? Lady Harrington, I'd be honoured to inform you that I am a certified witch and a daily practitioner of magic at the Merrycks Home for Witches and Magicians. Soon, very soon, you will deal with some peculiar experiences that will unlock your magic, and you will be escorted to a dark forest to train. This has all been orchestrated right under your nose without your nod of approval or consent.

I can't imagine Heather saying that, but the image of Ailis babbling a speech like that has me laughing. Then, I'd tell her about my elemental powers, of course. I can't even explain what I feel about my magic, let alone comprehend the fact that it is a part of me—always has been and always will be. It's mollifying and petrifying at the same time to be able to control the wind or make a fire with whispered words and frail hand gestures. If snapping your fingers could kill a person, imagine what clapping your hands in rage could do. Well, I do not want to imagine anything gruesome right now.

Thirdly, I'd illustrate Honour's stubborn habits, Caitlyn's fierce nature, and Jack's curious behaviour. Esther would be pleased to know that I am spending a considerable amount of time with the stranger I danced with on the night of her birthday ball. She would smirk and snicker and tease, and I would blanket my face in my skirts to hide the fact that I look like a living tomato and will look like a living tomato for the rest of my life, should Jack still be lurking in the deserted, secret passageways of my mind.

If I told her she deserved magic more than me, she would slap me and argue that I am the rightful owner of my powers and nothing can come between me and my path of magical enhancement. She'd be supportive. Kind and warm.

'Jessica?' Jack calls out my name, and I realise that he is standing right in front of me, looking at me while I'm gazing somewhere beyond, twirling the burning candle in my hand and being so overcome by thoughts of Esther. He waves a hand to bring me back to reality, and a disgusted expression crosses my face. I am genuinely confused by what he is attempting. Ah, recollection hits me. I'm supposed to be practising the breathing spell, not ruminating so deeply about things I'd tell my dead sister.

'Oh, I'm sorry, I'm a bit lost in thought-' I mutter, but then he cuts me off.

'Yes, I figured that out. The bell rang a few minutes back. Your next class is some emotional thing, a sort of therapy, I'd say.'

He looks nervous and scratches the back of his neck. I notice that everyone else has left the training ground and Jack and I are the only ones standing here, waiting for nothing.

'Well, I'll lead you to the class then,' he says and takes me to a cabin that I recognise. Wilting black roses and withered leaves adorn the footsteps. Behind the dirt-encrusted windows sits a woman with a neat black bun and serious eyes waiting for me.

'Jack, please, I'm too tired to deal with her,' I implore, but he seems ignorant of my pleas. With a flick of his wrist, the door opens, and inside the cabin, Ailis Millerwood stretches her muscles while relaxing in her armchair. A portrait floats gently next to her. My mouth drops open. What? Bad thoughts plague my mind. I clap my hand over my mouth to stop myself from screaming. My knees fall to the floor when I see the figure inside the portrait smile. Jack just stands behind me, one hand over the other and head bowed slightly.

I dare not look up because the painting next to Ailis is not of a headstrong, self-oriented Ailis. The portrait is of my mother, the exact same one in Marilyn Manor. This beautiful painting could be the source of a thousand secrets, questions, arguments, crying jags, and so much more. My mother died when I was five, and there is not much to remember her by other than summer outings, coffee-stained photographs, and Father's recollections of her. And now, the ghost of my mother is here to haunt me. First Esther, then Heather, then my mother. The three people I love most in the world cannot be spared from the peculiarities of this world. *Am I that cursed?*

I hate Ailis even more now. She promised that she would tell me everything there was to know about my magic when I first met her. I was wrong. She hid a secret from me then, and I am sure she is hiding a chest full of secrets right now as well. Can she have the audacity to look at me in such a discerning way when she can't summarise the story of my life?

'Take a seat, please, Jessica,' says Ailis, her tone void of emotion, anger, or pity.

My jaw clenches. I want to cut her open with a knife and see how well the blood flows out. I can't do that, so instead, my rage makes books fall, and the curtains whip back and forth. When she seems unfazed, I realise that anger won't help at all. I won't sit down on the chair belonging to this traitor, so I'll stand and receive answers from her, no matter how long it takes.

'Interested in knowing something more about the Harringtons?' Ailis chuckles wryly. Something more? I'm getting facts about my own family in bits and pieces?

'What do you want from me?' I say impertinently.

'Oh love, I want nothing from you. I just thought that you'd want to know that the Marchioness of Frances once trained with us, too, and that you're following her footsteps.'

This. This is the answer to the question I asked her before: Why am I magical? And what response did she give me then? 'Magic is your own power, the extraordinary things you do that others can't.' She could have just said that I inherited the power from my mother, but that would have aroused my curiosity and confusion by a greater amount.

'A great witch, so great, so potent, mentally and physically strong. The world loved her, the townsfolk for her politics, the Merrycks for her talent. We were never able to trace the exact reason for her death, but we believe a highly envious and begrudging magician killed her, probably out of drunkenness or malice. Another theory is that she was killed because of the newest reform she introduced, which allowed underprivileged women to vote too—'

'You know nothing about my mother,' I say, animosity and indignation flooding my veins, hot, slick, and fiery. She said my mother was a powerful witch. Well, Winifred Harrington's daughter is twice as powerful. With furious waves of my hands,

I throw ramshackle chairs and useless documents around the room, shattering glass, ripping paintings and curtains, and eventually tearing my cloak in frustration. I turn around to see what else I can mar with my blazing magic, but then I stumble the second I notice that Jack has been here the entire time. He remains calm and composed, like a lighthouse, while I am the raging, thunderous ocean waves, washing over everything as if it's all mine to soak. He looks at his shoes and fiddles with his fingernails. Sweat beads down his face, and the raven curls of his hair seem to stand on end, alarmed and shocked at what I just did.

I am abruptly embarrassed by my behaviour, but it is too late to apologise. Jack probably hates me now, and Ailis definitely does, but you can't blame me. Heather is a witch; I'm a witch, my dead mother is a witch. Witch, witch, witch. Esther should also have been a witch. Maybe she was, but she passed away before her magic could show. Father should also have been a magician, though he doesn't deserve it. The Harringtons. The Magical Marquesses. Wonderful.

A bell chimes, the only sound in the cabin amidst the silence prevailing amongst the three of us.

'Go to lunch, please. We will talk later,' instructs Ailis, and I am bound to obey. There's no telling what she can do to me now. Punish me, hang me, perhaps even take away my magic.

I stagger to the door sulkily, not even turning back to see if Jack is following me. The door closes quietly behind us, and we stand still on the rickety steps, the balmy afternoon sunlight bouncing off our shoulders. My eyes well with tears, and I felt like the wooden boards below me could collapse at any moment. The piercing knot of guilt twists further in me, cutting through and engraving itself in my soul. I don't want to cry in front of Jack, but I don't dare to meet his pitiful eyes full of sympathy.

He directs me to a bench, whose backrest is against Ailis's cabin. I'm lucky enough not to need to look at the furious woman inside the cabin, who is meticulously writing something down or sipping herbal tea from unwashed cups. She could kill me with a snap of her paper-white fingers. It's clear that her mammoth fury at my behaviour is mounting by the second, turning into hatred, later vindictiveness, and a desire to castigate me terribly.

I pathetically weep and sniffle, and Jack just looks somewhere deep into the forest, to a dark spot engulfed by pine trees, where there's no birdsong or peaceful rustling of leaves. I think about what that dark forested region could be home to—gut-wrenching screams begging to be rescued by brutish animals, the snapping of a twig echoing throughout the forest, whispers by knaves stealing children from their beds late at night, luring them into the depths of the abandoned woods.

Jack slaps his knee, a clear indication that he is vexed by my crying, and says, 'I'd love to show you my favourite part about this place.'

Oh. Oh God, he thinks I'm the kind of weakling that needs cheering up. Why am I like this? So feeble and irascible? I wipe the tears from my face briskly before Jack can try to hold a handkerchief near the streams of tears sluicing down my cheeks. I won't let him treat me like a child, but eagerness blooms like flowers above the sadness I've buried deep inside of me. I nod confidently so he can show me 'his favourite part about this place.' The only things I've liked so far about this place are the cheese-topped tomatoes and the poem. The poem! If there's one person who can decipher the meaning of the mysterious text, it's Jack, the master of all forms of magic, or at least that's what he told me he was. I need to know I can trust him first, and that feeling of trust should be mutual. One-sided relationships never end well.

We walk towards a small clearing, not big enough for a training ground, so I wonder where Jack's taking me. The pines are closer to each other and block out most of the sunlight. This area almost looks insipid, but then I lay my eyes on something inevitable. Oh my. My breath is taken away when I see a beautiful, black, grand piano in the middle of the forest clearing, shining in whatever little afternoon sunlight penetrates through the trees. Beside this beauty, multifarious string and brass instruments sit in their stands, among them a humongous cello waiting to be played. Blithe about what Jack has to say, I scamper to the piano and begin playing a swift, traditional piece that I'd play for Esther when she'd looked lugubrious after debates about pressing matters at the House of Lords. The piece would instantly cheer her up, and within seconds, she'd be tap dancing to the rhythm.

Jack snaps twice, and the other instruments are released from their stands. They hover in the air and play along with me. His favourite place in the forest is now filled with the euphonious sounds of the flutes and trumpets, the strings of the violin and cello, and the notes of my piano playing. If I were permitted to play this grand piano every day, I might just start liking it here.

The piece comes to an end, and the instruments enveloping me cease their playing, too. I brush my fingers over the piano, feeling every wooden key and the music that each one contributes to. Is my life like a piano? Black and white, with no shades of grey in between? If black represents darkness, then my sister's demise, my being pulled away from Marilyn, and being scared of God knows what—half the time—all come under it. If white represents the bright side, unearthing my powers from where they lay under the dirt and meeting, Jack are the positive things about being a part of the Merrycks. But is there a downside to my magic? A price I'll have to pay in the future?

I turn to see Jack, who is clapping his hands red, clearly pleased with my performance. I nearly pick at the threads of my grey dress as I breathe a thank you. I then ask him, while trying not to look him straight in the eye, 'Do you play? Any of these instruments?'

He sighs and picks up a violin, readying himself. He plays a sweet tune, a minor one, but it still fills me with so much awe. Charles plays the violin as well, but the way Jack does makes me want to cry. I fold my hands neatly in my lap and close my eyes. My head gets lost in the music, literally. It feels like calm ocean waves lapping at my feet, damp dirt between my toes, hushed secrets in deserted hallways, promises made late at night. There's a slight bit of tension in his violin playing; a piercing sensation of anxiety accompanies the tranquil, simple music. There's a twist in the piece now—sickeningly saccharine to melancholy and dark. Still, my mind is occupied with Jack's music and his music only.

The tension builds up and then dissipates, and now hope and optimistic melodies resonate throughout the forest clearing. Even some of the songbirds join in on the tune. He ceases his playing, and I applaud him. He shakes his head and says, "Nah, you're far more talented than me."

I narrow my eyes and respond, "Jack, we're both talented at different things. Me at the piano, you at the violin. If I attempted to play the violin, I'd probably break all the strings."

'I'll teach you sometime, and if you break the strings, I'll mend them over and over again till you're fully equipped with the skills to play the violin,' grins Jack.

Why does he smile so much? And look at me—the grim, stolid, irascible girl who does nothing but get easily triggered all the time. I'm still trying to figure out who I am, and becoming a witch certainly didn't aid my search. The conversation between Jack and I pauses, and an awkward silence fills the air. I pick at a loose hangnail until it pulls free, and as the blood starts to flow, a small weight is lifted off my shoulders, although I have no idea why.

If I'm not scared of injuring myself and bleeding, I'm not as weak as I thought I was. That's a relaxing thought.

The second I walk into the dinner lodge, I'm pulled straight out. I stumble and groan, my legs completely sore from all the running in the morning. I'm taken to the training ground, where fireflies trapped in jars hang from branches, and trees are wrapped in red and black bunting. Tables draped with chequered red and white cloth carry mouthwatering food, such as an entire, lip-smacking, succulent chicken, vegetables of various kinds dipped in melted cheese, fillet, fried grains, and six differently coloured drinks. Fiddles, flutes, and accordions hover in the air, playing a tremendously jumpy traditional song. Besides the instruments, children and instructors dance to the rhythm in an unusual way—some tap dance, twist and turn with complicated hand gestures, and take minute steps while holding their skirts. But the stars stay still in the inky night sky. The only potent, unwavering source of light, giving hope to the Merrycks.

When I tilt my head up, breathe, and fill my lungs with the piercing night air, something else emerges from the sky, not the stars. Even in the blackness, the red of that something is so easily distinguishable. For a moment, I believe rose petals are falling from the clouds.

But roses aren't being showered down on this forest floor.

It's blood.

It is raining blood.

The blood streams down my face and doesn't stop flowing until it reaches my neck, like a river that never runs dry. It gets into my eyes and makes my vision blurry. I try to scream for help, but everyone around me seems ignorant of my plea. I'm silenced when thick, hot blood pours into my mouth, making it impossible to speak. I look up, and blood continues to rain from the clouds, pattering on my skin staining it as red as wine. I'm drenched to the bone in blood. Blood shimmers on the surface of my cloak, my fingernails are caked with it, and my mouth is so filled with it that I feel like I've shredded an animal with my teeth. I wipe my face, but my hand comes back all red.

Soon, I find myself trembling. It's like I've committed a sin, and I can't wash myself clean. The blood on my hands scares me to death.

I'm so in tears that I don't realise Caitlyn has grasped me by the shoulders and is in a frenzy, trying to shake me back to reality.

'What on earth is wrong with you? You're looking as pale as a damned ghost!' she shouts. The look of concern on her face is genuine, her eyebrows furrowed and grimacing terribly. I look at my hands. Not a spot of blood on them, but they're shuddering. I wipe a hand across my face, and this time, it comes back clean, not at all bloody or sweaty. *How can this be? A second ago, it was raining blood.*

I look up at the sky and see no grey rain clouds drifting by, only stars staring down at me, probably wondering what the heck I was shrieking about. No one else is bloodied, and the ground is only mud and green grass, not a single trace of rain or blood. *So, was I dreaming?*

'No, nothing. It's fine, I'm fine,' I respond, confused and quivering like I could burst at any moment.

'Ah, don't worry. First day today, so I reckon it's the nerves. Anywho, this is our *Gathering*. A festival of sorts. A feast. Come along now, I'm dying to stuff that roasted barley salad in my mouth.'

Caitlyn grabs me by the arm and hurries me to a table where plates and plates of delectable-looking food sit. She coaxes me into eating a spoonful of pomegranate and tofu tart, a combination I wouldn't dare to try if Caitlyn wasn't with me. I almost spit the grossness of the tart out, but then down a glass of sparkling raspberry cider to mask the awful taste.

Cider contains alcohol. Do I care? No. Are there any elders here who care? Also no. Look at Heather. She's in a group of drunk women, bottles of champagne clasped in their hands and a flask of rum in hers. I've never seen her like this before—several hairs out of place, collar buttons half open, barefoot. Guess everyone is allowed a little fun in their lives.

I sit at a table where Caitlyn wolfs down fried barley and a chicken leg, and Averil, the girl from training, silently sips a miserable, single-flavoured tomato soup, unfazed by the obstreperous laughter and mania of everyone around us. Honour didn't join us, though; she's dancing in a group of girls with no boots on and boys with ruffled hair and shirts soaked with sweat. Among them is Jack, who is dancing and skipping with so much ebullience that he barely notices me staring at him while nervously picking at my food. But, as he turns around, waving his hands in the air, he does see me and gestures for me to join him. I, in my jittering state, mouth a 'No, thank you' and chuckle faintly. He nods sadly and returns to his dance. *I disappointed him, didn't I?* A lump rises in my throat, although I did nothing wrong and have no reason to feel ashamed or remorseful. It's just that I can't bear another person being disappointed in me, thinking I'm not worthy enough to spare time for.

I stand up from my rackety chair confidently but almost fall down because one of the legs is chipped and broken. So much for being confident. I take my cloak off and let the cold breezes caress my skin. It takes over a minute for me to find Jack in the crowd, but when I call out his name, he acknowledges me, and the corners of his lips turn up into a hearty, joyous smile, one I've seen innumerable times before, like it is a hidden part of him, just for me.

The song changes to an even cheerier, louder one than before, and bagpipes float out from a thicket of trees. People begin moving in a disorganised circle, fast, clapping to the rhythm. Some sing along, while others simply place their hands in their pockets and tap dance, briskly keeping the circle going. Everyone is so happy like all their worries have been forgotten, all because of the music, blinding lights, and food.

I wish I could be like that. Worriless and happy. *In another life,* an evil voice in my head snickers maliciously.

The euphoric dance continues, and my legs feel wobbly and unstable, like strawberry jelly. My fingers are wrinkled with sweat because of all the clapping. And that's when they start twitching again. No matter how I try to stifle it, my fingers are adamant. Unusual black smoke appears in spirals from my fingertips. I have to hide this from the partygoers. I don't want to be the centre of unwanted attention on my first day here.

I scamper into a thicket of trees until I'm well away from the festivities and collide headfirst with a person. I'm not sure if it's a person at all because I can't see their face in the darkness. It could be a massive, human-sized animal, too. One with pearly-white teeth, which have either been ruined after eating the food at the Gathering or from eating a Merryck alive. The latter option seems soothing. *What's wrong with me?*

I stumble back and grasp my forehead, pounding with pain. The black smoke stains my hands, making them look sooty and smudged. I consider rubbing my soiled hand over my face to haunt whomever I've collided with. I realise I don't want to do that, as the person's dreamy voice shatters the quiet.

'Terribly sorry, miss. Hope you're not hurt.'

Why is Jack everywhere? Eh, I'm starting to like him and his unexpected arrivals in my life.

'Don't worry, Jack. It's me, Jessica. And no, I'm not hurt. You?'

'Little collisions now and then with interesting people don't usually injure me.' Interesting people. Even in the low light, I can make out his fine features and a few new ones as well. His raven hair is as dishevelled as ever. A broken ring of alcohol circles his lips. The top buttons of his shirt are loose, leaving his collarbones exposed. Always smiling. *Smiling, smiling, smiling.*

'I didn't notice you stepping out of the dance,' I whisper, nervousness rising in my throat.

'Ah, my legs gave up, and I secretly slipped away to catch my breath. Fancy a walk?'

'Would love to, but I was just heading back to my cabin.' Heading back to my cabin? More like trying to stop my fingers from driving me insane.

'Allow me to walk you to your cabin then.' The offer is tempting, and I take it. We leisurely stroll toward the students' cabins, crunching pine needles and shrivelled leaves with our boots along the way. I try to rub off the soot on my hands but to no avail. The consequences of my own magic are here to stay. Permanent. Like the birthmark below the nail on my right thumb, black, in the shape of a very odd circle. This birthmark constantly got on my nerves when I was younger. Esther said that when I grew older, the mark would fade away, but it never did. It is the only permanent thing

I possess, something that I can remember when I'm in a hell-like situation. Knowing that the mark of who I am is still there.

The quieting flow of thoughts is rudely interrupted by the bloodcurdling cawing of crows, their razor-sharp beaks pointy as ever. I shriek and wave my hands around, trying to dismiss the horrendous, brutal, pernicious, hateful creatures that don't deserve to be called birds. Jack tries to steady me, but I'm so frantically jumping around like an idiot that I nearly slap him. I am half brought to my senses when he says, 'Easy now, Jess, seven crows here. They symbolise a secret, a mystery. Quite mystifying, don't ya think?'

What? I'm scared to death because of my encounter with the crows, who have flown away due to the dramatics I displayed, and Jack is concerned about what the crows symbolise. Well, the world is filled with arcane, hard-to-comprehend mortals. It is clearly not my fault I know a few.

We reach my cabin and stop at the steps that lead to the door. The sky is so lovely tonight, twinkling with diamond-like stars and wispy, feathery clouds. Moonlight lands on Jack's face and makes his freckles glow, making him look younger but yet so dignified. He smells so distinctly of alcohol, his Merryck's coat hanging off his shoulders. I left mine at the Gathering. Hopefully, there's a spare in the drawer; I'm drained and have no energy to go back and retrieve it. Also, I do not want to abandon Jack here, although I know he'd tag along to fetch the coat.

He exhales, mouth open, and a white puff of air hangs in front of his fine lips for a millisecond before dissipating. For a fleeting moment, I feel like he has leaned forward, but he hasn't. Jack is so tall he towers over me like he is the king on the chessboard, and I'm just the mere pawn. The two of us stand still, blankly staring into each other's eyes, neither daring to shift their body weight from one foot to the other. One misstep could shatter the fragility of this night.

'Speaking of secrets, Jessica, I think I—' He is unfortunately cut off by someone clearing their throat. I exhale and turn to find a tight-lipped Ailis, one hand in a pocket, the other clutching a lantern. I will hate her forever for ruining this moment. *What was this moment exactly?*

'Hmm, Harrington, tomorrow at seven, my office. I have an errand for you to run. Long story short, it is a part of your training. Further details will be provided at our meeting. Good night.'

With her instructions and brusque bidding of good night, she's off. I'll meet her if I can wake up on time, let the punishment for being late or failing to meet her be damned.

The thought of why I'm supposed to meet her in the morning nags me. I'm fidgety the entire night and stare at the ceiling till my eyes water. I look across the room at Honour and Caitlyn, who are literally snoring as I lie in bed, clueless, exhausted, and slightly on edge. Ailis could very well be informing me about the status of my punishment for my outburst in her office when I discovered that my mother was magical like me and that another intimidated magician killed her out of jealousy. What a nonsense theory. However, greed and power can do funny things to people, even those people who are always kind at heart and true to themselves.

When I finally do get sleep, I'm plagued with spine-chilling nightmares. In this particular horror, I'm bathing in a tub of blood. The soap bubbles are black, and smoke constantly emits from the bubbles in spirals. I choke on the smoke and cry for help. When the lady's maids arrive, they dress me in such a dainty white gown that I think this nightmare might turn into a peaceful dream. I'm proven wrong when a belt of daggers and guns is tied around my waist, and I see that needles and pins hang from the hem of the dress. I'm hurried out of the bath chambers and brought to the dining hall, where a bruised and beaten-up Charles Silasbury winces in pain on the floor, blood staining the carpet. When I embrace him, he is reduced to ashes, and despite my screams, I am pulled away from my old best friend, who is no longer in this dream.

In an unfamiliar, dingy room, I am forced to my knees, and my wrists and ankles are tied brutally with hard rope—the kind that bites into the skin and mercilessly leaves deep crevices that no anodyne can help. Someone takes a dagger from my belt and slits my throat in a neat circle. My head comes free from my neck, rolls across the room, and lands near the feet of a woman. She picks up my head, snaps twice, and I'm back in the tub full of blood. No black bubbles emitting smoke or knives digging into me. Just blood covering my whole body inside a bathtub. And it isn't even blood at all. It's water, with a myriad of rose petals giving it a red tint. Instantaneously, the creature that murdered my sister is inches away from my face, seconds away from eating me alive.

When I wake from my nightmare, my chest heaving and my fingers trembling under the covers, I find Honour by my bedside, a metal bowl of water in her hands and a cloth soaking in it.

'You've been burning with fever for over an hour. Do you know how hard it was to sneak water and cloth for you in the middle of the night?' she chirps.

I peer out of the window and wish the sun had risen so I wouldn't have to return to sleep. To my utter misery, it is pitch black outside. But, as long as Honour eagerly watches me like an owl while I whimper and shiver, sleep is an inevitable thing.

Honour places the cool, soaked cloth on my forehead, and I instantly feel relieved. Silence prevails between us, and neither of us is interested in deep, pleasant conversation. She whistles while darting her eyes around the room, snaps her fingers, and taps her toes on the floorboards, blithe about Caitlyn getting disturbed. Honour gets bored again, sighs, and gets up.

'If you need more tending to, wake me up.'

I open my mouth to beg her to stay, but she plops down on her own bed before I have a chance to say anything. I take a deep breath and shut my eyes, clutching the duvet tightly.

I consider thinking about Jack and imagine the curls of his tousled hair, glinting eyes, and tall stature. So far, so good.

Luck abandons me when he suddenly bursts into countless azure particles and completely disappears from my sight.

Leaving me all alone.

Chapter 11

Under the table, my right leg shakes uncontrollably, and my anxious eyes dart around the room. I'm obviously stressed. Not because I don't know what our meeting is about but because Ailis isn't even in her office at the scheduled time. I arrived well before the clock struck seven, and the archaic grandfather clock at the far end of her bedraggled room reads 7:07. I can't believe I made an effort to dress myself and slap myself into a state of consciousness, only for Ailis to be late. My roommates are still snoring their heads off, much to my displeasure, as they didn't need to drag themselves out of bed on a day free of training. The morning light isn't allowed to penetrate much through the uncleaned, rain-stained, murky windows, so I fix a used candle, with solidified wax clinging to the sides, into a candle holder and murmur, '*Sradag*'. The candle sparks to life. I blink at the flame, and though it provides only a meagre source of light, it still pleases me. The candle wavers completely when the door flies open, and Ailis waltzes in, a fresh cup of something I don't know in her hand. When she takes her seat in front of me, I realise the cup is of frothy, foamy coffee with cocoa beans tossed on the surface. She takes huge swigs and burns her tongue but doesn't react with a cry. Instead, she says, 'So, Miss Harrington. Remind me why we're here.'

This is why I find Ailis Millerwood vexatious. The woman didn't even inform me what I'm supposed to do for her and is literally asking why I am here. *Deep breaths,* I think. It's no use lamenting and losing control of myself for the third time since I've met her, so I reply, 'You had an errand for me—'

'Yes, that's right! To get your powers under control.' She takes a slight sip of her coffee, aware that huge swigs result in tongue burns, and continues, 'You're new to magic, and your magic is new to you. It's the same with all the others who've arrived recently. We send them on tasks, usually outside Abandoned Haeems, should they be above 15 years of age. These tasks are related to your powers. Today, in the late afternoon, you and the group you trained with yesterday will be going to the village fair in Walsh Vale to help raise money to keep Merryck's Home going. You kids will be representatives tonight, so you're expected to be well-behaved and follow precisely the instructions I give you. Each of you will have a stall or a tent where activities will take place. Averil is raising funds by being one of those entertainers who eats and plays with fire to amuse the common people. Then, Honour has beseeched me to allow her to utilise her creation skills and put on a show for the townsfolk. If she or any of you reveal your powers through your respective forms of entertainment, you can expect to be burnt, hanged, or chopped on a guillotine. But, as you see, you're using your powers in such a way that the folk think it's just those old illusions like card tricks. Now, what you need to do is ruminate on a way you can entertain the townspeople, raise money for the Merrycks, and keep your magic hidden. Questions? Keep it short.'

It is a bit obnoxious and selfish of Ailis, how she is ordering her own trainees to run around in the village outside the safety of the forest and raise funds for her own benefit. Can't she handle the accounting herself? Pitch her 'Merryck's Home for the Mentally Challenged' to investors in Aurelia. Had this actually been a mental hospital, I really don't think she'd be cajoling her patients into entertaining villagers to earn money for their own treatment. But this is not an asylum. It is a training camp, and Ailis is using us to her advantage. My chest swells with anger, but I keep these indignant thoughts to myself.

'First, there's a big fat chance that I'll be recognised at the fair,' I ask. *Let's see how she responds to that.*

Ailis grimaces. 'Oh, you have a list? This is Walsh Vale, of all places—'

'Yes, a place I've visited a fair amount of times. People will recognise me, and this carefully crafted errand of yours will burst asunder.'

'There's a spell to mask your true identity. "*Còmhdach*". Repeat it thrice, and no one apart from the Merrycks will know who you are.'

The next question makes me feel like I want to be spoon-fed all the time. But if I don't ask her this, I'll be staring at my cabin ceiling the entire day, blank and clueless.

'How should I use my magic at the fair?' Ailis looks at me, expressionless, like she is buzzing with ways to strangle me, pull my hair out, break my limbs, or slap me until red handprints cover my face. She lets out a disappointed sigh and says, 'That is for you to think about. You have the whole day to experiment and observe what others are doing at the fair. Come up with something creative but safe.' She pauses to examine some documents scattered hopelessly on her cluttered desk.

Without shifting her gaze from her work, she remarks, 'You may be dismissed now.'

Dissatisfied with her reply, I stagger to the door. *What the hell should I do at the fair? And even if I had an idea, how would I execute it? I have no supplies, no nothing. Only my elemental magic?*

How on God's Green Earth could the elements be useful in fun fair games? Other than fire eaters or those wooden water slides?

I consider sleeping the moment I step into my cabin. There's no use pacing the room and creating holes in the velvet carpet. Maybe some innovative idea will fly into my dreams. I hope I oversleep. No need to host a magical stall at the fair, then! But I'll be disappointing Ailis yet again. And if that happens, she might disown me from the Merrycks, and I'll be left to fend for myself in woods I'm undoubtedly not accustomed to.

The second I close my eyes, a pillow is thrown in my direction, smacking me right in the head. When I ignore it and turn around in bed, the blanket twisting and turning along with me, I earn another pillow to the head.

'Watch it!' I yell, jolting awake, examining the room to find out which girl had the courage to test my patience. Arms firm on her waist, her facial expression as furious as ever, and a slight smirk forming at the corners of her lips, Caitlyn stands at the foot of my bed, eyeing me up and down like I'm an antique at a museum.

I suddenly remember the inauguration ceremony of the Merlin State Museum of Natural History. Father, Lord Silasbury, and I cut the ribbon, inaugurating the museum. Charles and I walked through the hallways together, the walls reeking of fresh paint, and reached the section that contained different kinds of human skulls. Heather dragged us away from them, saying that there were far better things to explore than a decayed human head.

What the hell is he randomly doing in my mind all of a sudden? And that, too, an irrelevant memory of a museum inauguration with the Lords? They want me dead.

'Why do you look so lost all the time?' Caitlyn says with a groan, indicating she is greatly vexed by my random thoughts, as I am.

'I just have a lot to think about,' I say, pursing my lips.

'Well, it'll be far more beneficial for all of us if you think about what you're going to do at the fair.' She replies, her insolence overpowering her kindness. Never has she been this rude to me or to any friend she's ever known. Caitlyn has always been rough, stiff-necked, and slightly indignant, like a thunderstorm, but not towards friends.

I guess being with the Merrycks has only nurtured her flaming attitude more. I swallow all the rage and sadness I'm feeling, as being angry won't help at all in my situation, and reply with a heavy sigh, 'It's my second day here, and you think I can conjure up a tornado all by myself?'

'Most of us here are able to annihilate buildings with a snap within a week's time. If you don't hurry up and rack your brains, no one will think you're worthy of being here. Have fun being burnt alive when the townsfolk find out you're a witch. An awfully feeble one, I'm afraid.' She snaps and slams the door shut after stomping out of the room. How could she say all that? That's not the kind and affable crew hand I love and know. Knew.

Well, there goes our friendship.

I have two choices.

One, feel sorry for myself, wallow in my cocoon of self-pity, and eventually find myself on Ailis's list of troublemakers. Two, be productive. Think about a 'magical activity' for the village fair. And not just think. Do. I could practise the few spells I've learned and try to use them. Even though I only know the breathing spell and *Sradag*, something small is better than nothing at all.

Let's see. Elemental witch, am I? Fire, earth, wind, and water. I could do something with the wind, seeing as Averil has chosen fire. What could I do with the wind?

Spin the air? The spell Theodore showed me! *Argh, why Theodore?*

Anyways, what was it? Snapping? No. Something that involved both hands. Ah. Moving two fingers of my right hand in a circular motion above my left palm. I recall the gesture instantly, remembering how amazed I was when the spell worked on my first try. I stride outside, barefoot, wanting to feel the grass and mud under my feet and savour the moment.

My lungs are begging for fresh, cold air, and I breathe in quite deeply. Choosing a shady spot under a pine tree, I perform the spell, which, after a few agonising attempts, picks up a collection of lightweight stones and dried leaves. A miniature cyclone stares back at me, one that can't reduce buildings to rubble or steal innocent lives.

Spinning.

What activity involves spinning? A memory strikes me and brings me back to Esther's 13th birthday. Father arranged tickets to see that year's travelling circus, and as we went outside the theatre for the intermission, we came back in with huge fairy flosses the size of pineapples. I've always hated spun sugar, but I loved seeing the smile on Esther's face when she licked at the glossy, pink cloud on a stick. I could use this cyclone spell to create fairy floss at the fair and charge a pound each. I won't even need the costly machine—just a large bowl with sugar is enough, as my wind magic will do all the work. I'll only need someone to hold the stick when I carry out the spell, as both my hands won't be free.

I burst into Ailis's office without a second thought because making magical candy floss is the best I can think of.

'I need all the sacks of sugar you have, a heated bowl, sticks, and an assistant.' I demand after catching my breath, the run here having been arduous and excruciating.

I was barefoot. You can't blame me.

Ailis blinks at me for a few seconds, like she's still processing my words. Clicking her tongue, she asks, 'What are you planning to do, bake a wedding cake?'

'Spin sugar,' I give her a brusque reply.

Ailis shrugs and says, 'There's a notepad hung outside on the door. Whatever you want, write it down there. Now go and sleep. You'll need your rest for tonight.'

This excruciatingly annoying woman has a penchant for pausing right in the middle of giving instructions to do whatever she pleases at the cost of other people's time.

'3 o'clock, by the automobile.'

I'm standing next to the automobile that took me to Abandoned Haeems, and no one is here yet. I know I'm early, as I left well before the appointed time, hoping to be as far from Caitlyn as possible. Is avoiding her and showing her that I don't care the best option? Or will making peace with her and apologising help? I'm not brave enough to do either, so when the time is right, I guess we'll resume talking.

From the thicket of trees emerge Honour and Averil, as cheery as ever, some kids I recognise from training, some I don't, and... Caitlyn and Theodore? They couldn't stand each other, and now they're trotting down the hill towards the automobile, hauling a large steel bucket and a crate of wine-red apples. Honour has magicked long-taloned eagles to carry her crates. A brown-feathered eagle flies towards me and drops a crate at my feet. The contents of the crate disappoint me greatly.

Instead of a good supply of sugar, I've been given two meagre bags and a primitive cauldron and its stand for the bowl I requested. If I wasn't supposed to reveal my magic, why am I given a bloody cauldron in which witches brew? I peek into the bags and find that the sugar is green. That's an odd colour for fairy floss. At the bottom of the crate is a banner in carnival colours of striped red and white, with a pen tied to it. 'Ah, the placard for the name.'

What could I possibly name my stall? One look at the fairy floss, and you'll be emptying your pockets. No name or sign needed.

Witchy Floss. Green candy floss spun in a cauldron over a fire. Perfect.

Honour signals to me that it's time to make our way towards the fair. We trek down the forested hill until we reach the moorland. Then, it gets easier to walk as there aren't any more steep or slippery slopes. The moors give way to the cobblestone streets, and we arrive at the village of the Vale. Bunting and unlit lanterns are strung like washing lines between the houses, and the locals behind the shop doors are readying their crates with supplies for the fair. Bakers are bringing out pastries, sweets, and an assortment of cakes and arranging them on trestle tables. Trinket store owners are loading cardboard boxes with tiny wooden ships in bottles, toy bullock carts, and carved ducks, which are probably prizes for games. Seamstresses are setting up their best garments for display, from intricately tailored robes to feathered felt hats. I want to run a hand over the fine embroidery, but the rest of my group has already begun organising their stalls. Confused and slightly on edge, I look to Honour for answers.

'Darling, we're all doing entertainment-like shows and stuff, except Caitlyn and Theo, because I genuinely don't know what those two are up to.' 'Your candy floss station should be next to that baker fellow there.' She points to a man, inclined to be plump, who is multitasking by churning a purple batter of berries and cream and buttering croissants. Bet he could throw knives across his bedroom as a pastime and look after his family at the same time, too.

Before I approach the empty trestle table beside him, I recall the spell Ailis gave me to mask my identity. I whisper '*Còmhdach*' thrice and begin unpacking my crate. I write 'Witchy Floss' in bold letters and make swirly patterns at the letters y and s, like how Jack did at the Ball when he handsomely signed my dance card. I decide to set the cauldron first, but it weighs as heavy as a boulder that when I lose grip on it, it falls near my toes, and I squeal as a reflex.

'Need a hand?' A male voice says. Thinking it's the baker, I reply while hauling the cauldron again and wincing, 'I appreciate your concern, sir, but I am doing just fine here.' I put the sticks in a fancy jar and remember I am in need of an assistant for when I perform the floss spell. I haven't even tested it yet, whether the spell works with heated sugar or not, so my chances of triumph depend entirely on fate. But when I turn around after successfully setting down the sugar sacks on the table, the baker is busy tending to his croissants, and Jack is standing behind me, his usual smile spread across his face, hands in his trouser pockets.

It's like my thoughts have summoned him.

Chapter 12

'More than two, actually.' I joke meekly. 'Well, not only do I need an extra pair of hands for help, but I will also need a shoulder to cry on when this spell doesn't work.' I try to manage a smile to show Jack that I, too, am capable of being cheerful and worry-free all day, every day, like him.

'I'll give you my hands and the shoulder, but I won't have you crying over something so futile.' He says, lifting the cauldron and fitting it in its stand with only one hand, making it look so effortless. If I tried that daring stunt, the damned cauldron would land on my toes, and I'd end up in the hospital wing of the Merrycks Home if there is one. It's supposed to have one, or at least, that's what the senators and townspeople think.

I'll give you my hands. The former part of his words looms inside my head. I imagine us holding hands on a starry, wintry night, the heat of our skin providing the warmth we'll so desperately crave in the cold. Leisurely strolling through the pine trees, magicking little fires, controlling the wind, creating lilies and making them twirl merrily in the air, just like how we danced at the Ball. I wonder if he is imagining the exact same thing, too. *Learn to limit your thoughts, Jessica Harrington.* I bet he wants to say that because he isn't smiling at all while he pours a little sugar into the cauldron. Did Jack somehow read my mind and disagree with

their conditions improved, wages raised, and education provided. What has Mary Leigh been doing? Warming her seat? Because she certainly hasn't been looking after the welfare of these innocent, unfortunate souls. Marilyn has just lost their future Marchioness, and the girl next in line is learning magic in a forest, but if Esther were alive and saw this... ho ho ho, she would have been an ocean capable enough to bring a dam to bits of rock and clay.

I stifle the rage rising in my chest because if I burst here and mention my being a Lady, all is well and done. Jack looks like he is about to cry. I squeeze his hand and make a mental note to talk to him later about why he was on the verge of tears. Who wouldn't be? The state of these children could break the fiercest.

'Hi there, would you like Witchy Floss? Take how many ever you want, for I'm no dictator.' Jack greets playfully and even adds a rhyme. The girl giggles, but the boy stares into some far-off place only he knows about.

'Just one, please, sir. This is our first time trying it. Trying anything sweet at all. We don't get much at the workhouse.' The girl replies. I so desperately want to ask which workhouse she is employed at so I can register a complaint, but pestering her is the last thing I plan to do.

'How much for one? We have but a pound to spare.' says the girl while we create the candy floss. Jack almost falls when he hears this. Yet, he puts on a cheerful expression and exclaims, 'Tell you what, since you've never had it before, I'll make it ten pence for one big enough for two little sweethearts like yourselves.' He's—he's wonderful. I don't know any stall owner here who'd reduce the price to an amount that won't get you through a day just to see a child smile. The girl pulls out her money from her sooty pocket, and I see that the pound she has is pennies added up. *Not even proper pay.* I scoff and imagine chopping the workhouse master's head off.

Finishing the Witchy Floss with a dollop of hot caramel sauce on top, I hand it to the girl, who, in turn, presses a penny into my palm. The penny is rusted, but it doesn't matter because the boy takes a bite of the sugar cloud, and immediately, the corners of his lips turn up into a joyful smile. A sign of happiness that hasn't been felt in a long time. I ache terribly for these children, for if I were in their place, I'd definitely be dead. 'Enjoy the fair, and there's a magic show happening that I think you'll like very much!' I chirp as the twins skip through the cobblestone streets, hand in hand, getting out of our reach with every step. There's nothing I can do now to help them. I wish I was in my position again so some form of action could have been carried out. But, if I was in Marilyn and not here, how would I have come to know about their plight?

'You're so kind,' I say to Jack, tears forming in my eyes.

'You're awfully kind, too. You tore your dress for me.'

'I did what anyone could have done. You did the evitable.'

'I understood them. I'm a forest boy; it could have easily been me destroying my childhood at a poorhouse with no amenities at all.' This hits hard. Jack is from the village. I, from a rich family. I could never understand the folk as he does; no rides into Walsh Vale or regular scrutinies could help me. I feel so mortified.

'I wish, I wish I could do something.'

'Oh, my darl—.' *Just say it.*

'Oh, Jessica.' *And... he settles on that.*

He sighs and looks ahead, where customers are beginning to line up. I hand them the sweet and accept the payment, thinking that Jack is making more. But he isn't. He isn't even looking at the customers. Instead, he's staring at something beyond them or even beyond this realm.

What's wrong with him?

'She swears her vengeance, cold and sharp, like the penetration of her eyes.' He murmurs, his voice diffident and soft like he's walked through a ghost and is mentally scarred because of it.

'Jack? You're fine?' I ask, suddenly trembling myself. His face has gone pale, and his mouth is slightly agape. His limbs are unmoving and stiff.

'The child of Frances shall breathe their last. The son of Hecate shall rise.'

The poem. How does Jack know it? Oh, he knows a myriad of things and magic of all sorts, but the poem appeared on the page only when Honour made the book reveal its hidden texts. Has Jack done the same thing?

As swiftly as he entered into his trance, he drifts out of it. He looks at me, profound eagerness in his eyes, patiently waiting for me to spin the sugar in the cauldron. He looks completely unchanged. No shivers or stiffened limbs. No petrifying words pouring out of his mouth. Now, I'm the half-unconscious one, my nerves scrubbed raw by what just happened, fingers shaking and eyes watering. Jack puts a hand on my shoulder to soothe me, but in fact, I feel the opposite.

If Jack Fynn can get his hands on this mysterious poem I discovered just yesterday, erratically appear right behind me, and be a magician of tremendous powers, what else can he do?

Suddenly, I'm terrified of him.

Who or what is he?

Chapter 13

'Two cask ales, please,' Jack says to the keeper at the tavern. It's dark now, and our work at the fair is done, so we took a few pence from our earnings for ourselves. Jack assured me that Ailis always allows it. I've swallowed my suspicions about him and let myself breathe, filling my lungs to the top. No one has paid heed yet to who I am, and for that, I am grateful. Some time alone with Jack is what I need. To understand him outside of the Merrycks. Strengthen our friendship. Yes, friendship. Wary choice of words, alright?

'I'm underage,' I whisper to him. Realisation dawns on him that a 17-year-old cannot be exposed to alcohol. What I wouldn't give to down a flute of champagne without anyone noticing and act as if I'm permitted to swim in alcohol like a gambler in a card den.

He rubs his chin, either in nervousness or as a ploy to buy time while he thinks of an alternative. Since he is probably 18, there's nothing in between him and his journey into drunkenness.

'Really? I'll turn 19 in a while. Nevermind.' It flabbergasts me to know that he's older by two years. His freckles and tousled raven curls make him look so young, even dashing.

'A bottle of rum, then.' He tells the tavern keeper. The man who runs this drunkard-churning machine is as red-tinted as the baker beside our stall, save for the pencil moustache. Much merrier and jocund than him.

Jack places two gold sovereigns on the table that were definitely not a part of our takings. Another peculiarity to arouse my suspicion. A needle to poke me. But I know if I pick at this scab, I might lose him. Or worse, upset him and trap us both in fiddly silence forever.

He takes big swigs of his rum while we near Abandoned Haeems. The bottle is three-quarters empty when he asks me, 'Sip, uh, fancy?' I respectfully decline, as I have no interest in becoming a wobbly, mentally and physically disoriented, unstable drunk like he is now. But that's not his usual character. I mean, other times, he's decent. A voice in my head scoffs. *Yeah, Jess. Nineteen-year-olds are definitely decent. Well, you can't guarantee the sobriety of a boy that age.*

I hear people approaching from behind us. I make no effort to scurry away from them, whoever they are, because I have a bottle full of bitter rum that will burn even the strongest person's insides the second their lips touch the spicy liquid. But when I see Caitlyn trodding to my left from the corner of my eye, uneasiness weighs down on me. Dragging his feet behind her is Theodore. No questions asked, they join us on our walk.

What's my next move? Polite conversation? Brusque behaviour? I am at a loss as the two, both tired and affected by alcohol, begin squabbling when we're halfway up the hill. Forgetting my own skirmish with Caitlyn earlier, I intervene and half-drag, half-tug her away from a fuming Theodore. My efforts are in vain as Caitlyn wiggles free from my grasp and throws a punch straight at Theodore's forehead. He's about to retaliate when Jack grabs him and pulls him aside. Caitlyn looks like she wants to tear Theodore's eye out, so I cajole her into going back to our cabin. She gives him a long, painstaking glare and leaves him alone after that. I heave a sigh of relief, as I have no interest in watching and being a part of a fight between two drunk teenagers, with another drunk who is drinking more and more by the second and enjoying it.

Silence hangs heavily between Caitlyn and me. Neither of us sparks a normal conversation or begins to talk about what happened between us earlier. Her fists are clenched, and her muscles are tense, so I take a deep breath and pull her into an embrace. She doesn't flinch, thankfully, as I really do want to resolve our differences.

I can't have Caitlyn on the list of people I've lost.

'Forgive me, please.' She says so softly that it's almost like a hushed whisper.

'You have nothing to apologise for.' I remark while stroking her hair. She's far taller than me, so my arm begins to ache within seconds.

'I have to. Theodore was a complete arsehole and didn't contribute a little to our fair activity. He didn't take it seriously at all, and we came up with APPLE BOBBING OF ALL CARNIVAL GAMES! HE CAN ROT IN HELL FOR ALL I CARE!' She gets it all out and instantly looks relieved.

If I'm broken from the inside, she's equally broken as well. We were both at fault in our argument—Caitlyn with her bitter remarks, my not sensing the uncertainty nagging at her. However insolent she might've been at that time, it was my job to console her. If friendship is like fragile glass, it can break very easily, and those minute shattered pieces can pierce and cut wounds so deep. I'll repair the pieces with my own blood if that's what it takes to bring us back to a state of normalcy. Although we didn't speak for only a matter of hours, it is imperative that we bury the hatchet now before it escalates into something that has to be judged by the House of Lords.

I resume stroking her dark hair, bathed in moonlight, and she encompasses me back. I can give myself this: a small moment between two friends, one who absconded long ago, the other who recently ran away.

The distant hooting of an owl sends ripples of shivers all over my body. Although I know it's a nocturnal creature, I'm suddenly terrified of the forest. The leaves look like they've been smeared with ink, the ground looks like it has the tracks of a wild animal, and the clouds in the sky look ethereal, almost ghostly.

Then, in the distance, I see dots. Silver, to contrast the black of my surroundings. Dots. A myriad of dots. All in pairs.

In a split second, most of them turn into mist and disappear, but one pair is adamant. It refuses to move. Ringed by the silver dots are minute gold circles. Suddenly, the dots turn black but become silver again like a blink.

That's when I realise they are not dots at all.

Eyes.

I'm being watched. By something that is not from this earth. Not a branch of knowledge. Not a myth from a fairytale.

I find myself trembling. In the darkness, I try to reach out for Caitlyn's hand. Nothing. A wave of nausea ripples through me. My head spins with the knowledge of the terrifying truth.

If she's not here, then I'm all alone. And if I'm all alone…

No. I refuse to accept the possibility. I have magic. I'll fight it, like last time. Run. Just run. I heed the plain advice of a diffident voice in my head like a fool.

I traverse through the trees, which, in the shadows, look like monsters, and the branches resemble deathly elongated fingers. The weeds on the ground seem to grip at my ankles like the manacles in the prison building. The zephyrs in the air carry a taste of rain in them, but these fateful waters don't seem refreshing and tranquil.

Out of the blue, I feel a rough hand grasping at my shoulder. Surprisingly, I don't react with a scream. With every ounce of strength I can provide, I conjure a ball of fire and hurl it at whatever attacked me. I hear a burning sort of sound, and when I turn to uncover my attacker, I see a gigantic, bleeding hole in its stomach.

It has a stomach.

It has hands—crooked ones.

It has legs—distorted and more than required.

Headless.

My feet have gone numb. All the colour has drained from my face. I don't believe my eyes. I stopped trusting all my senses, in fact, when Esther died, when I unlocked my magic when I exercised it. But this is different. A feeling unmistakably unknown.

What did I do to deserve this? This punishment so heartless, this obstacle so dire?

I don't know the answer to that rhetorical question, but what I do know is that I am going to die. I'm serious.

As I'm speeding away from this grotesque creature, limbs trembling, forehead sweating, I trip on a cobblestone and fall flat on my face. Damp mud touches my lips, and the taste is horrid. I touch my stinging cheek, and my hand comes back shiny with brownish-red, sticky liquid. What a nice fall. What a nice night.

An ear-splitting screech tears through the night. Instinctively, I get to my feet and clamber through the forest, heedless of direction, unsure of my destination. I force my legs to carry me away from the merciless creature that is out tonight, hunting for me. I stumble upon a familiar path of withered leaves and flower petals and realise that it's the path to my cabin. Relieved, I continue on the path, careful to feel the crunch of the leaves so I don't veer off-course into the darkness.

Tired and panting, I halt and bend double when I'm just metres away from my cabin. I can see it in the distance, screaming to me to hide from the creature. Then, a thought pops into my head. *What if running away isn't the option?*

I instantly regret my choice, as the moment I turn around to face the monster, I'm greeted by an unpleasant sight. Its talons reach out for me, long, glinting, and pointed. Its legs kick dust into my face, and I start to choke on it. But one thing surprises me. Not the pure grotesqueness, but my ability to actually stand right there and not falter one bit. I'm not whimpering or trembling or begging my stars for favours. I'm facing it. I'm actually facing it.

The creature lunges forward and slashes its hands aimlessly in the air. I deflect and lose balance, but thankfully, I fall onto a patch of leaves, which diminishes the impact of the fall. I take my chance.

'*Sradag*!' Every morsel of willpower in my chest contributes when I ignite a handful of leaves and throw them at the attacker the moment they catch fire. Not even one leaf barely grazes the creature when it dwindles to ash like a mystical phoenix, and its entire being disappears. What?

First, it was a hand. Then, a malformed being. A whole new species of unnaturalness. Did I scare it away? I scoff at the idea. Even if I did, wouldn't it just retreat instead of turning to grey powder? I'm utterly perplexed right now.

Nauseated, I slowly get up from the forest floor and take wary steps towards the cabin, leaving the pile of dust and ash behind. My fingers freeze on the doorknob, and I swear my knuckles are so ashen white that I can see my finger bones. When I enter the room cautiously, overcome with the horror of what I just witnessed, I find a snoring Honour spread across her bed and Caitlyn standing in the centre of our room in her nightgown, arms crossed.

'Where have you been? She begins to chide.

Her eyebrows are furrowed, and she wears a grimacing expression on her face. *What the genuine...* How the hell does she get to rebuke me? She bloody abandoned me five minutes ago when I had that ordeal with that monster-come-phoenix. I should be the one asking that question.

'Where have I been?' I scoff, 'Fighting a monster all alone thanks to your wonderful accompaniment.' I snap. My soul begs me not to spark a fight with her, but the words come out of my mouth, uncontrolled and filled with venom.

Caitlyn tries to maintain her composure, unlike me, and responds, 'What mons—? Harrington, the last time I saw you, you were gallivanting with Jack without consent from Ailis across the entirety of the Abandoned. Have you taken leave of your senses?'

Is she playing some sort of joke with me?

'For your kind information, I was not gallivanting. It was work for the carnival, which I'm quite sure you had to prepare an activity for. Secondly, you completely deserted me and left me to fend for myself. I just dealt with an unnatural creature that burst into ashes before my very eyes. Forgive my petty soul if you think I've lost my mind!'

'Woman, you have lost your mind! I'm literally trying to explain to you how!'

'Oh, pray tell, the floor is all yours, madame. It's you who have taken leave of your senses by entirely forgetting that *you all* just participated in the Walsh Vale fair!'

'Jessica, there was no fair.'

Chapter 14

We stare at each other for so long that it feels like 10 minutes have passed. Agonisingly slow, long minutes that have passed at a speed slower than a snail's crawl. It takes me longer to process what Caitlyn has just revealed. What she has revealed justifies that I have gone mad.

First the blood rain on the night of the festival, then the entire carnival. Then, the monster. Then the monster reducing to ash without me praying or begging for anything to happen.

'Was the festival unreal, too? Was it my imagination?' I ask, trying to be assertive and firm, but the words come out as soft and broken as ever. She doesn't notice, but a tear strolls down my cheek.

'The Gathering was celebrated, I think, the day you arrived. But I'm telling you, there was no fair or carnival. Ailis isn't stupid to allow us to even step into the villages near us.' Caitlyn responds. Her answer doesn't pull me away from the cliffside of absolute fright and perplexity.

Shakily, we both plop down on my bed and begin to retrace the events that have happened to me so far, trying to differentiate between what's real and what's not. The latter is the hard part. I don't know what is real and what are just funny, sadistic tricks of my brain.

A part of me doesn't want to retrace our steps. Jack is there in almost everything that has happened to me. It's like my thoughts never fail to summon him. I couldn't begin to describe any of my moments with Jack to Caitlyn. Jack is my little secret. An ethereal, arcane secret just for me.

We're in the middle of a conversation about my life and death when Honour suddenly groans, 'Can you two stop moaning? I need my sleep, I had a row with Priscilla today!' Her whining is so high-pitched, like an alley cat, that I want to laugh, though I try to stifle my visible giggles.

'We're trying to sort out why Jessi's gone mad, alright? It's not like you're much of a help.' Caitlyn snaps.

'I'm not mad!' I squeak.

'Yeah, totally not head over heels for Jack, darling. It's evident.' Honour sniggers. The three of us burst into a fit of laughter. We're laughing so much that it feels like we're going to experience a coronary event soon. But it doesn't matter. We don't stop.

This is what I've always wanted. One room filled with friends who didn't care who I was, what I was, or where I came from. Friends who'd treat me plain and simple. Friends who wouldn't be consumed by the vexing, arduous thing called Politics. If Honour and Caitlyn are those friends, I'll be content for all eternity.

Although Esther was the older sister, only by a few years, there were certain things we could and could not do as Ladies. We had different governesses, different schedules, even at the age of five, and different interests. The time we had to talk dwindled as we grew older. Charles grew distant, too, quicker. My best friend in the whole wide world, with whom I undertook the daunting task of dance lessons, with whom I sauntered up to the heath whenever Father permitted us. I might have thought of him as more at some point, but I was grateful for the friendship we shared. And lo behold, he turned 19 and left me grieving in my shallows. Esther was always engulfed by paperwork, worthless men scurrying behind her with proposals, both formal and informal. It was like the two people I cared most about in the world were swept away by this ocean wave, leaving me abandoned and stranded on the shore. I don't know if that tide will come in again. I don't know if I'll want to be washed away as well.

My despondent thoughts are pounding in my mind, and I hardly notice that Honour and Caitlyn have been gawking at me.

When I look utterly dumbfounded and try to make sense of what's going on, they burst into laughter.

'See! I told you, it's true!' Honour tries to manage, slapping the bed and guffawing.

'Oh my god, she's like a walking strawberry, she knows he's there!' Caitlyn responds, equally convulsing with laughter.

I really cannot process what they are prattling about, but I turn around, and my heart starts racing.

Jack is standing in the doorway, a stack of dust-covered books in his hands and a coat hung from his right shoulder. Ah. It's my coat, the one I left at the Gathering. *But there are perhaps innumerable look-alikes with the same gold threading and dark purple hue. How can he be so sure that it is exactly mine?*

'Hiya Jess, here to return this to you. Don't worry, it was in safe hands, no damage done.' He sets the books down on the nearest desk, lets out a groan of relaxation, and hands me the fine fabric, covered in specks of dust and withered leaves but not a single thread loose.

'Boy, how are you absolutely positive that it's your sweetheart's?'

'My, my, Caitlyn, the guy sure knows the tiny details!' Honour snickers. Either she's a mind reader or just peculiarly engrossed in the insignificant pieces of information about my life. But what she said was partially inaccurate. *I am not his sweetheart.* He probably fancies some forest girl who isn't irascible and knows how to handle every wayward thing that's happened in her life.

'And I thought Silasbury was the ambitious one!' Caitlyn sniggers, and I'm baffled. *What are these two girls talking about? He was my friend. That was it. Her ability to assume outlandish ideas is beyond my comprehension.*

'You mean the Lord?' asks Jack.

'Look who's jealous!' snorts Honour, and Caitlyn follows. Both are in a laughing mess. They're slapping their knees and bending double. I think it's all the rum, alcohol, wine, whiskey, and whatnot stored in the cabinets of the Dining Hall—definitely not under lock and key. I can't take it anymore. Let Jack think less of me. Scoff every time we cross each other in the woods.

'ENOUGH! STOP! SHUT UP, EVERYONE!' I bellow, and silence rushes in like a draught through an open window. My voice is alarmingly commanding. Honour is still grinning from ear to ear like her life depends on it. Caitlyn's giggles have died down, and Jack apprehensively looks at his shoes. I'm immediately mortified by how I dealt with the situation. Jack wouldn't have screamed. He'd have joined in the fun. How do I know? Because that is who he is. Unruffled and mirthful. Warm like a hearth. Familiar like an old photograph. But I am not him.

I think that is what makes me like him so much.

A light-hearted spirit to balance a heavy-hearted one.

I peer at the books Jack brought. One with torn pages, one with a velvety spine, one the size of a pocket dictionary, one as grand as a palace. I wonder what his goals are in equipping us with an array of differently shaped books. 'Jack, what are those for?' I ask, pointing to them. He lifts them from the desk and spreads them out on the bed. We shift to accommodate the tomes. The books do not just vary in shape, but in content as well: *Caladh Buidseach, Sgàile agus Cnàimh, Bràithrean Teine.* I can vaguely make out the translations: Safety Rules for Witches, Shadows and Something, and Fire Brothers. I doubt that my translations are correct.

We aimlessly flip through the pages. Jack doesn't bother telling us the purpose of the books. He sits cross-legged on the bed, playfully whistling a cheery tune, his eyes darting around the cabin. If he wants us to make a discovery, it will surely be a troublesome process. While going through *Caladh Buidseach*, I catch a glimpse of illustrations that seem impressive at first glance, but when I take a moment to really study them, their gruesome secrets are laid bare. Pictures of witches being burnt in an accidental fire. There are clearly a few cruel men grinning in the background, pleased with their mischief. A witches' daily market selling curses, curdled blood, and crimson thread for dark magic. A cult of men obscured by a blanket of darkness, a tiny, almost unnoticeable orb of light illuminating their devilish faces. The man in the centre of the group cackles at me. Stares directly at me. I slam the book shut. I break into a cold sweat, and my entire body trembles with the newfound nightmares. I massage my temples, but the images don't seem to disappear. If one book could house such abominations, *what are my friends reading?* Caitlyn seems to be fine, monotonously turning the pages of the book about the fire brothers. Is it only me who is put on edge because of a few simple drawings? Though the illustrations were basic, with almost no intricate detailing, they still petrified me. It's funny how something so simple can have deep roots and take the form of something unfathomable. I wonder how lies work, then.

Honour, too, is unfazed by the elements of the book in her lap, *Sgàile agus Cnàimh*. She comes across a bygone technique of welding animal bone into the human body, and to my bitter misfortune, she fabricates the whole process, like a lecture by old governesses or long, insipid monologues by office-holders at the Lords. There was no need for me to know that a part of the host's body is cut off in order to accommodate the incoming flesh, blood, and bone. If the images weren't repugnant enough, I can loathe these remarkable magic spells, too.

'Ladies, allow me to tell you the real motive behind my bringing these tomes here,' speaks Jack, finally. Listening to an insipid monologue by Jack is far more preferable than staring at more sickening, head-spinning pictures. Though, I doubt whatever he says will be tedious. He knows how to make someone smile.

'Do enlighten us,' huffs Honour as she piles the books and hands them to Jack. He gestures for us to get off the bed so we stand at the edge, watching Jack do whatever he means to. He gets down on his knees and meticulously reorganises the books. Then, he flips to a page in each. The pages are blank. Blank. Like the book in the library, which contained that confounding poem none of us has dared to decipher yet.

Honour kneels down beside him and performs the same spell she did that day—the crossing-out action which makes writing arise to the surface. Caitlyn and I join them, and we read the texts inscribed. I know I shouldn't be startled, but surprise is the only emotion that reverberates inside of me.

'The poem,' Caitlyn whispers, her frightened eyes glued to the text. It overwhelms me to know that she is terrified as well. I always thought Caitlyn was stoic and bold, her relentless spirit undeterred by any challenge coming her way. She could navigate the most thunderous of seas, comprehend the most complicated of maps, and defeat the most rogue of pirates with a rusting cutlass. I guess even the greats have off nights.

The poem we discovered just a while back is everywhere. It's confounding. It's a work of literature, so it can be in many books, but books which have no relation to each other? One talks about mixing animal and human bones, and the other warns about men masked by darkness leading a petty cult. How can two contrasting entities have this in common?

I read the poems more carefully. Nothing different. All contain the same traces of mystery and a daunting threat that Hecate will shoot anyone who is better than her. For some ethereal reason, just reading them fills me with terror. The poems look more frightening, as though they are big rocks in the sea, threatening to fragment any ship sailing near them.

It is well past midnight, and I have been unfortunately introduced to a horror, one which few have the valour to face. I do care for poetry, but not when it becomes creepy and devoted to a goddess prayed to by some, feared by most. My body is aching and sore, and I've earned a considerable amount of bruises from all the falls tonight. I have faced enough monsters today. No returning to the battlefield.

Jack says, 'Technically, I was finishing off some holiday reading I planned while I was on break, and I came across this rather peculiar prophecy—'

'Prophecy?' 'Holiday reading?' Caitlyn and I ask in chorus, incredulously.

A stir of meekness ripples through Jack, and he sighs. 'Ailis is sending me on an errand that requires me to travel to Merlin. I'll be leaving first thing tomorrow morning. I wanted to catch up on reading but then stumbled upon this. I've been trying to research the poem for a while now. That is why I called you to the library that day to share my findings. But so far, my findings are fruitless.' He chuckles drily.

I want to ask, When will you come back? And why did you never show up in the library? but thinking that I will drift off-topic, I softly mutter an *oh*.

'Now answer the question, what prophecy?' prods Caitlyn.

'Look at the last two lines of the poem. "The Child of Frances shall breathe their last, and the son of Hecate shall rise." Someone in this district will meet their death at the hands of Hecate's son.' Jack remarks matter-of-factly.

'But who is that someone? And the son of Hecate? Only theology could give us the answer, but I doubt the library will have books on faith,' says Honour. 'Why not?' I ask.

'Books on faith maybe, but we aren't particularly followers of Hecate. We have always been taught that the goddess is primarily associated with evil. Worshipping her is not advised,' answers Caitlyn. What she says explains her uneasiness when Jack showed us the poem.

'Alright, you've enlightened us enough, Mr. Textbook,' fusses Honour, 'If you could move on now?' I start to get impatient, too, and pick at my nails because I want to get this over with. If Jack has revealed this to us so we can proceed with deciphering its secrets, the sooner done, the better. Although, a part of me itches to study them—not only because I want to finish it, but to grab hold of something material to do. An adventure of sorts.

'Oh, milady, move on with what?' he asks, cocking his head to the side. It's almost flirtatious, and I feel a pang of apprehension slice through me. Shush, I think. Focus on what is important. The decipherment. Comprehending the mysterious texts.

'How do we go about deciphering them?' I ask nervously.

'There's no need for that; the language is quite simple. Only the prophecy is important. Before that, everything is kinda fluff,' responds Jack.

We reread the texts. Again. And again. The poem rings like an earworm in my mind. It is like one of those evil voices at the back of one's head, prattling nonsense, brewing sadistic thoughts, cultivating an iniquitous mindset. The poem is evil, at least to me, no doubt about that. The line 'She will kill, control, protect Her own' gets on my nerves. Still, I am beginning to admire the Greek Goddess of Necromancy. Few women would have the spine to murder and manipulate for the safety of her own children. Her son.

What if the son didn't mean a biological child? She couldn't have had so many offspring. And she's a Goddess. Followers of God always look to Him as their Father. If prayer books and daily, unending church services have taught me one thing, it's that we are all God's children. I sound fervently devoted, don't I?

'Disciple. Children means disciple. There's no son of Hecate. It's disciple. The disciple of Hecate will kill the Child of Frances.' I say, stammering, trying to expound my point. I don't want to look like I'm mumbling rubbish, but the words come out slightly broken. Hopefully, they'll be able to fathom it, untangle the childish lisp of my words. I ache for them to understand my argument, praise it, and accept my views on this magical matter. I'm completely new to this forest, a witch plucked from the ranks of the Lords, a neophyte. And they've been here for so many, countless years that they could verily be immortal. They've been able to tame the flickering candlelight inside of them. Nothing can be more formidable than that. That makes them almost scary and intimidating. Their magic is their light.

I want mine to be my fire.

'With that logic, the child of Frances is also a disciple,' Caitlyn clicks her tongue.

'Now, who would be a disciple of this swamp?' Honour groans, irritation whipping in her voice.

'Marilyn is not a swamp!' I hiss. No one has the right to insult the city I belong to. *Some more evidence to prove you don't belong here. You're a Lady, attached to your land, a devout to the House of Harrington. Or was. My position in the State is entirely up to the Lords now. Have they forgotten to send the search parties? Am I really a matter of importance anymore?*

'A politician,' remarks Jack contemplatively, joining his fingertips together.

'What?' Caitlyn, Honour, and I ask in sync. A politician, a zealot? Well, they are passionate about throwing chairs around in Parliament House and deeply believe in empty flattery. Fanatics, then, you could say. Lunatics, even better.

'So, you're suggesting a politician is buried in prayers to Hecate?' asks Honour incredulously.

'No, I'm saying that a politician is devoted to his country, his state. A politician can be a Child of Frances like a disciple is a child of Hecate, a senator a Child of Frances.' reasons Jack. He's so clever. How he brings valuable suggestions to the table and is always right. How prophecies, theology and practical magic pique his interest. How a smile always manages to flicker on that resplendent face.

'That narrows it down,' I say, my eyes widening, the hair on my arms raising as the weight of his words settles on me.

'To the Lords and Ladies.' adds Caitlyn.

To me.

Chapter 15

This newfound knowledge is a great deal more terrifying than the poem. The undeciphered prophecy was a verse of sorts that just left a profound impact on you. Now that we've unearthed the real meaning behind it... the truth scares me to death. The Child of Frances. I am the youngest to have a position... so I guess 'child' can be the title for me. Someone is out to get me. And not just an ordinary someone. The goddamn son of Hecate, whoever that is. What did I ever do to that family? I've only just begun to use my powers, so my crime cannot be related to magic.

The poem did allude to how the child of Frances is suffering the fate of his ancestors, how there was one who neglected Hecate's superiority and thus was subjected to her wrath. It prophesied that whoever follows them will die at the hands of the son of the Goddess.

I followed after my mother. Ailis apathetically informed me that Mother was magical too, a laudable and powerful witch. I supposedly inherited my own power from her. But my mother was not immoral. I may not have much to remember her by, but I'm positive she was a gracious woman and an admirable Marchioness. How could she have stripped Hecate of her dignity and sparked a sense of revenge in her?

This is getting illogical. How is my mother related to Hecate? If I'm the child of Frances, how did my sister die then? That sinful creature which killed Esther that night—was it hunting for me? What did she have to die for? What was written in my fate, for which Esther took the fall?

I can't contemplate any longer. More questions will only aggravate my situation if I don't start searching for answers and proper explanations.

'This has taken quite a surprising turn,' Honour chuckles drily, trying to break the tension of the moment. Surprising turn? Illusions and monsters, figments of my imagination, hallucinations, unreal events, thought-provoking prophecies, daunting poems. I can't grasp anything that's going on, and life has taken a surprising turn. It takes everything in me not to burst out screeching. *Deep breaths. In and out. It will all be alright. I guess the spiritual mentors aren't correct after all. Breathing does not help.*

I want to get out of the cabin. Find out what Hecate wants. She's a Goddess, so there are definitely places dedicated to her, landmarks of worship. We could go there and research her history to see who in my ancestry wronged her. Finally, unearth the truth about Esther's death. Put an end to all this nonsense.

Go back home. The last desire is way far off. Will I even be allowed to return to Marilyn Manor? I was thrown in prison without a trial, so I'm already condemned for heresy. They think I killed my own sister, not knowing a monster was lurking around that night as well. If I'm even given the opportunity to step into Marilyn, I'm sure I'll be chained, hanged, or chopped by a guillotine. Even if I find out who killed Esther, they'll never have me back. And if the impossible happens and I am accepted, how will I live without my own sister? All the grief buried in the graveyard of my heart will return from the dead and haunt me. A ghost that no magic, no new people, no new memories will make go away. What new memories am I even contemplating? Picnics in the gardens with mum, strewing flower crowns, gossiping about Leigh and Duxubury and their secret relationship behind the walls. It is all gone. 17 years. Half of it was wasted on Politics and our individual duties as damned Ladies. If we did anything un-ladylike, you'd see both our faces stamped on the front page of the Times the very next morning. All we had were our walks, our conversations late at night, and occasional warm squeezes of the hand if one of us was anxious or on edge. At this point, I would commit murder to be ordinary, like a washerwoman of the village. Or even a servant in my household. A cobbler, a seamstress, a bird. A bird would be fun. Soaring high in the sky until a hunter shoots me. At least I'll be dead. I can meet Esther in the afterlife then. No. There's no possible way we will be together again, even after death. Hell is where I'm supposed to go.

Everyone senses my angst. I've broken into a cold sweat and started breathing heavily. A twitching sensation rolls over my fingers. They start drumming themselves against the cool sheet of the bed. I don't understand what is making me so anxious and apprehensive. We know the Children of Frances—my sister and I. And we know why Esther died. Well, not exactly why. She was 20, and I'm 17. I'm the child. I'm the witch. Esther was the heir of the estate; I was the heir of Mother's powers. If Esther is the real Child of Frances, whose life was ended by the son of Hecate because her ancestor—assumedly my mother—incurred the Goddess' wrath, then why am I alive and with powers? Shouldn't Hecate have me dead, too, so I don't go forward to make the same mistakes as the people in my past?

There is no end to this confusion.

I could pick my nails to injury trying to find an explanation. To my magic. To my sister's death. To why Hecate hates the Harringtons.

Did my mother really do something that sparked revenge in Hecate's eyes? And what do I have to give to extinguish that spark?

We know so much and yet nothing. I think that has me on edge. We know who the Children of Frances are, but we don't know who the son of Hecate is. We sort of know why Esther died, but we don't know why I'm still alive and what or who the murderer was. No one has any idea how the hell we are going about this hellish situation.

Caitlyn reaches forward to squeeze my arm. She wipes a fresh tear from my cheek. I didn't realise that I'd started to cry. I look so weak. Flinching would make me look pathetic. God, please.

The four of us sit in silence. The solemn kind of silence that prevails during mourning or when something deeply forbidden has happened to someone, and the others have just decided to leave that something unspoken. Jack breaks the silence and says, 'I think I know what to do next.' In a few slow words, he has grabbed the attention of the room. My head shoots up, my teary eyes glowing with the barest glimmer of hope. Sweet, smart, peaceful Jack. Of course, that beautiful brain of his has started untangling the mess we are picking at.

'Scour the crypts,' says Jack. 'They have stories of the gods carved into the walls. If you're lucky, you'll find accurate ones. Start your search from there.'

'And Fynn, how exactly are we to know what's accurate and what's folklore?' asks Caitlyn accusatorily.

'Whatever matches the poem is what you focus on. You might just find what you're looking for.'

Honour gets up and walks toward her wardrobe. She pulls out a dark woollen coat and wraps it around her shoulders. The three of us exchange confused glances. She throws us a narrow glance as though we are all idiots.

'Well, come on!' Honour squeaks, her exasperated arms waving violently in the air.

'Come on, where?' I ask. My head aches. I have neither the energy nor the excitement to travel to wherever Honour intends to take us.

A wicked grin flickers across her lips.

'Midnight clue hunt?'

'You're stepping on my foot.' A high-pitched voice squeals. It must be Honour. Darkness has filled the forest this late at night. Neither of us can see anything, so we're all relying on touch alone.

'No one told yah to stay so close to me. Not my fault you're afraid of the dark.' A raspy voice, like charred bricks on brick. Caitlyn.

'I'm afraid of the dark?' Honour asks incredulously. 'You're the ruddy one who sleeps with a stuffed toy in the shape of a fish.'

'Reminds me of home.' Caitlyn grins sarcastically. 'And if I sleep with a fish, what do you cuddle, your own magical creations?' She guffaws, and her laughter has me bursting into chuckles too. Honour magicks a rock and makes it hurtle toward Caitlyn. It hits her, but Caitlyn just grins viciously, clearly unhurt.

'A pebble! What a witch you are. Use common sense and pick one from the ground.'

Honour seems unfazed by Caitlyn's brashness. She cocks her head to the side, winks, and says, 'Would've missed my magical touch.'

A hole burns into Caitlyn's shirt where the rock had hit her. With a wave of her hand, Caitlyn creates water to wash the burn. She then sends water gushing toward Honour, drenching her but not washing off the devilish cackle on her face. I step back, warily and absolutely terrified by both of their powers.

'Stop fighting, both of you,' says Jack, trying to put an end to their nonsensical argument. His voice is as clear and sharp as a blade, piercing through the black of the night.

'I agree,' I manage, despite my trembling and surprise. They look at me like I'm a pathetic weakling.

'Fight? This is called fun,' says Caitlyn, looping an arm around my shoulder.

'Fun', I marvel at the thought. It's been a long time since I was allowed to succumb to gratification.

'Don't worry, you'll receive plenty now that Jack Fynn's in your life,' laughs Honour, pointing toward the sweet little boy to my left. I blush. Jack's face turns red, too, and a grin dances across his face. *He's probably just angry and laughing at the stupidity of what Honour said.*

'We have two walking strawberries, Caitlyn!'

'Time to empty our pockets!'

'A wedding is on the way!'

'What?' exclaims Jack, incredulously.

'Ignore them, I beg you,' I say. How mortifying can one night get?

'If the two of you have stopped fighting and are on good terms, shall we head to the crypt for our research?' I ask, sounding as firm as I am able.

'Jess, I best get going... I have Ailis's errand tomorrow morning.' Oh right. The smile has disappeared from his face. He looks almost solemn, stolid. *Goddammit.* Curse Honour and Caitlyn for mentioning a wedding.

'Safe travels, Ja—' He walks away, hands in his pockets, before I can even say that beautiful name of his.

Caitlyn claims she knows where the crypt is. She says it's beneath an abandoned church, hidden somewhere in the woods. A few supposedly religious girls had gone there to ask for blessings and came back with dust on their hands and ash on their faces. Caitlyn thinks they scoured the crypt that day. I pray that it belongs to Hecate.

We walk through the dark, almost daunting woods, carefully, noiselessly, not stepping on branches that will crunch with a loud snap. The silence destroys me. I don't like this. Caitlyn leads us. Honour trails behind me. We all walk in a slow, silent file, ready to face whatever awaits us in the catacombs.

And there we see it. A grey structure covered with green patches of either moss or vines. If it is moss, then it's growing at a deadly rate, spreading like a plague all over the walls. If it's vines, they need to do a better job of looking snake-like rather than bushy and grassy like moss. Whatever has made the church distinctly green, it is peculiar and deathly terrifying how we're able to spot it despite the dark sky practically falling down on us. Iridescent. In a different way, I suppose. An array of multiple shades of grey. The old church. Hopefully, of Hecate.

Hopefully, fingers crossed, this small building houses the secrets of my family, my bloodline, my future, my magic, and my own sister.

Of why she died, who was responsible, and why they did it. Why would they kill a Marchioness because of some past skirmish?

The three of us cautiously move closer. The church has two twin columns on either side, covered with velvety moss. Stone steps lead to the door, and bricks surround the structure, forming a sort of wall. What's the point of a wall behind the church and not protecting the front? Hooligans will attack from the back?

I'm the first one to ascend the steps. Honour peers behind Caitlyn, her eyes struck with panic to see if I've arrived at the threshold. Wow. The girl who technically planned this escapade has her whole valiant demeanour crashing down like the prison building. *God, you need to stop bringing that up.* Another thought instantly pops into my head. *If someone as effervescent and fearless as her can be reduced to a diffident child, what on earth will happen to a naturally shaken person like me?*

Breathing in deeply, filling my lungs with the wintery night air, I reach out for the doorknob. My hand drops. I try to feel for any handle or grooves on the stone door, but nothing. Then, my fingers brush against an uneven surface in the stone. I brush my thumb over it, and it dawns on me that it is a carving. Intricate. A symbol etched in stone.

'Girls, look at this,' I hiss, still keeping my fingers on the carved image.

'Look at what and how exactly?' complains Honour. This girl. Picturing an orb of fire, I conjure a minuscule one to give us light with my left hand. Didn't even need to use an incantation. Improvement.

I shine the light on the intricate symbol, hoping the girls will comprehend what it means and somehow get the door to open so we can scour the crypt. Caitlyn speaks up first, 'The better part of my brain tells me this is a bloodlock. I've seen loads of these during my time on Dying. They're usually used to seal treasure and keep it hidden. Pirates did that sort of stuff often.' Caitlyn bites her lip. A momentary wave of remorse rolls over her. She misses her old life. I wonder, in time, perhaps, will I too?

'A bloodlock,' I whisper slowly, letting the word fade on my lips, understanding its meaning. 'Is there a way to open it?'

'Easy. The blood of a successor has to be smeared on the lock to get the crypt open. Wrong blood, and we incur the wrath of the Gods. Earthquakes, dancing sheep, clocks that tell the time wrong. Fun things, really,' replies Caitlyn, with a laugh at the end. *Her sense of humour is scarily unique.*

'Blood of a successor? If the crypt is Hecate's, we need her offspring. We have the faintest idea of who her son is. Where do we get the blood from?' says Honour.

'What if…' I start.

'What if what?'

What if my blood works, too? I'm the Child of Frances, and my witch mother 'wronged' Hecate. Maybe, just maybe, my blood will open the lock?

I feel too foolish and small to tell them the specifics of my plan. I slash my finger against a sharp groove in the stone door. The blood starts to flow.

I press my finger on the lock. Caitlyn and Honour's eyes widen in disbelief at my rash actions. Then, a ring of fire encircles the symbol. In the light, we can see what the symbol etched in stone really is. A banyan tree, one cut open but still standing erect. The ring expands and consumes the door. We recoil, thinking that the holy place will catch fire and diminish to dust.

But, it is the fire that extinguishes, crawling back to the symbol from where it extended. The lock clicks open.

My mouth drops agape. Shivers crawl down my entire body. It seems as if new cool breezes have started to blow. Unsettling zephyrs.

'Does that mean you're Hecate's evil spawn?' asks Caitlyn.

'Hell no. It means we were right before.'

This is definitely the crypt of Hecate. My family is definitely associated with hers somehow.

And underneath this old church lies buried my family secrets.

Secrets of my magic.

Of my sister. Of my mother.

The truth of who I am.

Chapter 16

As the lock of the church door clicks open, a large slab of stone slides to the right, revealing a poorly lit hallway illuminated only by a candle stuck to the floor. Wax drips from the nondescript white candle, but when it reaches the ground, it disappears and doesn't solidify, as though it has evanesced into the ground itself. *Well, this is the crypt of Hecate, after all. Scattered shards of glass, crimson threads, and pyres are just the beginning.*

This time, Honour is the first one to move. I guess she's resumed her unwavering demeanour. Or maybe she's realised she can't be weak in front of us. Usually, friends are comfortable with being vulnerable around each other. Perhaps her ways are different. *Different like this deep, dark place that's reckoned to be holy...I would think otherwise.* Is this a sacrosanct church or a dingy cellar? Cellars are peaceful and house interesting things, like rum, archaic books, or forgotten family heirlooms. Churches are known to have an environment of repose. This particular church dedicated to Hecate is everything but tranquil.

Honour's high-pitched shriek breaks my chain of thought. Even in the darkness, it's clear that she's disappeared. *But where*?

'H-hole, d-don't step forward, Honour slipped down it,' Caitlyn speaks. Fear resounds in her confident voice. My mind races with horror at what she's just told me. There can't really be a hole in the middle of a church? I slide my foot to check if the floor really is floorless, and I almost go careening downwards. Caitlyn catches me in time.

'Is this the only way to—?' I gulp, eyes wide, body shivering and trembling, with the realisation that there's a hole and not a staircase leading to the underground crypt. That explains why the girls who came here left all soiled and sooty. *How did they climb out?*

'Want to sit and slide down or make a jump for it?'

'You decide.'

'Jump.'

'What if we land on Honour?'

'She deserves it.'

Abiding by Caitlyn's wish, we count backwards from three and jump into the hole. Never thought I'd be doing that in my entire life.

I feel like my stomach is galloping inside my body. Sliding down the steep slope, I scream, terrified, but next to me, Caitlyn guffaws cheerfully like she's been waiting for this moment. If I had the heart to move my hand, I would have punched the air out of her. Then again, there isn't really any space to breathe here, so any movement other than sliding down would aggravate our already distressing situation.

'Yes, we've landed on Honour!' squeals Caitlyn, excitedly, when we reach the end of the slide. My nerves rattle under my skin, and sweat streams down my forehead.

'What?' I exclaim incredulously, colour draining from my face.

'Might want to recheck the body you're currently lying on,' chuckles a voice, not too far from us. I've landed away from Caitlyn, thankfully. Honour emerges from the shadows of the crypt. Caitlyn shrieks, scrambles, and shoots up. My gaze drops down at the body she landed on.

She was lying on a corpse. One with blood seeping out from numerous places, and wretched stitches on the eyes. Instinctively, my head turns away to avoid the grotesque, unappealing sight.

'You evil boar,' scowls Caitlyn.

'You really think I'm that stupid?'

'I don't *think.*'

The corpse begins to ebb and gradually disappears, leaving no trace of blood behind. Honour had created it.

'Thank your stars, if you have any, that it was just a figment of my power. Could've easily dragged a real one here, alive too.'

'Joke's on you, I've been on top of loads of people before. You're the one missing out.'

'I don't indulge in petty pleasures, like you. Abandoned pirate. Not interested in time-wasting.'

'Cruel hag,' Caitlyn curses, brushing the dust off her nightgown.

'Heartless marauder,' Honour returns, malice laced in her tongue, her fist balled, ready to land a punch.

'You two really need to stop squabbling,' I rebuke, hands on my hips, attempting to look serious and dignified. Failing miserably because they don't seem to be listening to me, and are more concerned with folding out the creases in their dresses.

This time, they don't say it's fun.

A pair of ornate pillars come into view. As we move closer, I catch a glimpse of symbols, similar to the blood lock, carved into the pillars. The banyan tree split right down the middle, an ancient species of willow, the branches growing at odd angles, several pine trees, carved upside down. *I wonder what religious symbolism they indicate.*

There are actually four pillars, surrounding a *casket*. Wilting black roses and candles that give off a strong, rather unpleasant odour adorn the sides. Judging by the size of the casket, it seems as though it's occupied by a woman. *But shouldn't Hecate's tomb be more grandiose, bigger?*

This part of the crypt is lit, though—dimly, but more illuminated than the church entrance. The lamps throw light on writings inscribed on the walls. I warily take a step forward. Breathing in deeply, knowing all too well what's written on the wall, I turn to my left and move my hand over the fateful words.

The prophecy is written all over the crypt.

Another confirmation, convincing me that the story of my life really is etched in the stone of this church of Hecate. *Another slap in the face.* Shivers slice through my veins.

I wanted to know who I was, and if I belonged. *But not like this.*

A single tear rolls down my cheek, my heart burdened by unavoidable pathos.

I press the heels of my palms to my eyes, trying to suppress the tears. Caitlyn and Honour aren't in an amicable state of mind right now, so it's best that my crying remains a mystery to them.

'Why can't we just get a History book and find out who the son of Hecate is and end this painstaking ordeal?' I bellow, mustering all the pain, suffering, and fiery anger that has lived in my bones for so long. The torches get extinguished. There is no wind to make the dust particles stir, yet they dance in a whirlwind. A quiet sort of nostalgia touches me. *The strange, peculiar experiences.* For some strange, peculiar reason, it brings a smile to my face.

'We've gone over this before, Jessi… our kind considers her malevolent. And we're still not sure whether it's her real son who is the murderer, or a disciple,' says Caitlyn, attempting to soothe me, squeezing my hand, a pitiful spark in her eyes. *Pathetic, pathetic, pathetic. When will pity be the last thing on someone's mind when they think of Jessica Harrington?*

'Then why did we find the poem?' *Why was Jack curious about it, too?* Well, who wouldn't be curious about something arcane that disrupts your holiday reading?

'Your sister died rather abruptly.'

'Rather abruptly?' I bellow incredulously.

'You needed to know why and unravel your family history. The poem says that someone wronged Hecate and she killed her off. That person's child must suffer too. Now, we concluded that the child of Frances is…' She scratches the back of her neck. 'Well… you.' *That did not need to be said with such hesitance.* 'If your mother had a rift with Hecate, and her child must die too, it should have been you. But instead, your sister took the fall. Jessi, we found the poem because of this. To understand what forces are at play and who really is behind this.'

'Then how do we go about this? There's no possible way we can get that witch's son to reveal himself by flicking our fingers!' I storm. *Plaintive, piteous, pathetic.* Like a child. Asking too many questions, not getting a satisfactory response, and sending a wave of annoyance drenching everyone in the room.

'With time, I think everything will reveal itself.' Yeah, time. Just a few more days and the Army of Frances will be here, to burn the woods down and chain me in shackles. The dilapidated prison building will welcome me with open arms, and I'll be forced to collapse into it. Esther will never come back. We will never find her killer. Hecate's wrongdoings won't be stopped. My past, present, and future will remain a tangled ball of yarn that was never unspooled. Actually, the future is quite certain. Unequivocal execution.

What's the point of all this? Being infuriated and imagining tragedy won't help anyone.

My anger dies down because I know being indignant will only earn me some nice glances brimming with sympathy. I don't need pity, I need answers. Answers this godforsaken tomb cannot provide. A voice scoffs in my head. *And you thought you were going to get your family secrets, understand the truth about yourself.* Maybe I never will.

'What are we doing here then?' I ask, my voice breaking and quivering with every syllable.

'Midnight adventure?' laughs Honour as she loops an arm around my neck. Caitlyn's hand circles around my back. Three friends smiling in front of a *coffin*, wrapped in each other's arms. I guess everyone's unique.

'We haven't failed, Jessi, and we certainly aren't giving up,' reassures Caitlyn.

'We may be no investigators, but the three of us will untangle this. We'll hunt down Hecate's evil spawn, rope him, gut him, and throw him into the graveyard of Fin'Olinn. Locals rumour it's haunted, and the dead talk to each other,' says Honour, nonchalantly.

'Something where I'll gladly collaborate with you. Always wanted to be an undertaker.'

Honour laughs. Caitlyn chortles in response. A simple chuckle escapes from my lips.

'Girls, enjoyed your little venture into death itself?' A woman booms behind us. Achingly familiar. I don't dare to turn around. The disappointment in her voice is as clear as dark ink on fresh paper.

'What punishment are we bequeathing to them? Running up the slope? Meeting with Ailis? Oh, my favourite: no magic lessons for a week and being locked up in the isolation cabin. What do you feel about the kitchen—'

'That can be decided later, Priscilla. Right now, I'd like to chat with the Lady.'

I turn around. Heather's eyes are trained on mine. Dark pools of discontent. She glares at me with an intensity not even Priscilla could match. With my night escapade, I've let her down. I've done one day of training, and here I am, gallivanting in the most threatening part of Abandoned Haeems, scouring forbidden churches and reading forbidden texts. Disappointing Heather is like disappointing Mother. Chagrin twists like a knot in my chest. *God, please, not her. Throw me in the bad books of anyone except her.*

The writings on the wall stare at me as I'm led out of the crypt, as if they knew I'd make this mistake. *Pathetic, pathetic, pathetic.*

Chapter 17

'What were you thinking? Were you even thinking?' rebukes Heather. She has never raised her voice like this. It was always motherly warnings or warm advice. She was never one to chide. *That was when you had a title, you're a witch girl in a forest now. Anyone can highlight your flaws as per their wishes.*

I don't answer her, because the truth is, I wasn't thinking. I didn't think what it would mean to hunt down clues about a Goddess, to visit her abandoned crypt, to engage myself with bygone, forbidden, prophetic poetry.

'Just because you're no longer under the protection of the Manor Guards, that doesn't give you the liberty to traipse around the Abandoned.' How I hate disappointing her.

'Heather, it wasn't her fault, I suggested leaving the cabin,' Honour stands up for us.

'Well, the rest of you went along with it,' snaps Priscilla.

'So what if we venture out into the woods for one night? There aren't any leopards in this area, we've done it loads of times before,' groans Caitlyn. *Loads of times before? Where, in the library? Is there comfortable bed linen hiding behind the bookshelves, or is all the suspicious stuff done on the cold hard ground itself? Oh, the things people do for love.*

'You've what? Well then, Heather, how should we deal with them? The morning training session, I'm thinking a good run will be fun,' Priscilla snickers. It's funny how a magical instructor can be so sadistic.

'I suggest… we let them go this time, on the condition you three girls never do this again. I know I can't control your unbridled curiosity, but I can give you warnings, and I assure you that the consequences will be unpleasant, should this incident repeat itself.' All of Heather's motherly tenderness disappears as she delivers her warning. *You shouldn't have done this. The one person who believes in you now thinks you're a disappointment.*

We follow them out of the church, shuffling in a silent file towards our cabin. I assume Caitlyn and Honour to be sulking after being admonished but their lively spirits seem to be untamed. They're guffawing at the top of their lungs, something about Jack and me. They never fail to continually tease us, do they? And I never fail to continually have him invading my mind. But Jack isn't an intruder. He's an effusive shade of forest green that blends with my thoughts.

The homely, rustic cabin comes into view. Dried leaves and fallen twigs crunch under our feet as we walk to the threshold. Priscilla, clearly exhausted, leaves us without bidding us goodnight, while Honour throws open the door and hurls herself prostrate on her bed. I hear snores. Sound asleep. I don't remember the last time I slept without apprehension poking at me like pins and needles.

'May we talk for a moment, Jessica?' asks Heather. Her characteristic familial softness has returned. She cocks her head to the side and a tender, warm smile flickers across her lips.

Will you rebuke me for my irrationality tonight? Or will this be a nice motherly conversation? One we've had countless times before, but perhaps might never do it again because of our given circumstances? We're in a bloody magic camp for God's sake. And I just uncovered a deadly prophecy and how I was supposed to die, and that the Goddess of magic is linked to my family. I don't really feel like talking for a moment.

I should say yes, walk with her, apologise for my blithe behaviour.

I should decline, avoid any emotional conversation, step inside, slip into a nightgown, plunge into bed, and comfort myself with the feathery duvet. Even Caitlyn has retreated to the tranquillity of our little cabin. But it's better if she knows if I'm adapting to this new realm. If. Well, I've made a great many discoveries about myself, my family, a vindictive Goddess who hates the Harringtons for some weird reason. So, yes, in the most sarcastic manner possible, I am coping, rather enjoying this magic camp. Such fun.

I scratch the back of my neck and reply, 'Of course, of course… do you prefer a walk or something—'

'I think sitting down would be good.' She says, folding her arms across her chest.

She never cuts me off like this.

Heather leads me to a bench beside my cabin that I didn't even know was there. I swear it was magicked somehow.

'How did you find your first few training sessions?' she begins. This feels more like an interrogation than a warm chat between a lady's maid and a Lady.

'We had to run,' I grin.

'That's there, but apart from that, did the powers come to you naturally? Did you have to force them?'

'They answered me after a few attempts. Perhaps, with practice, they'll heed my calls?'

'Well done.'

My eyebrows furrow. Perplexed, I ask her, 'What for?'

'Treating your elemental powers as if they were living, breathing creatures, who followed their master's orders. Well, in this case, mistress.' She chuckles. I grin too.

'That is the first step to becoming a Merryck. Here, we don't treat our magic as a trait, a gift. Yes, magic is the expression of one's soul, but in order for it to be tamed and guided in the right direction, you need to listen to it. Keep it happy in the growing stage, like when you cosset a child. Let it release itself from the cage of your chest whenever it feels like. And then when it is an adolescent, like yourself, that's when you start the conditioning. You are harsh to it. You keep it in line. Never, never let it get the better of you. A witch who violently unleashes them and lets the wildfire devour everything in its path—everyone suffers from the aftermath. It's like hot metal with acid. Vigorous, pernicious in the long run. You lose control of your powers, you'll lose yourself.'

I gulp. If magic is a buoyant force, cheerful and lively, untamed, it can prove to be ruinous. What if I do lose control? I am an elemental witch, so my diverting from the right path would be destructive not only for myself but for the forests, the skies, the winds, and the very matter that constitutes this earth.

'Has there… been any Merryck who has… lost control?' I ask diffidently, my fingers trembling. The incessant twitching has come back to haunt me.

'Must we speak about losing control on such a beautiful, serene night?'

'Sorry.'

'I'll narrate a happier tale, though I warn you the ending is rather… sordid.' She gulps at the last word.

'I thought this was supposed to be a beautiful night.'

'My mistake. Apologies for being so untoward—'

'Tell me anyway.'

Heather inhales and exhales, calming herself, and preparing to begin her story.

'There was a girl once, who thought she could change the world.' Heather's face lights up with memory. A happy memory. 'Thought that with magic, she could help the people of her State, use her powers for the general good, have a purpose. And she was a praiseworthy witch. Trained every breathing second of the day.' Her eyes fill with tears. 'She was a beautiful girl, golden tresses for hair, dark pools for eyes, a clear-cut, strong voice that told stories. Adored by everyone. Oh, what a witch she was! I remember one time when three students were suffering from scarlet fever. She brought the temperature of the whole forest down to liberate the kids from the fever. The instructors were initially planning to do that, by controlling the wind speed, the rain, God, and the loss of heat from our own skin. They failed. No one knows how she did it. Incredibly powerful and ardent.'

This girl seems awfully lucky, to be blessed with a power so divine, to have such purity echoing in her soul. I imagine myself with that kind of magic, that kind of strength and confidence, required to change the world.

'Eventually, she grew to be so powerful that the Merrycks started comparing her to Goddesses of magic, to prodigies who had made history in the art of the elements, creation, clairvoyance, divination, casting or even entering dreams.' Heather pauses. The smile that stained her countenance with happiness fades away. A remorseful, wistful expression crosses her face. A shift in a story. The protagonist, enjoying a happy life with the people she loves, but then one day it's all gone.

'What happened then?'

'What happens to every committed girl who wants to achieve greatness?' She places a gentle hand on my knee. 'There is always someone who'll trim you down, Jessica. Someone who'll clip your wings, make you believe that the walls surrounding you are your barriers, your limitations.' Heather's voice breaks and quivers, as if she's unable to even think of the next words of her story.

'What happened to her, Heather?' I urge, unable to keep my own tears from flowing.

'Hecate.' She breathes. A single word, a whisper, yet it carries such a deeper meaning. Malice. Diabolism. Envy.

The woods go silent. The pines refrain from swaying. The nocturnal creatures stop their chittering. The forest holds its breath as the forbidden, deadly word is exhaled from Heather's lips.

'That woman, not worthy to be called a Goddess, killed her. And not just that girl. Every other witch or magician who she saw as a threat. Who was really at fault? Some say it was the girl, she shouldn't have grown too powerful, too powerful for her own good. Others say the Goddess needed to tame herself, and bless the witches who were passionate about magic, not dismember their spirits. Now, everyone puts a limit on their magic. When they think they might be growing too potent, they stop training. Run away. No one wants to incur her wrath.'

Heather stays silent for a long time until she speaks again, 'You dare not make the mistake of letting anyone condition you to believe that you aren't fated for succeeding in the mastery of your elemental powers. You've only just begun your training. There's a long way to go, but you are mentally prepared for the fog of obstacles obscuring your path. Understood?'

With a sigh, I remark, 'Understood.'

What need is there for conditioning?

Do I believe I can be a good witch?

Will I ever shake off the timidness that seizes hold of me, the uncertainty that comes with every thought, every word, every action? Will I ever be confident, brave, and hold my head high? I'm not even sure if Frances wants me back. To them, I'm a murderer and a heretic. Then how did Mother survive with them? Did they know? Was she really killed by Hecate, or did she die at the hands of the senators, for being too wonderful?

Too many unknowns.

To the Merrycks, I'm a novice. With only a day of training, I'm traversing through the woods, seeking information about Goddesses, scouring ancient crypts, reading forbidden poetry, and doing it all with two carefree spirits who don't mind inviting danger to tea.

Where do I belong? What am I doing here? What am I to become?

Witch, witch, witch. An assertive voice reassures me.

Ha, you? No way. Another sadistic, perhaps right, voice scoffs.

The voices inside my own head are engaged in an argument in their own little council. I, like a small kingdom, suffer due to the nature of their revolt.

A rose growing to my left droops and wilts. Soon it will shrivel up and wither to nothing. *Something in common.*

Chapter 18

Run. That was what the instructor said. *No, bellowed.* Run away from what? A shadowy creature lurking in the woods or the instructor's cane?

Barefoot, I scurried through the thickets of pines, unaware of direction, unsure of my destination.

Run. Mercilessly, she ordered us on. I bent double, hands pressing on my knees, trying to catch my breath. My drenched hair coiled and clung to my skin, the strands looked like a hundred deranged snakes. If I wasn't so frightened already, I might have shrieked at the thought of reptiles slithering in my hair.

The instructor produced a whip from her coat sleeve and lashed a blow across my back. I convulsed backwards in pain, knowing fully well the shape of the scars that would form—long, deep crevices, like grapevines spreading across a wall.

She whipped again, tearing my dress and skin apart in the process. I let out a single groan, then a shrill scream—so high-pitched that owls flew from their nests, wings flapping, voices creaking. I was going to die tonight.

My eyes clouded with tears, and I felt blood gushing down like a perennial river from a glacier. The instructor slipped past me, and I caught a glimpse of her face. *His face*. It wasn't a woman at all. His dark, tousled hair was streaked with blood. The leather whip, a lethal weapon, was clutched in his hand. It glinted like a thousand gems, with the shiny, thick red blood smeared all over it, dried and fresh. *My blood.*

Jack was here to save me, right? Surely he wasn't the instructor who was beating me until my body disintegrated—damaged nerve, bone, and sinew. He wouldn't harm me. I knew that in my bones, or what was left of them.

Then again, the quirt was in his hands, and he too, like the deadly leather whip, was painted with blood. *My blood.*

As the realisation of his deeds sank in, I fell to the ground as he hit me for the third time.

I wake up with a jolt, hyperventilating. My brain searches for something tangible to confirm that last night was nothing but a terrible dream, a phantasm that would only haunt me when I closed my eyes. My sheets are twisted around me like a cocoon. It feels impossible to breathe. My head throbs painfully. The heat in this room is unbearable. Sweat pours from my skin, and I realise I am perspiring at an abnormal rate.

Last night's horrific events sink in, driving their claws deep within me, making the hair on my arms stand on end. *Running. The whip. Blood. Practically dying.* And in the middle of all the chaos, Jack. The boy I'm beginning to feel something inextricable for.

Part of me believes that I am still in that grotesque nightmare—running for my life, being lashed, every bone snapping and muscle tearing with each blow. How could Jack be the malicious instructor who was whipping me in the dream? Surely it wasn't him. Maybe a look-alike. I refuse to accept that he'd do such a thing in reality.

'Oh thank goodness, you're fine!' exclaims Caitlyn. *Why wouldn't I be fine? It was a nightmare, with Jack Fynn as the unexpected villain. Or was it actually real?* Ever since the annual carnival in Walsh Vale, which doesn't exist according to the girls, I've lost all sense of what's real and what's fantasy.

'You sweated out the fever, good. My, you were burning last night! I had to dump a bucket of ice on you to bring your temperature down.'

'Fever?' A single word escapes from my lips. I gulp. Not only was I witnessing a lurid nightmare of Jack wanting to kill me, but I was also suffering from a fever. Maybe the fever messed with my head and caused me to have such false, unnatural, twisted dreams. *Now you're just looking for an excuse, an explanation for last night's ghosts.*

'It's all good now. You missed breakfast and the first session. I don't know what your group did in your elemental training, but the next class involves both fire and water witches. At 10. Join it. It'll do you good to get up on your feet and exercise your powers. Keeps your body alive and functioning properly.'

At least I slept through the actual morning running session. That gives me some comfort.

I see that my other roommate isn't in the cabin and ask Caitlyn, 'Where's Honour?'

'Oh, she has some creation thing today. Her session lasts till lunch.' She slips out of the room, like an autumn leaf carried by the wind.

'Where are you going?' I shout out to her, but she doesn't respond. I make it a point to forget about the night's ordeal and begin afresh. When I fling my legs off the bed, I see a bit of paper sticking out from the folds of the feathery duvet. I tug at the paper, which is, in fact, a piece of writing parchment, with words scrawled lazily, ink splattered everywhere. The writer must have either been in a hurry or simply didn't care if the receiver could comprehend the note or not. I unfold the parchment, stained by ink and browned by coffee, and read the contents of the note:

3 days from now. Under the big willow tree. Theodore will show you the way.

Yours,

Jack.

Shivers prick me like needles all over my skin. I just had a nightmare about the boy, and now he's asking me to meet him under a willow tree. The last time this boy told me to meet him in secret, he ghosted me and left me dumbfounded. What's to happen this time?

The handwriting doesn't seem like his, either. At Esther's birthday ball, he signed my dance card in impressive cursive, not uneven scrawl. And why does he want a clandestine meeting with me? That too under a willow tree. They provide paramount privacy, though…

Stop having these scandalous thoughts when we have bigger problems at hand.

Moreover, he wants Theodore to take me there. Why not Caitlyn or Honour? What sort of esoteric intentions is he hiding? *He isn't hiding anything. It's just an illicit meeting. Let's hope it's romantic. I don't mind a bit of forbidden kissing.*

My heart hammers inside my chest, and my brain refuses to think about this convoluted matter anymore. I need food.

I change out of my silken nightgown into a white cotton tea gown. It's simpler than what I am used to, and for that, I am grateful. No need for traipsing around the forest in heavy skirts and restrictive corsets. But the embroidery of the tea gown is gorgeous. The thread is woven in patterns of leaves, twigs, and clusters of flower petals. I wonder where they get such exquisite beauties from!

I pull on the thick purple and gold Merryck's cloak and admire myself in the mirror for a few, stolen, brief seconds. Gone is the girl with a title and servants, and here comes the witch who has powers beyond her wildest dreams. My hair looks dishevelled. Dark circles loom under my eyes, but my eyes are full of fire. The fire with which I will bring down Hecate and that infuriating offspring of hers. The fiery passion with which I will unearth my family's secrets and the reason behind my magic, my *existence*. I may make mistakes along the way, and earn a few burns, but aren't scars a reminder of all we've survived through, of who we have grown to become?

As I fasten the buttons of my cloak, a memory slips into my conscience. Jack knowing that the cloak exactly belonged to me, Caitlyn and Honour teasing him because he knew the dimensions, the 'tiny details.' I bite my lip to suppress my blush. I remind myself that I am alone in the cabin and have no need to hide the silly blushes that creep across my cheeks. What if I'm being watched? What if Jack himself is watching me and can enter my mind and read my thoughts? He does have myriad powers, and I think mind-reading is one of them. I do love the idea of him watching me, giving me a furtive smirk, and me boldly smirking back. I imagine him slipping into the cabin silently at night, doing scandalous things that society would frown upon, kissing me on my forehead as a temporary goodbye, then returning the next night, the night after that, and the night after that. We're in a forest after all, and magical things could happen.

I beg you with all my heart. Shut up.

The forest clearing that acts as the training ground comes into view. The wind whistles as it flies through the pines, shaking the branches with a force too minuscule to completely snap them. A small creature skitters next to my feet, and I shriek in response to its brushing against my ankles. Unbalanced from the chittering little animal, whatever it was, I stumble backwards and bump into someone.

'Ahem.' That someone coughs behind me.

I turn around to apologise but immediately consider giving him a glare because, yes, God decided that I should collide with Theodore today—the very person I don't want to see right now. I think he should bottle his arrogance and rudeness and throw it into the ocean.

My lips press into a tight smile. 'Good morning.'

The tiny civilised part of him replies to my greeting, though in a monotone, flat voice, 'Morning.'

'Isn't this a session for the fire and water witches? I thought you had wind magic.'

'Well, someone needs to control the fire if it gets out of hand,' he mumbles. I don't care that he doesn't take pleasure in speaking to me. But he is the one who will guide me to the willow tree where my clandestine meeting with Jack is supposed to take place. It is imperative that I make polite conversation.

'Isn't water supposed to put the fire out? Doesn't wind usually accelerate the flames?' I ask, trying with all my might to sound courteous.

'In this particular experiment, we're going to take the air out of bodies and use it to douse the fire. Why does a candle get extinguished by exhaled air? We're going to help scientists one day! Sorry, I meant we as in the *Merrycks*, not the filthy Lords.' He snaps and walks off. I swear I heard him laugh devilishly.

The audacity.

I have half a mind to conjure a ball of fire and throw it at him, but the more logical part of my brain tells me to calm down and not waste a modicum of my power on that complete idiot. I poured over a great deal of scientific papers in the Manor library and can specifically tell him which gases support burning and which don't.

I hope a mammoth amount of oxygen is in the room when I set fire to your arrogance, Theodore.

'Partner up!' An instructor booms.

Thankfully, Caitlyn is here too, so I quickly walk to where she is standing.

'Hello to you, Jessi.'

'Hiya, Caitlyn.'

'Alright, I hope you have partnered yourself so that each pair has a fire and water witch or magician?' The instructor says.

Everyone else rearranges themselves, but Caitlyn and I don't need to because of my fire magic and her ability to manipulate water.

'What's the instructor's name?' I whisper to Caitlyn.

'Allena.'

Allena continues with her instructions, 'We all know the spell for a fire spark, *Sradag*, and that concentration helps to make fireballs, creatures, and all manner of things. Well, today's spell is *teine na loisg mi*, a spell that is used to burn objects or people, but will not burn the witch or magician who recites the words. So you will inflict the flames on yourself; they won't harm you, and the partner will douse the flames with their water. Simple enough?'

The syllables of the Gaelic words feel difficult to pronounce, but soon, I'm able to do it, and I've 'burnt' my hand in a matter of minutes.

The sound of the flames flickering soothes me. I feel their warmth, their tangible presence. If I touch the palpable fire that I've created, would it burn me? I know the spell isn't supposed to harm the creator, but would my own flames betray me? I smile at the flames as they begin to spread. It evokes a sense of euphoria in me that my magic, like the flames, is growing stronger. If my magic does grow more potent, I think I could truly learn to be content, even if Esther isn't here anymore, even if I don't have my old life back.

I hear a hissing sort of sound, the sound that you hear when water and fire have a union. Caitlyn has exercised her water abilities and doused the flames. My hand isn't the slightest bit charred; not even a scar marks the surface of my skin.

I wish life could be as easy as this spell was. I know magic is an inextricable, untamed creature that needs careful attention, but sometimes it can be truly liberating. I wish living were synonymous with that. Forbidden poetry, ramshackle crypts, and Goddesses add a tasteful flavour and a dash of colour to life, but doesn't one crave simplicity and love in the end? You sound pathetic. It is treasonous to be contemplating faraway, foreign notions such as simplicity and love. You know you're never going to get it.

As Caitlyn and I practise again, and *teine na loisg mi* gets engraved in my memory like a carving in stone, I imagine what life would be like if my life didn't contain midnight clue hunts, rustic wood cabins, family secrets, prophecies, mysteries, and Jack Fynn's easy smiles.

Have you gone positively mad?

The last one, I can't surely live without.

Chapter 19

I'm wearing a resplendent evening dress that surprisingly isn't ankle-length but stops at the knees. Though, I'm required to wear stockings. It doesn't even matter because the stockings are made of the smoothest satin that is surely lighter than a bunch of feathers. The hemline is gorgeous, packed with intricate lace and ruffles. The dress is adorned with elaborately embroidered puff sleeves and a bodice that is a forest green so dark it looks obsidian black. I'm going to blend in with the woods and be a pine tree.

Tonight is the *Witching*, a sacrificial festival dedicated to prodigious witches and magicians who were once part of the Merrycks Home. We're all expected to toss an object we hold dear into a bonfire to pay our respects and practise our magic wildly. But, I arrived here with nothing other than my nightgown, so I don't have any keepsakes from home. *Home*. The word tastes like vinegar on my tongue—acidic and putrid. It's only been a few days since I left, and I feel like Home is a stranger.

I instantly feel the weight of my crescent moon necklace, dangling there like the real moon suspended in the starry night. *The realisation* slaps me in the face. The necklace is a possession I hold dear to my heart. A sacrificial object.

No. It's all I have left. I can't and will not give it up.

Honour said she would meet with us at the festival celebrations directly. Apparently, she is at some girl's cabin, with the excuse that she needs that girl to help her dress. I haven't seen Honour all day. Even during lunch, she wasn't present in the dining hall. I inquired about her to a few acquaintances, who said she was off with the same girl somewhere. I wonder what they might have been doing, that took them the whole day.

Caitlyn is dressed in breeches, and a long linen shirt with a V-shaped collar, lined with ruffles. The cuffs are secured with gold cufflinks, which are shaped like minuscule banyan trees, split by lightning. *Where have I seen that before?*

The bloodlock of the crypt.

The symbol etched into stone.

I falter back and grip hold of the furniture closest to me, which is the bedpost. *Why is everything so connected? Why does Caitlyn have cufflinks that match the bloodlock?*

Why did my blood open the lock?

I push all thoughts aside, pests to deal with later. The *Witching* is a festival I hope to enjoy. Caitlyn promised me there would be rum. Although I am underage, I will savour every drop of alcohol before the search party, if there is one, finds me and I'm chained within the walls of Marilyn Manor.

It saddens me that Jack isn't going to attend the *Witching* because he is running an errand for Ailis in Merlin. I remember his exuberant dancing during the Gathering. He looked so full of life. A ring of alcohol circled his lips. The upper buttons of his shirt were unfastened, leaving his collarbones exposed. His raven curls were more tousled than ever, shining in the slivers of moonlight that penetrated through the pines.

Jack Fynn was truly breathtaking and still is. A part of me begs God that he graces us with his presence at the *Witching*. But the more rational part of me knows that is impossible. Even if he were here, he wouldn't care to dance with me. He left brusquely without bidding farewell properly. Caitlyn and Honour had jokingly hinted at a 'wedding' that was, according to them, going to take place between Jack and me. Jack turned red and walked away. I didn't hear his melancholy, mystifying whistles.

Good God, I hope he was blushing because he was positively delighted by the idea.

We walk out of the cabin and into the serene night, painted with the light of the stars. We don't engage in any conversation during our stroll, but a friendly silence prevails between us. Amicable, peaceful, and friendly. Silence like that is so easy, it's almost painful. A friendly moment of quiet between two friends who know they're going to spend a lifetime together, grow old together, and reminisce about the theatrics of the past. It would be absolutely wonderful if I had that with Caitlyn.

The forest clearing is filled with trumpeting, stentorian folk music. Groups of bunting in the classic Merrycks' colours are strung between pine trees. Witches, instructors, students, and magicians wander around, downing casks of ale, and exchanging objects like crystals, ivory-handled knives, bejewelled mirrors, and all manner of trinkets and charms. Even crimson threads and beads. Those must be the sacrifices. I am yet to decide what my offering will be.

A bonfire crackles in the centre of all the joyous effervescence. A group of witches, cloaked in dark capes, their faces masked, surrounds the bonfire. They twirl and dance around it, singing hymnals, casting luminous will-o'-the-wisps and letting them traverse through the trees. Like a small cult, they hold hands and dancc like each swish of their skirts is their last.

Caitlyn leads me to a group of girls and a few boys, which Honour is a part of. We greet her, and she grins widely. She stumbles a bit, but a girl grabs hold of her hip, preventing the fall. I think this is the girl she was probably bedding in the afternoon. Everyone is affected gravely by alcohol. The instructors do need to stop giving adolescents the highly intoxicating—but, *Good Lord*, electrifying—drink.

I take a couple of swigs of the exhilarating amber liquid myself. I tilt my head back and let the music absorb into my mind. I hear the distinct, sanguine sound of fiddles, and the lilting tune of a choir somewhere in a thicket of trees, lifting my spirits higher and higher. The people surrounding me are overwhelmed with merriment. Caitlyn, who is clearly enjoying herself, enters into a challenge with one of the strapping, well-built boys. The challenge entails swigging two bottles of absinthe in less than three minutes. Averil begins the countdown. Caitlyn swallows three bottles in two and wins.

I wish Jack were here to witness how carefree and utterly invigorating this night is unfolding. I would love for him to catch a glimpse of my mirthful state. I feel lighter than I have in years. It feels as though my soul is borne aloft so tenderly by the wind, carried by the wings of its breeze.

I think I'm in love with Jack. His mysteriousness. His heart. His beauty. His whistles. His curls. His soul.

Snipping the thread of thoughts of a boy I've grown to fancy is Ailis, who enters the forest clearing and proceeds to a small wooden platform, built a few metres away from the central celebrations. She wears a content smile on her face, and she seems genuinely happy. Ailis exercises the gliding joint in her wrist and the attention of the entire forest snaps to her.

She clears her throat and begins, 'Merrycks Home for Witches and Magicians. I warmly welcome you to the *Witching*, the sacrificial festival held every five years to pay our respects to the prodigious individuals who have marked their names forever in our history.'

The music dims to a low folk song, one that is played during the funeral processions of deceased Lords. It is peculiar and confusing why they chose to play this today.

'Tonight, I would like us all to acknowledge the ineffable contributions of one particular witch. To the townsfolk, the House of Commons, and the Lords, she is officially known as Lady Winifred Harrington, the late Marchioness of Frances. But, she will forever be remembered as Winnie of the Willows, to us.'

I swear my heart stops beating. This night is commemorating Mother. Mother. Witch. Harrington. Witch. Mother.

'We all know her to be a potent witch who was passionate about her powers and trained to assist the people of her State. Not just politics. She yearned to improve the lives of the commonplace and look after their welfare. Anyone else with a power so strong as hers would have misused it, and walked down the wrong path. But, our Winnie did otherwise.'

Mother truly was remarkable.

'All good tales come to an end. Her life was ended by the unspeakable Goddess, whose name we shall not take on such a sacrosanct night.'

There it is. The confirmation that Hecate really butchered my mother to death and completely abhors the Harrington clan. She couldn't contain her jealousy, could she?

Hecate killed my mother. Her son killed my sister. I knew that, didn't I? What I didn't know was that everyone knew. The girl in Heather's story was my mother. Heather knew. The powerful witch Ailis just described was my mother. Ailis knew too.

Mother was not only a remarkable Lady but a remarkable witch as well, her power so great and divine that Hecate killed her.

My mother was a powerful witch. So utterly, painstakingly powerful.

The realisation carves a hole into my heart. If Mother possessed such magic, am I destined to be as magical as her too? The thought sends me reeling.

'Although Winnie was killed by the Goddess, her magic resides in her daughter, who is with us, who shall join us in our journey to honing our abilities to the fullest. Tonight, let us bear in mind the achievements of darling Winifred. Let her life not evoke a sense of loss and sorrow but inspire us to unleash our powers and soar above and beyond the boundaries that the malicious create. Magic is the expression of one's soul, and let us portray that expression to the best of our capabilities. Never will we let the vindictive Goddess take the life of one of our own again. We will be well-prepared and equipped if such an atrocity should happen.'

The Merrycks knew. How nice. People who aren't even remotely related to Mother know everything about her. I, her daughter, have information as diminutive as a microplasma in a petri dish.

'Let us go ahead, continue to practise our magic freely and wildly, and grow to our full potential. Let no chains bind us, and no ordinary men or women despise us for who we were born to be. This festival commemorates Lady Winifred Harrington, the late Marchioness of Frances, and hundreds of others like her, who were subjected to Hecate's wrath. Let Hecate's name not make us recoil back to our homes, but empower us to step out into the open and embrace our powers doubtlessly. To Winnie of the Willows.' Ailis concludes her speech and lifts her sacrificial offering, a sovereign. I espy a bird carved into the gold.

The others raise their objects too, as though they were champagne flutes.

I feel like bursting into tears and absconding. The pieces of the puzzle are finally fitting in, but in a more gruesome way than I imagined.

Hecate hates my family because Mother was a witch more powerful than the Goddess herself.

She killed her, using Mother as an example so no one would dare to 'neglect her superiority.'

Her son killed my sister the night of her Birthday Ball. Ideally, I shouldn't have been slaughtered because I have magic and Esther didn't. Unlikely as it is, Hecate wouldn't want her rival's child to grow more powerful than her.

All roads lead back to the son, or rather, disciple of Hecate. Whomsoever he or she is, I am determined to find out.

Against my will, tears threaten to spill down my cheeks, and I let them. I have uncovered too much in the past few days. Never would I have thought that life could get so inexplicable in a matter of evanescent moments. One day you're riding through the Vale in a carriage with your soon-to-be-Marchioness-sister. The next you're a witch in a forest, doing all sorts of wild, improper things. Will this tangled ball of yarn—of life, hope, love, and family—ever get unravelled? Or will I get twisted in the knots myself?

I toss my necklace into the fire. The flames reflect my tear-stricken face.

Chapter 20

Breathe. I inhale the fragrant forest air and fill my lungs to the very top. *It's going to be fine. You're going to be fine.*

I have my meeting with Jack right now. A clandestine meeting. In his note, he informed me that Theodore would be escorting me to the willow tree.

And he isn't here yet. I awoke well before sunrise today and have been standing in front of my cabin ever since. Jack failed to specify what time he'd like to meet me. I only left the cabin for breakfast. The most delectable egg rolls and cheese-topped roasted vegetables were served today. The steaming food almost burnt my tongue but made my mouth water even more.

Ah, there he is. Theodore comes charging towards me in his usual surly manner, stomping his feet, hands in his trouser pockets.

'Come along now, I ain't got much time.' He remarks brusquely.

Despite my wishes, I follow him, a repulsive expression spread across my countenance. *He is only taking you there. You're going to meet Jack. It's alright, you can murder Theodore later.*

'Y'know sweetheart, you are actually quite pretty for a Lady. I thought all of them were just pleasure-seeking, good-for-nothing harlots who married for money,' Theodore says, looking smug and self-satisfied. I stop in my tracks. *Is Theodore trying to flirt with me? Oh, hell. I feel like slapping him until his face burns red.*

I maintain a slow pace behind him because I fear if I were to walk beside him, he would try something scandalous that I do not want. He is several inches taller than me, and I'm not sure if I would be able to defend myself.

'Ladies are far more capable than you think. All ladies. Not only the political kind.' I try to keep the venom in my voice as minimal as possible.

'You look even prettier when you get all defensive about your species.'

'Are you calling women another *species*? In that case, men are a stain we must wash our hands clean of.'

'I enjoy the idea of you touching me.'

'Theodore, that's enough.' A male voice speaks. Jack emerges from behind the willow tree, looking dashing in a parchment-beige shirt with lantern sleeves. Sunlight reflects off his face, giving it a golden, mysterious glow.

'Just trying to court a girl, mate. It's about time I—' Arrogant Theodore tries to defend himself, but Jack cuts him off.

'I think Jessica is perfectly capable of managing this meeting herself, Theodore. You may leave now. Thank you for your assistance.'

The conceited magician walks off, leaving Jack and me alone. My heart thunders inside my chest. We're standing right under the willow. Ailis had addressed my mother as 'Winnie of the Willows.'

Did Mother lie down under this tree, create sparks of fire, read books, and talk to the people she loved?

Jack shifts closer to me so that he is right in front of me. A lock of hair covers his right eye. I want to reach out and tuck the stray curl behind his ear. But I don't, because he does it himself, looking painstakingly beautiful while doing it. The wind plays with another curl of his tousled hair.

'Good day, Lady Harrington,' he says and smiles convivially.

'How many times have I asked you to call me just Jessica?' I respond, sounding as playful as possible.

'Hello, Jess then. May I call you that?'

'Jess is perfectly fine.'

'I think we should ruminate on a fun nickname for me, too,' he says, pressing his fingertips together, acting all philosophical.

'Oh yes, what would you like me to call you, Mr Fynn?' I laugh.

'Darling is fine.' He tilts his head to the side and smirks mischievously. I don't mind calling him darling. In fact, I want to.

My fingers start twitching again. Red sparks emit from my fingertips. The zephyrs blow more speedily than before. The leaves rustle more intensely. It is as though the whole of Abandoned Haeems feels the same emotions as I do.

'Wonderful. So, darling, how was your errand in Merlin?' I don't know where the confidence and courage to say such a scandalous thing came from.

'Sorry.' He chuckles. I'm confused.

'For what?' I ask.

'For the flirtations. I knew you wouldn't like it.' He looks down at his shoes.

'I don't like it when Theodore does it. With you, I like it very much.' *Where on earth is this confidence coming from? I must go to that place and pray there. Maybe read a few hymns and rekindle my lost piety. I'm a heretic for being magical, aren't I?*

'Are you saying that you fancy me?' His eyes light up.

'Maybe I do.'

A small sort of quiet hangs between us. He looks at me, content in his eyes. I smile back at him. Anything could happen at this moment. He could close the space between us.

'Shall we get on to the purpose of the meeting? Courting was one part. There is something else that I would like to discuss with you. It's related to the prophecy,' he says.

We begin walking side by side, moving away from the willow tree. We step on a path of withered rose petals and pine needles, which crunch under the weight of our boots and turn to dust.

'There are stories all about your mother's lineage and her magic. She was a powerful witch, and her powers incurred the jealousy and inevitable wrath of Hecate.'

'I know that.'

'How?'

'Ailis revealed it yesterday, during the *Witching*.'

'Oh right. It is pitiful that I missed it. I look forward to the *Witching* every quinquennial. How was it? Was there rum?'

'More rum, alcohol, absinthe, and whiskey than you've ever laid your eyes on.' I chuckle.

'I love ginger ale the best. Casket ale. Sorry, cask ale. I think murder and coffins and death have imprinted themselves into my mind.' He tilts his head back and laughs heartily.

'I'm only seventeen. I don't know anything about how these alcohol-based drinks are made. Father would have my head if he discovered I've been mere inches away from rum.'

He stops walking and stands in front of me, so swiftly and sharply that it catches me by surprise. *I almost collapse into him. Collapse into his arms.*

He exhales, and I feel his warm, pine-scented breath on my skin. He locks eyes with me. God, Jack Fynn's mouth is so dangerously close to mine that one wrong move would press us together.

'Jessica,' he breathes out again, saying my name like it's a sacred word. I feel his hand brush against my hip. *Good God, his hand is on my waist.* It lingers there for a moment too long.

I want to say his name too. I want his name to become muscle memory, a special word always floating on my lips. Jack Fynn. Beautiful, kind, magical Jack Fynn.

I take a wary step forward. The distance between us is close to an inch. I still feel his delicate fingers tracing the curve of my waist. My heart flutters. Heat pools in my core. My entire body burns with the telltale pink. This time, no biting lips or closing of my eyes can hide my blush.

He senses it and smirks slyly. A crooked smile, the corner of his lip tilted upwards to the left.

I gather the remnants of my courage and tuck the stray lock of raven hair behind his ear. He shifts. It seems like he is blushing too. Enjoying this fragile moment between us.

If this romantic moment we're sharing is more evanescent than a heartbeat, I might start to cry. What we have isn't glass. It won't break. It won't be beyond repair. Never.

'Mhm.' I will drive ten swords down Theodore's spine. I will hang him and let the vultures hack and dismember him till his raw insides are out on display.

But the intruder who cleared their throat isn't Theodore. Isn't a student at all.

'It seems like I always have errands for you to run. Especially Jack. Terribly sorry. But this one's important. My office. And no immorality and indecency shall be tolerated then.'

It's Ailis, and even with my back facing her, I can tell that she is positively horrified by the sight of me wrapped in Jack's arms.

Jack lets go of me. I instantly miss the warmth and comfort of his hands around me. This moment really was glass. It lies in irreparable shards on the forest floor.

At least this 'errand' that Ailis needs us to run requires both Jack and me. Although, I think Ailis is going to reverse her judgement and send someone else to either of our places because of the indecent situation she caught us in.

God, I hope there are many more indecent situations to come.

Chapter 21

I plop down in the leather armchair farthest from Ailis's desk, eager to avoid the weighted gaze of her beady eyes as much as possible. Her fading black hair is tied in its usual neat, immaculate bun, not a strand out of place. Ailis Millerwood might be in her late sixties, yet she still looks regal and strikingly imposing in her impeccable Merrycks cloak. Stone-faced, strict, and majestic on the outside, she hides an overflowing, bubbling cauldron of secrets inside. All of them tucked away in a hopelessly tangled ball of yarn, waiting for me to unspool.

She knows about my powers, my mother's powers, and her rivalry with Hecate. I knew none of it, yet she didn't even bat an eye.

And then, she expects me to dutifully follow her instructions and run the errands she somehow always comes up with.

I want to conjure an unstoppable, forceful wind to ruin that superficial beauty of hers and make those strands of hair go awry. But I'm worried that, if I do, I'll be testing her patience and might end up receiving a punishment instead of an easy errand.

The work that requires *both Jack and me* is the only thing keeping me from magically and physically strangling her.

I bury my fury and give Ailis one of my most courteous, lady-like smiles. She smiles back at me, then bends down to retrieve a folder of papers from a drawer. I sit up straighter in my seat to get a closer look at the contents, my curiosity piqued. As I shift in the shockingly comfortable leather armchair, my knee knocks against Jack's, and his gaze flickers to mine. He gives me one of his dashing smirks, *which I hope are reserved only for me.* He's sprawled out in his threadbare chair, arms resting on the armrests and legs alarmingly close to mine. He's casual and blithe about his sitting posture in front of the infuriating and rigid Head of the Home. I like this nonchalant attitude of his.

'Harrington, you are aware of the etiquette, dances, and all that royalty, I hope?' Ailis says.

'We're estate keepers, not royalty. And yes, I am aware of the etiquette, dances, and *all that nobility*,' I reply.

'Yes, whatever, all that sugar fluff. But let's get to the real business.' She presses her fingertips together and stares straight at me as if her dark pools of eyes want to examine my insides. I feel timid and exposed under her gaze. I silently pray that this meeting is short and swift without any display of emotion from showing on my face.

'The reason I've called you both here today is because of the Annual Community Local Business—something—God knows the blasted name—that's being held at Lord Duxubury's residence in Aurelia. It's one of those resource-depleting, money-destroying dinners that the two of you will be attending.' Ailis continues, blithe about the impact her words have on me.

The details of the errand slap me in the face. What the hell? What the actual hell? Ailis Millerwood, in all her golden glory, is literally gifting an absconded lady with supernatural powers to the House of Lords. They will surely recognise me and have me executed during the party itself. The senators will drink my blood as punch and chew my flesh as if it were roast chicken. I can't go back to Frances. Not yet. The reality of Esther's demise hasn't sunk into my skin yet, and I don't have the strength to face any of the Lords. Not Father. Not Charles. What will Charles think of me when he sees me? Will he see his best friend or a witch and a murderer who deserves to be burnt without a trial?

I am a murderer to them, condemned for killing my sister, who was going to be the Marchioness of Frances as Father stepped down in favour of someone younger. They will never accept me. Nothing will ever be the same again. I'll never hear Esther's carefree laughter, walk within the walls of Marilyn Manor, or have picnics in the meadows and swim in streams with Charles. Those pleasures are long gone. Buried in the graveyard of my chest for eternity.

'No. Absolutely not.' My disagreement comes out more defiantly than I expected. Ailis doesn't look surprised. She has the audacity to keep her gaze fixated on mine, inspecting my entire form up and down.

'What are you so afraid of? You know the spell to mask your true identity. *Comdach*, if you need reminding. No one will know that their mischievous little Jessica Harrington is in their midst, breathing the same air as them. Now, these papers contain biographical information on each of the notable professionals and Parliamentarians who will be present, with whom you'll have to make chaperoned conversation. And if you're wondering who has the bitter misfortune of chaperoning you both, it is Priscilla. I do pity her for having to witness the indecencies Fynn and you indulge in.'

'I am perfectly aware of the things that fascinate each and every Lord. I do hold a position and did frequent these events,' I snap, ignoring her comment on the *indecencies*.

'Then tell me. Practice makes perfect.' *Well, your bun won't be perfect anymore when I rip those hairpins out and poke your eyes with them.*

'Well, Lord Harrington really likes strict discipline observed when it comes to propriety and etiquette. He likes it when you talk about norms and rules like you're some governess. Conversations about the weather and the latest news can earn you an invitation to his parties.

I could go on and on about Father and his immeasurable desire for things to be prim and proper at all times.'

'Then, with Lord Duxubury, you should talk about the latest sporting events, especially dressage and hurdle-jumping shows. Raven Thorn is a stallion of the East that he very much covets.'

I gulp. I don't want to give her information about Charles. Things he likes are interests that we both share. They are personal, and Ailis doesn't need to know the intricacies of our friendship.

'Char—Lord Silasbury enjoys talks of gardening and carriage rides in the meadows. He is an avid reader and an assiduous Parliamentarian and likes to converse about books revolving around world wars and foreign politics.'.

I give her half-truths. Charles does like gardening but enjoys walks in flower gardens with Esther and me more. He does like carriage rides in meadows but enjoys them more when we're there with him. The last bit I completely made up. I have no idea what Charles likes to read. He always hid the books from me, saying, 'Oh, it's too scandalous. You ought to know it in the future only. I'll teach you.' God, I miss my old friend. I might miss him with all my heart, but seeing him physically after everything that has happened is too much for me to bear.

'I didn't know you were such a well-informed lady. Mary Leigh here just warms her seat and orders the peasants to get on with their work in hazardous conditions which she doesn't bother to inspect.' Mary Leigh is a different scenario altogether. But I, on the other hand, did get my share of training in polite conversation and the language of dance.

I take a few deep breaths—breathing in, breathing through, breathing deep, and out. One breath at a time. Letting all of today's horrors sink in. *I'm going to a ball. I'm going to see the Lords. I'm going to the place where I am most definitely not welcome.*

'Did they do the funeral yet?' I ask, choking on the tears that are threatening to spill.

'Of whom? Leigh? She died? How wonderful! That donkey doesn't give a fig about the welfare of Haeems, let alone the Abandoned.'

'My… sister.' It takes all of me to let the words pass my lips.

'As far as I'm concerned, you Lords indulge yourselves in actual *state matters.*'

'The funeral of a late Marchioness is a state matter!' I scream, tears making their way down my cheeks. I had prayed to all my stars that I wouldn't descend into a tear-stricken mess in front of Ailis and Jack. Prayers like that are dangerous. They might just grant you the opposite.

'Jessica, I have given you a job to do. You must be proper at all times and adhere to the etiquette. I did not call you here for a lecture on the House of Lords. I think the press is good enough for that. You may go. Jack, I will steal a few more minutes of your time so I can explain your role in the errand and other intricate details that Lady Jessica Harrington cannot know until the day of the ball, which will take place on April 5th. Her female constitution deems her unworthy of carrying the full weight of it all just yet. She needs time to deal with the fact that she will be experiencing all that nonsense, fluff, and royalty once more before the Lords hang a nice, tough rope around her neck.' A smug, conceited expression mars her meretricious countenance. The self-satisfied smile she wears so proudly almost goes along with the rest of her composition.

My female constitution? Ailis Millerwood, a woman herself, who lives to see witches ascend to glory, is commenting on my female constitution? And I thought it was the archaic patriarchal system that needed to be purged from this world.

Even with that overflowing pot of secrets she continually stirs, Ailis has made one thing perfectly clear: my job is to remain proper at all times. It maddens me how she is using my knowledge of etiquette for her ulterior motives—motives she isn't revealing to me. *When does she ever?* The full details are being disclosed to Jack, and him only. Well, he is a sole part of the Merrycks. It was Jack who came as the representative of the Merrycks Home at the Birthday Ball. Now, he is going to another one, for God and Ailis know why. And I'm tagging along with him.

I don't want to spend another minute in the proximity of this aggravating woman. I look at Jack before leaving the cabin, and he glances back at me. The corners of his lips turn up into a smile, and it is almost pitiful. *My female constitution deems me unworthy of bearing the full weight of the errand.* I scoff at Ailis's remark and waltz out of the cabin, my fists balled, ready to throw a punch at her if she passes one more remark on my female constitution. My ears catch the telltale hissing sound of candles extinguishing as I leave.

Instead of walking back to my own cabin, I settle down on the bench against the right wall of Ailis's office. I'll wait until Jack comes out and hear every minute detail of the errand that is being intentionally kept from me.

My right knee moves up and down. The hair on my arms stands on end. I haven't the faintest idea why I am so on edge and anxious to hear about instructions given by Ailis Millerwood of all people. Time passes agonisingly slowly.

After what feels like a painstakingly long hour, Jack emerges from the cabin and walks down the serpentine path leading deeper into the pines. He completely ignores my presence.

I get up and start walking behind him, but he doesn't look back or acknowledge me. His pace is several times faster than mine. I realise I will either have to shout his name or tug at his jacket collar to get his attention. I choose the former.

'Jack!' I call out. He turns around to face me, his face filled with bewilderment as to why I shouted his name.

When he doesn't move, flinch, or give me any signal that he is actually listening to me, I sigh and stomp towards him. Stopping more than a foot away to maintain appropriateness, should Ailis be watching us, I ask, 'What exactly did Ailis tell you? About the job? Why am I undeserving of knowing the technicalities?'

He sighs, hands in his pockets, and replies, his lips almost pressed together as though he wishes he were doing anything but speaking to me, 'I am not at liberty to say. Don't worry, Ailis has good intentions. On the 5th of April, I will explain all the particulars.'

'But, I *am* going to be doing a major part of the job—that is, maintaining conversation with the Lords and making sure nothing goes haywire… I should know everything beforehand.' I cross my arms over my chest and assume a defensive posture.

'Lady Jessica, I apologise. Most sincerely. But please understand when I say that I am not entitled to disclose anything just yet. I do regret my inability to help you further.'

I study him for a while, and he keeps his eyes trained on mine. I didn't think that Jack could be like this—cold and remote. I had really started to think that some invisible string was tying us together, destining us to march into the *future together.*

Perhaps I should stop hoping so much. Maybe these flames are meant to be put out.

'Alright then, Mr Fynn. Farewell to you.' I snap, filling my voice with as much venom as I can muster. *He wants formality and decency from me? Oh God, he's going to get so much of it. He hasn't seen the dim and distant Jessica that you meet when you've angered her greatly. Oh God, that is the only Jessica he's going to see from now on.*

I walk past him, praying that my indignation radiates off my skin like a bright light. He starts walking too, though down another path, probably towards his cabin. *Let's walk different ways, Jack. Let's go down separate journeys away from each other and never turn back.* I hear his whistles as he skips down the crooked path, trying to avoid the copses that grow at random. *He can crash into one for all I care.*

I was hoping for a nice indecent situation where I'm in Jack's arms, and our lips are inches apart.

I think it's wise to bottle up hope, store it in a dank cellar, and never get drunk on it. I guess it's easier that way.

Chapter 22

The carriage bounces up and down the gravel-laden path as we traverse the forest hill and into civilisation. Goodness, I'm leaving the forest after a week or so. I'm not quite sure what I feel. Euphoria that I'm going to a ball. The trepidation that the people who want me dead are going to be there. Melancholia that no matter how much I try to search for Esther in the throng, I'm not going to find her laughing, her cheerful expression, her eyes filled with mirth, life, and light-heartedness. Excitement, anxiety, and sorrow. A deadly combination.

The thought of not finding her there makes my heart sink. I feel my chest heaving; it's hard to breathe. My legs feel still and cold, and my fingers start twitching. This time, it's almost painful. Unnatural. Each bend and flick is an excruciating spasm. My angular fingers emit bloodshot red sparks that turn black when they fall onto the burgundy silk of my dress. I realise they are little sparks of fire, diminishing to ash. *I am creating fire without command.* Usually, when my fingers twitch, they effuse some sort of trifling substance that evaporates into thin air. This is strange and frightening, and I don't want Jack to find out. I hide my hands in the folds of my travelling cloak and turn my head to the window. Green patches of forestland pass us as our carriage carries us to Aurelia.

We could've travelled the entire journey by the Merryck's automobile, allowing us to take roads that horses can't travel by. But Ailis insisted we travel by horse-drawn carriage. The open, roofless vehicle exposes me to the prying eyes of the townsfolk. Does she want me to be recognised and butchered on the spot? I think her heart would fill with sadistic, malevolent pleasure at the sight of me lying in a pool of blood, hacked and dismembered by a throng of bloodthirsty locals, resenting me for my impiety and crimes. *Why is she making me go?* Esther isn't here anymore, and I am not wanted in Marilyn, Aurelia, Merlin, Haeems, or even the Abandoned. I'm too murderous for the Lords and too inexperienced in magic to gain the respect and acceptance of the Merrycks. I'll never fit in right. Like a puzzle piece with a corner chipped off. Imperfect, unwanted, and piteous.

To aggravate my misery, Jack Fynn is sitting right in front of me, looking resplendent in his immaculate obsidian black suit, dark waistcoat, and gibbous-moon-shaped freckles. It's hard to be furious at him and then practically faint at seeing how beautiful he is. *No, stop.* His pulchritude can't hold an advantage over my emotions. I won't give in. I glance away but find myself looking right at him. Jack Fynn is so heartbreakingly beautiful and infuriating at the same time.

When he catches me staring at him, the corners of his lips turn up into a bold, charming smirk. I give him one of my most contemptuous glares, but his grin only deepens.

'Oh Jessi, darling, tell me, why does a cloud of melancholia float above your head, pouring down on you and drenching you? Let me liberate you from your sorrows. Do tell, what is troubling you so relentlessly?'

'Do you have a death wish?'

'Whatever do you mean?'

'Are you so smug and sly that you wouldn't stop to think that *you* could be the source of my troubles?' I snap, my voice laced with venom.

A wave of hurt rolls over his features, dissipating quickly. My remark might have been more caustic than I'd intended.

'If you're angry about my not disclosing the particulars of the errand, I'm keeping your interests in mind. I'm not revealing anything just yet for your own protection.' The tide of pain recedes and a new wave of concern rolls in. I bet his affection is pretence.

'Protection?' I scoff, 'I can protect myself just fine. Do you think this is an act of heroism on your part? That you're going to save Lady Jessica from hearing anything that will be too piercing for her soft, female heart?'

'Harrington, it isn't like that. I assure you—'

'Oh, so now we're on a last-name basis? When we left Ailis's cabin, you treated me with such an air of formality that it was as if ancient Lords were observing us! We were in a secluded forest clearing, for God's sake! You can call me by my Christian name!'

'Oh, forgive me, Lady Harrington, if I was just trying to show some respect. Next time, I'll keep in mind that you prefer being addressed as a concubine.'

'A con—mind your words! How dare you?'

'Oh, so now you want me to mind my words? You female species really are a confusing, bewildering lot.'

'*Female species?* Are you Theodore? Forget it, you're just like everyone else. Haughty and egoistic, proud to be born in a world of men.'

'And maybe you're just—well, leave it. No point in voicing my opinion. You're just going to contradict it.'

'Oh no, please, do tell me what venomous insults you have in mind for my species.'

'I don't want to sacrifice evanescent moments flirting with you, so I'm going to keep my mouth shut.' *The gall.*

'Good luck, because you already have.'

'At least I got a chance. Poor lad Silasbury couldn't even pull you close enough. And he's a Lord. I wonder how he'll get a wife. Oh right, the House will find him a nice, graceful girl. Maybe it'll be you.'

'What on earth is wrong with you?' I bellow.

'Why do you have to treat me like a stranger just because I will adhere to my duty?' he asks, almost trembling. Jack's booming voice suddenly dies down to meek and diffident. A single tear rolls down his cheek. This is the first time I've seen him cry. And I'm the cause of it.

'Because—' I pause. Tears threaten to spill. He pities me enough as it is. I look down at my hands and pick at my skin until it bleeds. The flowing blood gives me comfort. I don't feel like facing him. I feel like unlocking the carriage door and bolting out, so I don't have to give him the real reason. Why did I hate him so much after he expressed his inability to help me with Ailis's instructions? Why did I think he'd betrayed my trust when he really was just following orders? He was not at fault. It was me who was being unreasonable and uncooperative.

'Because why?' *Because I love you, Jack. I love your curls, your freckles, your smiles, your laughs, your kindness, your affability, your everything. I also love how you argued with me like we were a married couple, facing the challenges of married life together, marching into the future as though you and I are fated to be together. Oh God, Jack. Jack Fynn.*

His questioning gaze is fixated on me. His hands are on his knees, his face mere inches away from mine. I wasn't aware that he'd leaned closer. I was too engaged in our argument—a fruitless brawl that I began by calling him words he most definitely was not.

He has every right to scowl at me; instead, his eyes are filled with empathy instead of fury, and his question isn't laced with malice but concern.

I gather the remnants of my courage and look at him, breathe in deeply, and register his features. He suddenly gets up and shifts closer to me. Now he is no longer in front but right beside me, pressed against my nimble form.

'Jess, I am terribly sorry, oh please, please forgive me. I don't know what evil has worked its way inside my mind, what seed it has planted, but I couldn't bear the idea of you being mad at me and distancing yourself. I swear, the guilt has been eating me alive. That was the reason for my cold behaviour earlier. I didn't know what else to do.'

His confession sinks into me. I feel terrible and aghast for my behaviour towards him. A simple apology on my part won't repair the weak, broken tether binding us.

'I, I apologise too. I was being unreasonable. I shouldn't have badgered you like that.' *What happened to not giving him a simple apology? I thought I was going to confess my undying love to him as an apology. 'I was being unreasonable' isn't enough.* Well, my courage was spent on our argument, and I don't have the temerity to say I love him. If my feelings aren't reciprocated, the chasm dividing us will only deepen.

'I truly am sorry,' I say. It comes out quieter than I expected.

'It's alright. All good.'

He grins widely and takes my hand in his.

Chapter 23

A sensation of heat burns in the pit of my stomach then spreads like vines to every other part of my body. I don't move, for I risk him withdrawing his hand. *Good Lord, he's holding my hand. Jack Fynn and I are— My God, I can't fathom this.* I resist the urge to pinch myself to check if this is a dream.

I remain motionless in quietude. He doesn't look at me, but his hand is still pressed into mine. We sit together side by side in comfortable, *affable* silence. *Friendly and compassionate.* Not at all romantic. *Oh sure. Not at all romantic?* An insolent voice in my head urges me to confirm with Jack whether this moment is a symbol of courtship or not. I tell that foolish voice to keep its opinions to itself. I decide to remain silent and still, lest he move his hand due to a shift of any limb or spasm of muscle in my body. Jack clasps my hand more tightly.

'Ailis warned me this would happen.' An impassive voice says. *Priscilla. Our chaperone.* My eyes widen, and I feel every hair rise. *How could I not notice that Priscilla was in the carriage the entire time? Scrutinising our every action, taking note of any indecencies to report back to Ailis Millerwood?* Jack and I just argued like a married couple and then held hands to make up. He's older than me, and I am a *17-year-old girl.*

Emphasis on girl. There's nothing more unfortunate than that. If Priscilla communicates this outrageous, flagrant display of impropriety to Ailis, the consequences might range from punitive to pernicious. I might never be permitted to see Jack, let alone run errands with him.

Jack and I immediately withdraw from each other. I hide my hands in the pleats of my silks, and Jack's hands find comfort in his trouser pockets. An atmosphere of awkwardness and reticence envelops us. Priscilla's beady-eyed gaze is unwavering. She stares us up and down through her spectacles with such relentless fierceness that I feel like she has cut me open, is examining my raw insides, and placing them in specimen jars for further scrutiny.

'Uh—so, when will we be reaching?' I ask, with visible timidity. My fingers twitch and tremble.

'About a few hours. Till then, I have to deal with whatever this is.' Priscilla remarks clinically. She waves her hands airily in front of us, gesturing that *we* are the 'this' she has the misfortune to deal with.

'I promise— you have nothing to worry about, it was momentary, it will never happen again, I assure you.'

'If you're afraid of my tattling to Ailis, *you* have nothing to worry about because I couldn't care less that the two of you are out to soil and tarnish your reputation. It's not like you have one anymore anyway, so it wouldn't matter.'

My stomach twists with burning rage, and my blood begins to exert furious pressure on my veins. But, I suppress the anger, as it is the wisest thing to do. Priscilla and Ailis are just the same. Like twin sisters. Condescending and disdainful.

I wonder if they might actually be biologically related. Their similarities are remarkable.

Jack bends his head low and whispers into my ear, '*Momentary?* Will it never happen again?'

'I was talking about the argument,' I respond in a hushed tone.

'What about the other part? I'm assuming there's a next time?'

'Of course.' An indubitable and confident response comes out of my mouth, but as low as a mutter to prevent our improper conversation from reaching Priscilla's ears, then Ailis's.

Maybe Jack disappoints me sometimes when our lips don't brush, or he adheres to Ailis's instructions like her darling pet, or he acts all secretive and abstruse like he's hiding something. But above all that, he's just a 19-year-old boy who I've grown to fancy and perhaps love ardently. There may be a deep chasm separating us, but we could build a bridge together, cross it, and find solace in each other's arms. God, I hope my feelings are reciprocated. Well, he has held my hand and flirted with me multitudinous times, even in front of the Merrycks' instructors. If I'm wrong about his fancying me back, I might as well be the biggest delusional fool in the world. But I don't want that to be the case. Ever.

When I look at Jack, I see his dashing smirk plastered across his dashing face. I want to look at that face forever.

The carriage leaps across the metalled road that runs through the village and into the numerous counties that lead to Aurelia. Tonight will be filled with dancing and song, and hopefully more *indecent situations*. But Jack will be explaining to me all the particulars that constitute the errand, so there may be less dancing and song, and more of whatever sinister or benign scheme Ailis has planned for us. Whatever it is, it rests like a dormant, sleeping creature, locked inside a cage, waiting to be awoken and revealed to the world.

Chapter 24

As the colossal Mariborough Manor comes into view, chills run their icy fingers down every inch of my skin. An invisible hand tugs at my hair, slowly, almost lovingly, stroking my dark locks. The temperature drops, along with my plummeting confidence. Lord Duxubury's garish estate home suddenly looks taller, as though a devil's shadow had been cast against the sky. The Manor looms over our carriage as we skitter by like a timid mouse being stalked by an intimidating cat.

My breathing becomes laboured. I didn't realise I was so apprehensive about attending this ball. The people in bejewelled coats and polished shoes who want me dead are going to be there. *Charles* is going to be there. *Father* is going to be there. And *Esther won't be there*. I can't guarantee that I'll be completely mentally stable the entire time. I might just break into uncontrollable tears and weep until my gown is soaked.

As though he can read my emotions and sense my anxiety, Jack squeezes my hand and gives me an assuring glance. I smile demurely, but even physical contact with my sweetheart doesn't calm me down. He tucks a wayward lock of hair behind my ear. I don't know whether that makes my racing heart hammer thunderously inside my chest or lower its pace.

I want nothing more than to dance the night away with Jack Fynn. But Ailis has a mission for us to accomplish, an imperative job for which I don't have the details—details that Jack has to reveal to me, but hasn't as of late. That makes my skin crawl all over again. When will he let me in on the secrets Ailis is hiding? Will I be able to stomach her ulterior motives? Do her intentions take into account the *well-being* of the Lords, or is our mission purposely plotted against them? She does loathe Mary Leigh and her pleasure-seeking attitude. Who is to say she doesn't hate the House of Lords as a whole? She could even have a rivalry against the Harringtons, if she despises Lady Leigh of Haeems so ardently.

We descend the steps of the carriage and make our way toward the entrance. The grandiose ornate double doors are flanked by identical flower vases, with bright pink gerberas, magenta baby mums, and violet orchids—each twice the size of my person. Twin pillars stand behind each vase, with similar flower garlands strung around them. A crimson carpet, the colour of blood, runs from the lowest step to the threshold of the baroque doors. Excessively embellished wonders might be waiting for us behind those walls. Lord Duxubury *is* devoted to luxury, pomp, and circumstance.

Before we reach the steps, Jack pauses and turns his head to the right. Confused and curious, I stop walking and look at where Jack is glancing. A man tips his top hat, revealing his flame-like red hair, as a gesture of greeting. The act is quite ominous as he doesn't smile, grin, or blink. Jack nods back at him. Well, Jack is well-known as a noble representative of the Merrycks. Maybe this acquaintance likes to be an emotionless stone.

Unable to control my piqued curiosity, I ask him, 'Who was that?'

'Caius. Caius Felicks. Part of the Merrycks.' He replies matter-of-factly.

At the doorway, the footman greets our chaperone, Priscilla, and asks for our invitation cards. She produces two golden envelopes from her coat sleeve, embellished with silver swirls at the edges.

The footman politely procures the invitations from Priscilla and reads the contents aloud: 'Mr Edward Phillips and Mrs Elyza Phillips. Representatives of the Merrycks Home for the Mentally Challenged.' He grimaces as his eyes catch the word 'Merrycks' printed on the invite in bold. Eyes drifting to the second card, the footman says, 'Miss Ivy Addison, Deputy Head of the Merrycks Home for the Mentally Challenged.' Once again, a frown briefly crosses his features, then disappears. For the love of God, what aversion do the people of Frances have to an asylum for the mentally unfit? The differently-abled are not outcasts of society but only possess characteristics lacking in the average man or woman. Although the Merrycks Home isn't exactly an asylum but a secret training camp for witches, the townsfolk don't have the right to whisper cruel remarks about their own people who are different from the rest.

If the world is indifferent to the sufferings of those considered cerebrally weak, how will it react to a cult of witches and magicians practising their magic in peace, enveloped in the safety and serenity that the woods provide?

My mind rummages through ways I could lecture the citizens of Frances, and I fail to realise how the footman addresses me. My real name has not been listed in the invitation. My identity for tonight is someone completely arcane. *A woman called Miss Elyza Phillips. Mrs.*

I'm going to be playacting as Jack Fynn's wife tonight. A blush creeps across my face, and my cheeks redden with the telltale pink. Jack himself looks flustered as the realisation dawns on him as well. He flashes a grin at me, more bashful than cheerful and mischievous, like his usual smirks. It's a shame that we're only pretending to be each other's wedded partners. We argued, held hands, and shared our innermost thoughts like a real, plausible couple in the carriage. Maybe one, halcyon day, years into the uncertain future, I'll see Jack standing at the altar, our families surrounding us, and we won't be pretending then.

You've known the guy for a little over a week, stop trying to pretend that you've known him for a lifetime. But how can I stop trying when it feels like I have?

Jack did magically appear in my life, like an eerie figure emerging from a cloud of mist. I'm familiar with the saying that people come and go, and there's a big chance he might be one of those people. But I'm done with the incessant, horrifying echoes of the memories in my mind, all the voices talking to me scornfully and telling me I don't have a purpose. For once in my life, I want something tangible to hold on to. A palpable bond. Something that isn't as elusive and esoteric as a ghost. Something that is solid and true, a living thing that breathes life into my actions, someone I can touch and seek reassurance from when troubled by phantoms at night. Someone I can express my love to physically, be it a brush of lips, an embrace, or even something more. Someone who is *physically and actually* wafting through the corridors, calling out my name and smiling convivially when they see me. And it isn't a figment of my imagination, an illusion to compensate for the loved ones I've lost. It is real. It is tangible. My love is living and breathing, and they're with me for eternity. But that's only wishful thinking. An embrocation called Hope that is more intoxicating and pernicious than any alcoholic drink in the world.

I always thought that people were forever, but after Death snatched Mother and Esther away from me, I realised it was only the memories that were obligated to stay.

Tears threaten to spill, but I threaten them back. The kohl around my eyes has already smudged from my argument with Jack. I won't let my emotions ruin anything else now. Maybe that is why Ailis didn't explain all the particulars to me before. *My female constitution. My emotions. My feeble nature.* All the things I'm made of are working against me. It is as though I am against my own self. The thought brings a wave of nausea and pure horror crashing down on me.

I whisper *Comdach* under my breath and slip through the double doors, quietly and unemotionally, like a shadow. My thick lace skirts sweep the floor behind me as I enter the opulent hall—into the arms of those who had condemned me as a murderer.

Perhaps, into my death itself.

Chapter 25

The scintillating chandelier hanging from the ceiling lights each face in the magnificent ballroom. The glittering fixture takes my breath away. It resembles a heavenly body, casting bands of yellow light all around the room, illuminating every nook and corner. Dark floral brocade wallpaper lines the walls, giving the room a sombre and murky atmosphere. The melancholy clouds enshroud the sun in their mist. The sun, the source of hope and light, tries to peek through the thick cover, but to no avail. Light is killed by Darkness. Joy by Sorrow. Life by Death.

Mariborough Manor is a contrast in itself.

I walk towards the centre of the room, memories of past experiences here seeping out of my subconscious and into my present state of mind. I remember Esther and I had once attended a ball in this room, not too long ago. I was 14 then. Charles was there too, and we all unanimously agreed that Charles should be the one to try the punch first. It looked like blood to me. I remember being plagued by nightmares from that incident. The thought of Charles drinking blood like Prince Dracula made my own blood curdle and churn inside my veins.

To worsen my misery, I espy a crystal bowl of red cider on a table to the right of the room. I gulp as a nauseating feeling gnaws at my stomach, imagining my friend relishing the drink like some feral. It wasn't the thought of him drinking *blood* as though he were draining it from a body that made spiders walk on my skin—it was the idea of *him* doing it. Charles is so soft-hearted he wouldn't dare harm a fly. Yet, for some arcane reason, my mind doesn't relent, and the image burns itself into my memory. I feel as though I'm about to collapse and vomit on the plush carpet, when Jack steadies me. He lays his right hand on my right shoulder, pulling me into a small embrace. A guest nearby glares at us with fully widened eyes. Jack's hand immediately falls, and he steps back a little. His comforting gesture may have been momentary, but it certainly gives me the reassurance and confidence I need to face my monsters. Or, rather, fight the monsters that I see before me.

Lord Harrington, Lord Duxubury, and Lady Leigh are huddled together in their own sort of congregation, glasses of wine in their hands, gaudy suits clinging to their tall, imposing statures. They're all dressed in neat, ironed suits, black so dark it resembles charcoal. Not a hair is out of place, slicked back to the superficies with probably the latest gel. Well, all except Lady Leigh. She is adorned in jewellery that was probably stolen from the East, and cream-coloured skirts, the front of which drape down in neat folds to the ground. If the Manor isn't ostentatious enough, their extravagant clothing certainly overdoes it. The shoes, too, are embellished with glinting gems. Father's black loafers have pure gold metal running the length of the shoe, while Charles's are more modest. He is the youngest of the Lords, so perhaps he has to prove his mettle until the elders can reward his performance with tawdry finery.

It takes all of me not to wave at Charles and run into his arms. I wonder what his reaction would be if he knew I was here. Would he be delighted to see me, or would his now ebullient expression morph into a pale look of horror at seeing the ghost of the witch-girl who murdered her sister and took to the woods?

Jack seems to be enjoying himself, engaging in polite conversation with respected members of society, trying his hand at flirting with a girl or two he meets. Apparently, he's uttered something terribly hilarious, and all the girls are surrounding him like crows around a piece of hacked meat.

Jealousy's footsteps echo in the corridors of my heart. A dagger of envy twists inside my stomach, wrenching itself deep inside. *I hope the look of disgust at seeing Jack flirt with anyone other than me doesn't show too evidently on my face.*

Yeah, right. Even if it doesn't show, the master of magic can still sense it. Jack's head whips around, and he catches a glimpse of my disgusted expression before I beg all the envy to fade away. I force my lips into a tight, sweet smile.

'Oh, sweetheart,' he begins.

'What?' I bite the inside of my cheek.

'Are you jealous?'

'No.' It comes out as a timid lie, like a child lying to his father that he didn't eat sugar at midnight.

'You are not to worry. My heart belongs only to you.'

'I wasn't worried, just, well—'

'Ladies and Gentlemen. Presenting, Her Highness, Lady Harrington, the Marchioness of Frances!' The announcer booms, and the crowd bursts into thunderous applause. For a moment, my heart skips a beat, as I thought the spell had worn off and my name had been called out so they could send their armies after me.

But then the words echo in my mind.

Marchioness.

My mind clouds with confusion and disbelief. Maybe they changed the gender of Lord Harrington? No. I examine the crowd. The exuberant throng isn't looking at Father. They're clapping for someone who is beyond the group of Lords, someone I hadn't noticed earlier.

As the crowd parts into two and moves to either side of the ballroom to make way for the guest of honour, I glimpse familiar light, sandy blonde hair combed into a bun. A beautiful, cheerful grin spreads across smooth, fair skin. The face I thought I'd never see laugh again.

Memories flash through my mind as I hear something scream internally. A shrill, blood-curdling cry of panic. I'm not sure whether it is a voice in my head or if an actual shriek escapes my lips. I bend double, trying to focus on the plush white carpet, but all I see are spots of dried blood, marring the perfect surface. I try to focus my attention on something else in the room, but when I look up, I see her face again. Living. Breathing. Laughing. As though the monster that night had never really slipped into the room.

'Jessica?'

'Mrs Phillips?' I don't know who utters what. All I can hear is the cacophony of voices inside my head, echoes of memories from the past, warnings telling me to find a haven and run to it.

I reach out for Jack, trying to find his arm to hold on to, but my hand dangles in the air, catching nothing. All I can see is the girl in front of me. *Marchioness, marchioness, marchioness.* Another scream rips my throat apart, although I don't think I made a sound. But who knows? At this point, I have no idea what's fiction and what's fact. I think everything is a figment of my imagination. At this point, *I can't think.* My features slowly morph into what I feel is a look of holy terror. The room blurs in and out of focus.

Because I don't believe my eyes.

It's the carnival night all over again. Except for this time, I think I'm ready to admit that I have truly spiralled into insanity.

My sister has literally risen from the dead.

Esther Harrington is standing in front of me, like a phoenix risen from the ashes. Like a corpse that has climbed out of its grave to haunt its loved ones. But I know Esther isn't here to haunt me.

But what if she is?

Everything is a lie. Esther died the night of her birthday ball. It was the monster's doing, but since the wisp disappeared before the guards knocked the doors down, I was condemned as the killer, for there was no other logical explanation for Esther's sudden murder. I scoffed. *Killer of my own sister.* And because of that, I was taken to the Merrycks Home as my powers 'unlocked' the night of my sister's passing. I had yielded my magic to fight the monster, which had undoubtedly taken my sister's life. But here she is, living and breathing. Alive. *Did I imagine her death, or am I imagining now? If she didn't die that day, what am I doing here? Were the past days all a nightmare? Is right now a dream? Nothing seems real. Everything is a lie.*

They say a person goes pale as though Dracula has sucked blood from their body when something frightful happens, *as though they've seen an apparition.* Whenever I'd read a scary story at night and tremble with fear and uneasiness, Esther would say, 'You look like you've seen a ghost.'

I think now, I understand the poetic phrase's meaning.

Because tonight, I really do see a ghost.

Chapter 26

Words are lost in my entangled thoughts. I can't separate fact from fiction, reality from imagination. I am more than overjoyed to see my sister again, but I can't help but wonder what it means: *If she didn't die that night, how am I here? How is Jack here? Why are we here, and how did everyone get here? The events that have been taking place are due to the fact that Esther Harrington is no more. But if she's alive, how did those events unfold? The laws of the universe have been changed somehow. Everything is a lie.*

Someone is behind this. Someone killed my sister, brought me to the Merrycks, showed me the forbidden poem, and made me believe the prophecy—that Esther died when death was really written in my fate. Then someone brought her back from the dead. What is true, and what is false? Does the prophecy still stand? What is the prophecy? If Esther's alive, is Mother breathing in here somewhere too?

Someone. Someone. Someone. Hecate. Hecate really does abhor the Harrington clan with all her heart, doesn't she? Is this all an illusion? A ghastly nightmare from which I'll wake up, drenched and sweating in a twisted cocoon of bedsheets, with Esther right beside me?

Illusion.

This is all an illusion.

The carnival was an illusion.

Esther's death is too, somehow—although my theory might be too convoluted—an illusion. Right now might be an illusion, but I am sure as Hell it isn't. Everything looks lively. Everyone is laughing as though I wasn't hit with a crashing wave of deadly realisation. Their happiness seems tangible. I don't know where Jack is. Maybe he realised too and is descending into madness just like me. Someone has been conjuring illusions all this while.

There is only one truth delicately woven into the fabric of this deceit.

My sister is alive.

And it changes everything I know and don't.

Chapter 27

'Jack, Fynn, Jack, we need to get to Abandoned Haeems this instant. I think I know who the son of Hecate is.' *Or rather, daughter. Evil spawn.* I'm surprised how some words don't fail to elude me, and my demand to Jack comes out with confidence.

I take a moment to breathe and calm myself. *My sister is alive.* In the midst of my confusion and terror, I allow myself to take a deep breath and compose myself. *Breathe. It's alright.* Esther, goddamn Harrington, my beloved sister, is standing mere metres away from me, and it takes all of me not to dart across the room like a bullet and wrap my arms around her.

For a second,

I find myself bolting towards her. I can't fight the fresh wave of tears. I grab my skirt and halt right in front of Esther.

I never thought I'd be seeing her again.

My chest heaves up and down from the exhaustion of my run here, but I tuck stray locks of hair behind my ears and attempt to look presentable. I want to make a good impression on my sister, because tonight she isn't seeing Jessica Harrington. She's going to meet Mrs Elyza Phillips. Mr Phillips'—or rather, Mr *Fynn's*—wife.

A reunion of two sisters, and here, one sister is a complete stranger to the other.

I never want Esther to be my stranger.

'Good evening, Lady Harrington. An honour to be graced by your presence.' I give my most lady-like bow, trying not to collapse as I examine the whole of her. Real, breathing, alive.

Even in death, Esther can never lose her abiding qualities, her radiance. Even if this is an illusion, I'm grateful for these few last moments I get to spend with her now.

'Good evening, Miss—?'

'Jessica—Phillips,' I hiss. *You're going to give away your identity tonight. You're going to end up in the Prison Building again.*

'Jessica? That was my sister's name.' Tears spring in Esther's beautiful eyes.

'Was?' Nausea tickles my skin.

'Assuming that—something terrible has gotten hold of her. She fled the state a fortnight ago. We're doing everything we can to locate her and bring her home.'

A fortnight ago? They think I'm dead? A fortnight ago, I didn't know magic existed, I didn't know Jack Fynn existed. Why on earth would I have fled? For what purpose? Has Hecate's child beguiled the entirety of Frances with some deceptive fantasy? A fantasy in which I'm the villain?

'Lady Harrington, you have my sympathies. Is there anything the Merrycks Home could do to release you from your worries? I assure you, we don't mind at all.'

'Lady Harrington!' Jack interrupts my little reunion with my risen-from-the-dead sister. He stoops down low and presses a kiss to her hand. He lingers there for a moment too long, slathering her with passion. I scoff. The scoundrel chooses my sister, of all women, to flirt with.

'A pleasure to meet you, Mr Phillips. How are the proceedings at the Merrycks? Fruitful, I hope?' My sister greets and smiles brightly.

'I must say, because of the fund provided so generously by the magnanimous benefactors, the physically and mentally challenged really are asserting their position in this world. Just a month back, we had a survivor of traumatic disorder attend a seminar on public relations,' says Jack, laying emphasis on the words *magnanimous* and *fund. What a businessman.*

'Anyway, Your Grace, I must take my leave, the champagne calls out to me heartily. My first love. Goodbye, I wish you well.' I wonder who his second love is.

'Mr Phillips, you do know how to make anyone's day a little bit brighter.' Esther chuckles.

During Esther's birthday, she hadn't the faintest idea who Jack Fynn was. Now, she's making jokes and conversing with him as though they're ardent companions.

I bid goodbye to my sister, hesitantly. This can't be my last goodbye. I make a mental note to meet Esther one last time and possibly embrace her before leaving Aurelia. Possibly take her with me. I'll secretly kidnap her if I have to.

I don't get a chance to capture her joy and radiance in my memory, as Jack grabs my arm and ushers me down a hallway.

'Jack, what the hell?' I snap, resisting, but to no avail. His grip is like iron.

'Shush, stay quiet.'

He leads me down a serpentine corridor, twisting and turning like the body of a slithering creature. I never knew Mariborough Manor to have such snake-like hallways, but I guess that's just one of the many secrets these lords hide.

We stop at an ornate door, which Jack unlocks by using the pulling action Heather taught me when I first arrived at the Merrycks. It was a little more than a week ago, but it feels like aeons. Not ungently, Jack pushes me into the room and locks the door behind us. I recognise the room as the Frances State Archives. All information about any firm, any criminal activity, and any commercial interaction is tucked away here safely in the drawers.

'Would you like to explain yourself?' I scowl, my chest rising and falling, anger boiling in my throat. No one gets to drag me around. Especially not Jack.

'You want to know why we are here tonight?' His voice is dark and deep, a complete contrast to the cheerful, light-hearted tone that he always saves for me.

All the defensiveness I had donned as a mask melts away. Now, anticipation grabs hold of me. Jack is going to reveal all the particulars of the errand that Ailis was intentionally keeping hidden from me. The way Jack says *you want to know* makes me feel as though I shouldn't have asked in the first place. A secret that's too dark for my soft heart. A game too dangerous for me to play.

'Yes. The whole of it.' I cross my arms against my chest, begging God that an air of confidence encompasses me, that I don that cool mask of defensiveness again. But Jack only grins, breaking my weakly built façade.

'You know the spark spell? The breathing one?' he asks. His fingers begin twitching. The windows suddenly open with a loud bang, and books fall from their shelves. A cold, unwelcoming zephyr rushes into the room, bringing a cold, dry wave of fright along with it. The wind starts howling, echoing a child's cry.

'*Sradag*?' I whisper. My own fingers start twitching, too. I hear the sky tear open as thunder growls distantly. Rain begins to fall. A soft, steady thrum.

The candles snuff out. Darkness fills the room. The central table crashes to the floor, books abandon their shelves.

'Jack, Jack, what is happening?'

'Why is everything so—?'

'Unnatural? Listen to me, Jessica. You need to stay calm for this.'

'STAY CALM? What's this? What do I need to do? Why are we here?' The room starts spinning. Jack blurs in and out of focus. I see waves of brown and black where solid bookshelves should be.

'Look around.'

'What?'

'Look around and tell me, what do you see?'

'Darkness.' I gulp.

'And how do we get rid of the darkness?' He lays his hands on my shoulders.

'*Sradag*,' I mutter.

'That's it now. Keep saying *Sradag*, more confidently each time.'

'And what are you going to do?'

'Accompany you. Jessica, there's been a lot of darkness in your life. We're going to light the candles, and it'll all go away.'

His words sound oddly familiar. Like an old saying.

Light a candle in a dimly lit hallway, and all sorrow will go away.

When there's darkness, find the light.

Here is the darkness.

Create the light.

I heed his words and steady myself.

'*Sradag.*'

A feeble flame plays on the wick of the nearest candle.

'*Sradag.*'

The flame grows bigger, brighter. I see my tear-stricken face reflected in the fire.

'Close your eyes, it'll help you concentrate better.'

I close my eyes and picture a flame. The imagery suddenly morphs into a forest. A girl in a nightgown. A boy with tousled hair. A lily floating above his palm. A crooked smile playing on his lips. A distant bell ringing in the background. The smell of roasted chicken flying through the breeze. The boy commenting that I'm going to love it. Maybe even grow to love him too.

'*Sradag.*'

I hear the fire crackling beside me.

'Easy now, you're doing just fine.'

Jack's reassuring words echo in my mind. The wind whips the pleats of my skirts, brushing by the hem.

'*Sradag.*'

Warmth travels up my arms.

'*Sradag.*'

My nose catches the smell of burning paper. But maybe it's just my imagination, or I've lost my senses.

'*Sradag.*'

Heat hits me like a thousand bullets from all directions. *My God, I smell smoke.*

When I open my eyes, I immediately wish that I hadn't.

The Archives room is burning.

And I helped create the fire.

Chapter 28

'Jack, there are people inside this Manor.'

'Yes, that's exactly why we need to burn this Archives Room.'

'What the actual—burn? We?'

'That's what Ailis wanted us to do.'

'I'm sorry, WHAT?'

'There are records here that the Merrycks Home is not an organisation benefitting the mentally challenged. Therc's evidence revealing who we really are. We need to get rid of it. Of it all. Otherwise, the entire Abandoned is at potential risk.'

'Why can't we just grab hold of those archives and burn those separately? Why the entire room?' *Why are you doing this? Why am I doing this?*

'Jessica, the Lords need to know that whatever they throw at the Merrycks, the Merrycks can do twice as much damage to them. We've spent our lives living in the Abandoned, being called sinister creatures, monsters, curses sent from the Devil. We're just people who were born different. With different abilities. That doesn't give the Lords or the ordinary people the right to want us dead.'

'So we're burning the GODDAMN MANOR DOWN?'

'Not the Manor, we're controlling the fire. Only this Archives Room will bear the brunt of it. Or even you and I might. We need to get out now.'

'I'd rather burn here alone than potentially kill a couple of hundred innocents.'

'Jess, listen—'

'JACK, MY SISTER IS IN HERE. WE ARE NOT—'

'*Oi*, open the door!' A chorus of fists bangs on the wooden door, which soon splinters. Panic seizes hold of me, its icy fingers piercing my skin, making me hyper-aware of my surroundings.

We're going to get caught burning the goddamn Archives Room down.

Forget getting caught, we're burning the goddamn Archives Room down.

How could Jack do this to me? He isn't heartless. I know in my own heart that he isn't. I glance at him to analyse his composure, to check if he has reacted to our situation yet.

All I see is a blazing fire in his eyes, ready to burn down everything he gazes at.

But I know he isn't heartless. Jack knows my sister is here, my father, my Charles, the Lords, innocent people, staff members, cooks, scullery maids. Maybe Ailis injected some dark toxin into his blood or cast an incantation on him that caused him to abide by her horrible decisions.

How on Earth can Ailis Millerwood even contemplate setting her enemies on fire? What will she do if her loved ones wrong her?

My heart thrashes against the wall of my chest. The room spirals in and out of focus. The pounding at the door rises to a crescendo, then diminishes, then reaches the zenith of its roar again.

Snapping me from my partial unconsciousness is Jack's strong and steady hand holding onto my arm. But it isn't a forceful grasp like last time. It's comfortable and reassuring. A physical, tangible piece of assurance, silently portraying, *It's going to be alright, I'm here, we'll get out of this. Get out of the trouble that we've caused. We don't deserve an escape. We deserve to burn in the fresh Hell that we've created.*

The flames whip around the room, begging, pleading for us to do something. We have two choices: stay here like stoic soldiers and let the guards come in. All of us will end up charred pieces of meat. Or run *and escape in time, and let the guards end up as charred pieces of meat.*

I don't know if I'm soft-hearted or downright evil, for I choose the latter.

'Three.' Jack breathes.

'Two.' I reply, my skirts clenched in my right fist, my left reaching out for Jack's hand. My fingers intertwine in his. 'One.' We speak in unison. Two voices uniting to form one. Two powers joining together in a holy union of souls to form a potent force to reckon with.

I don't need my brain to send a message to my legs to run. They carry me past the burly, angered soldiers, through the spindly galleries and into the Hall where the party-goers are frolicking around, completely unaware of the horrors taking place just a few corridors away.

A million faces snap to us as we scamper through the room, hand-in-hand. One of them is Esther, a mask of bewilderment covering her face. Maybe the *Comdach* spell has worn off. Maybe realisation has dawned on her that it's her runaway sister gracing Mariborough Manor, leaving a whole lot of trouble and destruction in her wake.

I want to scream at Jack.

I want to scream at Ailis.

I want to scream at Hecate.

I want to kill.

A dormant creature awakens inside of me. I urge it to return to its sweet sleep, but it softly threatens to wake up. It feels like a dimming light going on and off in the pit of my stomach. A faint, feeble glow. A tiny little dark seed which just needs the right conditions to grow. I don't recognise myself. This new version. This witch, this heretic, this potential murderer. This isn't me. I thought coming to the Merrycks would help me find an identity and a purpose. But it only baffled me more.

I shove my scattered thoughts into a mental pocket and focus on the weight of Jack's palm pressed into mine. I hear guttural screams and frightened shouts as we practically fly through the Hall. Esther's petrified and confused countenance drifts through my memory, twisting a knife of regret in my stomach. I disappointed her tonight. I failed her in life. I failed her in death. I failed her in the resurrection. I've put the entire aristocracy of Frances in danger tonight and look at me, I'm literally running away from all my destruction, leaving them to suffer because of me. Esther will die again tonight and this time I'm the murderer.

Stop saying that. Esther will be fine. Only the Archives Room is burning, and the soldiers are smart enough to put the fire out before it engulfs the whole Manor. Esther is alive and breathing and well.

Alive. She's alive. I'll find a way to come back, without arousing curiosity and questions about any heresy on my part. *I'll find my way back to her. I promise.* But who am I promising? The chances of me returning to Marilyn with my head intact seem hopeless.

A single syllable of Gaelic leaves Jack's lips when we reach the grand double doors, and a gust of wind forcefully opens them. We're out of the Manor before the door even opens fully. Not slowing our pace, we clamber down the steps, I trip, and he catches me. We continue to run until our carriage pulls up, we climb into it, and the driver cracks the reins over the horses, signalling them to trot, no, skid back to Abandoned Haeems.

We started a goddamn blaze and we're escaping.

What sort of devils are we?

And this was all Ailis's plan? Is something genuinely wrong with her?

Fire and wind, opposing elements, worked together tonight, to conjure a great, potent fire.

What sort of dark wizardry is this?

Chapter 29

'I'm sorry,' says Jack, biting his lip, his head hung low. The carriage jumps up and down the gravel road as we exit the Aurelian border and enter the Vale.

'It's not your fault,' I say, keeping my gaze away from him. I decide to stare out the window and watch the trees as we leave them behind. The wind flows silently through the leaves, making the trees sway to and fro in a melancholy, mysterious dance.

'It may have been Ailis's plan. But I went along with it. I didn't convince her otherwise. And I treated you brusquely. Surely you can't forgive me for that,' breathes Jack, his voice trembling as the words leave his lips. I say goodbye to the dancing, dark trees outside and lock eyes with him.

'But you didn't have a choice. And besides, I think it was for the best. At least now the Lords don't have any evidence against us. And they know what we're capable of.' *Us. We.* Single syllables uniting me with the Merrycks, marking me as theirs, and tying me to the ethereal cult. I want to return to Marilyn and live with Esther again so ardently, but what if I've become more witch than Jessica? Is the old Jessica buried somewhere in some dark, forgotten corner of my heart? Is the new Jessica, the witch, all that's left now? I practically revolted against the entire House of Parliament today, in favour of the Merrycks. It's us versus them.

Which side am I on?

'I promise no one got hurt.' Jack's eyes are fixated on me, unblinking, unmoving. It's like he's examining me like a keen scientist, observing even the slightest form of movement, a twitch in my mouth, a lock of hair going astray.

I ask him the question that's been lingering in my mind, 'How can we know that, though?'

'It was only the Archives Room, I promise. And I'm positive they'll rebuild it in no time.' He chuckles.

'Yeah, like the prison building.' I snort.

'What?' His features morph into a look of confusion.

'When they thought I killed Esther…' I choke on the words but feign courage and continue, 'I was held prisoner there, and then Heather crashed the Merrycks' automobile right into the Prison Building and, well, it's a pile of bricks and rubble now.' He guffaws and slaps his knee at my reply.

'Well, that's just how important you are for the Merrycks. We'll demolish and burn everything in our path for you. You really are valuable.'

'Really?' My eyes light up with the hope of being something, being purposeful. Having something to wake up for every day. If the Merrycks can give me that, maybe my return to Marilyn shouldn't be a priority. *Maybe, just maybe.*

'You know, I still don't find it plausible that the Merrycks and the Lords hate each other so much that they'd be willing to kill the enemy without batting an eye.'

'I guess then, you learnt how the world works today.'

'Communal riot? Divide and rule? Seeds of dissension between communities who would thrive if they tried to resolve their petty differences?'

'Exactly.'

'When did you learn?'

'Not too long ago.' He crosses his arms against his chest. His gaze strays to my lips.

'When?'

'The 23rd of March.' He breathes.

'Esther's birthday? Why?'

His cheeks flush with the telltale pink. He fiddles with the loose thread of his jacket. I sense his toes wiggling inside his polished boots. The corners of his lips pull up into a nervous smile.

'I learnt that a forest boy could never have a Lady.' Jack's whole demeanour changes, his knee bumps against mine, and his eyes are filled with a longing I haven't seen or matched before. He intently looks at me and studies me up and down. It's as though his keen gaze is enough to completely fluster me.

'Well, I'm not a Lady anymore.' I try to make it as flirtatious as possible, cocking my head to the side, maintaining a steady gaze on his lips. I think my efforts are enough because he leans forward and presses his lips on mine.

His kiss is slow and sweet. It tastes like cinnamon buns slathered in butter and sugar. It smells like pine cones and petrichor. I want to memorise it. *What if this doesn't happen in the future again? But I don't want to think about the future right now.* My mind is focused on the present, his kiss that sends fire through my veins, and his hands that wrap around my waist, pulling me closer.

I tug at the collar of his shirt, deepening the kiss. His grasp around me tightens. I suddenly feel light-headed and breathless. A wave of joy washes over me. I want to get lost in this feeling, this ocean tide of merriment, and I think Jack wants to get lost too. We'll get lost together, in the woods, and no dark monsters will be able to threaten us, no shadows will be able to stalk us, and no nightmares shall plague us. We'll be together, we'll set the world on fire like we did the Archives Room tonight. We'll start a blaze in the darkness that engulfs my reality.

His touch brings forth an incandescent glow, tarnished in the scandal that I somewhat hold a position and he's a magician of the forest, but still, so grand, so homely, as the Universe fated this to happen.

We pull away together, slowly. Jack steals a last lingering kiss. He chuckles.

'That was nice.' I say, smiling, our hands finding each other, fitting together like broken shards of a wine bottle.

The carriage flies down the road leading to the Abandoned, bouncing up and down on the gravel. Jack's fingers interlock with mine, and he holds my hand firmly but comfortably, as though the unstable hops, jumps, and skips of the carriage could separate our hands.

As we walk the leaf-adorned path leading to the cabins, my entire body screams out in pain with every step. I think it's tonight's epinephrine rush causing such excruciating pain, making me regret all that running and spell-casting. My eyes feel heavy, as though they're being weighed down by metal. My bones feel stiff and rigid. I start to sweat beneath my chafing embroidered collar and find myself suffocating from my too-tight corset. *God, what a trying night this has been, and I still have a ballroom of a ballgown to aggravate it.* I hope I can get out of this dress and burn it. I begin walking swiftly towards the cabins, hoping to escape this torture. Jack, too, picks up his pace to match mine.

Our walk comes to an end, and we promptly arrive at the threshold of my cabin. *How I wish Jack could sneak inside with me and... No.* My bravery has been spent for the night. Seeing Esther alive, burning a part of Lord Duxubury's Manor down, evading the scene of the crime, and *kissing Jack goddamn Fynn* is more than enough to fulfil the requirements of a trying day.

Before I perform the pulling action at the doorknob and unwillingly abandon Jack, he speaks, so softly it's almost a whisper. 'Jess, what did you mean when you said that you...knew who the son of Hecate was?'

The hair on my arms rises. My heart throws itself around my chest, hammering nails into my ribcage. I was so overwhelmed by my clandestine moment with Jack that Hecate and the whole—well—drama slipped from my mind's grasp. But tonight opened a new door of logic and unearthed a secret intentionally left buried. And there are people in this forest, who smile, but have in their hearts, I fear, millions of mischiefs.

I breathe in the fragrant pine-scented air, hoping, praying, begging God that my lungs absorb confidence and chivalry, too.

'Jack...I think—I... it's not... son.'

He cups my chin with his hand. 'It's okay, Jess. Breathe. You can tell me in your own time and—'

'Honour Blackbell.'

Chapter 30

The door of the cabin creaks open, sounding almost like a yawn, as though I've rudely woken it from its slumber. I take one step forward. Then two. Slowly and tentatively. One foot in front of the other. Another foot in front of the first.

I told Jack to return to his room. And now I'm standing here, in the middle of a place I share with two people I've grown close to, about to accuse one of them of treason and hexing.

This is something I need to do alone.

I take a deep breath and calm my nerves. I close my eyes and envision a stronger version of myself, a Jessica capable of many great things. *The girl in my mind smiles devilishly at me and crumbles to ash.* Taken aback and disappointed, I force my eyes open and literally jump when I see the Daughter of Hecate right in front of me.

'Honour,' I hiss.

'Hey, Harrington. How was the Ball? Did the Lords sense anything suspicious about you while you were there? I swear to God those Lords can't leave anyone alone—'

'You killed my sister.' It comes out a little more high-pitched than a whisper, but still audible. Honour's audacity to even comment about the Lords right now fuels my anger. My fingers begin to snap on their own.

'I did *what*?' She blurts, bewildered. A hint of venom laces the single heightened syllable.

She looks genuinely baffled. I scoff. What a trick. Does she really think *she can fool me?* I don't care what she has to say. Honour is an illusionist. She created the illusion that my sister was dead. Honour conjured the phantasma that a carnival was being held. She magicked the monster the night of the false carnival and the night of my sister's murder. She is devoted to this ethereal cult in the woods. She had the means and the motive. Honour is Hecate's daughter. She has to be.

'You really think I had something to do with the death of Lady Harrington? Wait a minute. You think I am the daughter of Hecate? My mother wasn't a witch and she died a natural death birthing me. We lived in Forest Plains. Hecate is the Devil. Her worship is considered equivalent to treason. I'm not her disciple, let alone her daughter. How could you honestly think that?' Tears well in her eyes. Her lower lip trembles. *What if she is telling the truth? Which killer admits to murder?*

'Then, how do you explain the carnival? The monster that killed Esther and that almost killed me? That nasty gash down your arm you flaunted the night I arrived here? All the illusions, creatures, timelines, Honour, *everything* leads back to you.' I scream. The air gushes out of my stomach. My breathing becomes laboured. I want answers, and I want them now.

'Jessica, I am telling you. *I don't know what happened with that carnival*. There is no such thing as the annual Walsh Vale fair. I didn't make it up and put you there. My powers are limited. I can't create a whole goddamn evening. As for the monster, I don't know what you're talking about. I do remember you bursting into the cabin, blurting nonsense about a demon, but I didn't do it. I didn't kill your sister. I've never left Abandoned Haeems. I have no idea what's gotten into your head that's feeding you such rubbish.'

'I—I, Honour, there's no one else who could have done it.'

'Seriously? Are you listening to yourself!? My only intention is to train my powers, not at the cost of lives. I promise you, *I am not that wretch's daughter*.'

'How can I know you're not lying?' My mouth trembles as the words escape my lips. *If Honour really is telling me the truth, then...I've just ruined whatever scrap of a friendship we had. But who else could have done it? Who else hated the Lords enough to kill them?*

'You know, I was just starting to like you. But it's fine. Believe what you want,' she snaps.

'Honour, I—' With a flick of her fingers, she disappears. I stand, dumbfounded, staring at nothing. She's gone. And I am the reason why.

I think I have a passion for ruining my own life. Time and time again. Sometimes I'm too soft and timid, other times I'm incredibly wrong and stupid.

I should have thought twice. Honour was my friend. She never once gave me a reason to distrust her. She even helped me with my findings. If Honour really was the daughter of Hecate, she would have done anything in her power to prevent me from getting too close to the truth.

Another life ruined. Another friendship burnt to ash.

Like autumn leaves, tears fall, one by one. My soul unravels with every droplet of sorrow that forms. My heart tears open. A guttural scream rises from the pit of my stomach to the gate of my lips, ripping my throat, and leaving it raw and numb.

I don't want to see the light of day again. I don't deserve to. I deserve shattered dreams, unrequited love, bitter friendships, and the world's darkness and horrors. Monsters created by my own undoing and wrath.

In the midst of my unravelling, a tiny seed implants itself into my thoughts. Another prospect. A person who could have very well created the illusion of Esther's death, who could have hated the Harringtons enough to bring the worst fate upon them.

Hope blooms, slowly and tentatively, like a shrivelled flower uncurling after being tormented by torrential showers and thunder.

There is still one person left here, brewing a cauldron of secrets, hiding something they pray I will never find out.

Chapter 31

I burst into her cabin like a forceful zephyr. My dark locks of hair form a halo around my angered face, demanding answers. I know I'll be right this time. She is definitely hiding something behind that stoic façade.

'Good morning, Jessica. I gather that the ball didn't go as per your liking? At least you got to spend time with—'

'MY SISTER IS ALIVE AND YOU DIDN'T THINK TO TELL ME?' I scream. My throat is still raw from last night's crying ordeal. But that was all a mistake, a misjudgment. I know that the woman before me is dangerous and sinister. If I don't confront her, she will never stop harming me or those I love.

'I knew you'd find that out in your own time. On another note, I have another errand—'

'You can take your errands and throw them out the window for all I care. You manipulated Jack last night. You planned... AILIS, AURELIA MANOR IS A CHARRED PIECE OF MEAT RIGHT NOW BECAUSE OF YOU. How are you so—so malicious? How did you, even—the audacity to contemplate killing the Lords? Ailis, *my sister could have died again.*'

'Jessica, you will realise in—'

'Realise?' I scoff. *She can't be serious. Ailis Millerwood wants me to realise that bombarding the Lords is humane.*

'Admit it. You hate the Lords. You hate the Harringtons. All you want is their downfall and your ascendancy to glory.' I snap. Poisoned insults rise in my throat, threatening to spill in the form of tears. I force them back down. I will not cry. I will not lose my temper anymore. I force retorts to dissolve on my tongue. If Ailis can remain annoyingly emotionless, I can be composed too.

Ailis remains silent for a long time. Her eyes are trained on the surface of her table, her fingertips pressed together. She appears as a philosopher, meditating on the futility of the argument that I pose. And then, she speaks: 'Since aeons, the Lords have oppressed the witches and magicians living in Frances. All we wanted was to live in peace and find solace in our own sort of education. It wasn't our fault that we'd been gifted by the Divine. It wasn't our fault that we were born different. We started off as a minute cult of young girls, making camp on the edge of Forest Haeems, practising our magic quietly in the peace of the woods. And then they came. They robbed us of our bare necessities, stripped us of our cloaks and our dignity, and chained our hands so that we wouldn't conjure any "demons" or unnatural "curses". They called themselves chivalrous. But really, they were just cowards. Afraid of us. Fearful of what we might do if they hadn't bound us in their chains. We could burn them to the ground. Instead, they burnt us, tortured, tormented, and hanged whatever few "harridans" they could catch. Some girls fled just in time. The Merrycks Home you're a part of today is the legacy of those few who bled and cried, their nerves, bone, and sinew exposed to the elements, their skin rubbed raw, their throats blazing with thirst, their minds fatigued by torture and exhaustion. They walked and walked and walked till they arrived at this haven, and formed the Merrycks Home. The others who sacrificed themselves were tossed in a pyre, and set aflame.

The world isn't kind to women who possess power. Those Lords think that magic is this unnatural entity, a Dark Art, that demons possess. They believe it isn't of this world, that it is an illusion, crafted meticulously by followers of Hecate, whom our kindred does not worship. But the truth, Jessica, is this: To burn a witch is to admit that magic exists.'

I didn't know. I— I didn't know that the Lords did this to them. I can't even imagine—with all their welfare schemes and promises for a brighter future, they couldn't protect people who were born different. They eradicated powerful women from our world, women who could have helped Frances progress if they'd been given the chance.

I don't know who the Devil is here. Hecate. Or the House of Lords. Or me.

'Ailis... I—' My breathing comes in raspy, uneven intervals.

'You didn't know. The Lords didn't know. No one knew. They killed us. But Jessica, I didn't kill them. I merely had their Archives Room burned down, which contained records that the Merrycks were a cult and not an asylum for the mentally challenged. You have no idea the lengths I've gone to, to try and protect the remainder of us. Faking documents, attending balls and conferences, sending delegates and representatives to convince them that nothing ethereal and otherworldly is happening within the tranquillity of the pines. Because if they find out, you, I, your beloved Jack, everyone here, and perhaps even your sister, will never see the light of day ever again. Whatever you're suggesting that I have done, other than the Manor fire, I have not. I promise. All I have ever hidden is for your own protection. Your mother's powers, your sister's resurrection, everything. I don't know yet the peculiar story behind your sister, but I assure you I will get to the depths of it and inform you the moment I come across a development. Understood?'

Ailis is innocent. Ailis goddamn Millerwood, the vexatious, infuriating, egregious Head of the Merrycks, has nothing more to hide. All she ever hid from me was for me only.

It wasn't Honour.

And it certainly isn't Ailis. She despises the Lords but not enough to kill them. She doesn't hate the Harringtons in particular, and she certainly wouldn't have aimed at killing me out of jealousy of my powers, because she wants to protect the witches, including me.

Everything hurts. From my head to my toes. Like a thread on fire, heat courses through my body, slowly igniting the most minuscule parts of me. My whole body moves like a pendulum, to and fro, to and fro, lulling me into a state of unconsciousness.

I gather my skirts and pick up the broken shards of my courage. I will never find my sister's killer, the person who was supposed to kill me. I will never condemn Hecate's child to death, the person responsible for my unravelling.

I magick a gentle breeze, and the door creaks open, groaning as it awakens from its slumber. As tears well in my eyes, I step over the threshold and rush out into the woods, because I will not let Ailis Millerwood see me cry.

Chapter 32

My face is stained with dried-out tears. I've been walking for hours. Beyond me is an endless stretch of green. Thickets of pine trees and a few spindly oaks surround me. I don't know why I'm so overwhelmed. Esther is alive and well. I should be reassured by that fact.

I stop in my tracks. In the distance, I spy a stone structure, engulfed in patches of moss and crawling ivy. Hecate's church. *What will I even do here? Pray to the very monster who created this all, for some clarity?*

I scamper up the stone steps worn out by time. The bloodlock is clearer in the daylight. The banyan tree split right down the middle, the ancient willow, the upside-down pine trees. As my hand rests on the bloodlock, a thought creeps into my mind—*what if I could find answers here?*

The slide down from the church to the underground crypt was thrilling. A sense of exhilaration amidst the dreary darkness.

I dust off the dirt that has clung to my dress and flatten the creases of my skirts. Garnering my strength, I take one step into the crypt, into secrets and unsolved mysteries, into a history of enmity. Hecate's crypt. Her coffin lies here in the heart of the catacombs.

Suddenly, my ear catches the reverberation of muffled voices. My head whips around in alarm. *Someone is here*. A deeper, possibly male voice replies in anger to a female one. *Not one someone*, but two. Blood runs cold through my veins. Fear quietly settles and makes a home. Its branches of apprehension, uncertainty, and trepidation spread around my heart like vines.

Warily, breathing in and out, one foot in front of the other, I take another step into the depths of the crypt, hoping that whatever—*whoever*—I find will not pose a threat to my life. *What beautiful wishful thinking!* A malicious shadow in my head whispers sadistically.

As I near the crypt where Hecate's coffin is placed, the distorted chorus of voices turns into clear-cut words. White sparks of light emit from my fingertips. A knife of nausea drags itself down my spine, tearing my skin open and leaving me raw, exposed, and numb.

'I DON'T WANT TO DO THIS ANYMORE!' A man bellows. His booming voice hits me in the chest like a thunderous blow. The boyishness of his tone is utterly familiar. I realise that I am at the threshold of Hecate's tomb, and I immediately recoil back into the darkness, behind the wall that separates me from the horrors beyond.

'YOU HAD ONE JOB—TO KILL HER—AND YOU COULDN'T EVEN DO THAT? HOW USELESS AND PATHETIC CAN ONE NINETEEN-YEAR-OLD BE?'

'MOTHER, I LOVE—'

'SON, SHE IS THE CHILD OF FRANCES, HOW COULD YOU POSSIBLY—'

Without a second thought, I shift from behind the stone wall and reveal my timid self to the people inside, hoping that at this moment, they will perceive me to be anything but.

My eyes widen with the most apparent surprise, and I'm sure that they've rolled to the inside of my head. My jaw drops to the floor. My entire body shakes with panic. The sight before me is a lie. It's definitely an illusion. It's the only thing I'm sure of in this world enshrouded in uncertainty.

Because before me is Jack Fynn, standing next to a woman wrapped in black, with decaying skulls hanging from her fingers like engagement rings. A gold chain encircles her waist, from which sharp daggers hang. Obsidian ink in the shape of moons and torches ornaments her skin. It feels as though the indelible marks are welded into that ashen white. Blood-red lipstick stains her lips and the skin around them, as though she gulped down a whole wolf before coming here. *Or perhaps a human.*

I don't know how, but *I know* the paranormal woman before me. An old friend. A forgotten whisper. A forbidden familiar.

The killer of my mother.

The orchestrator of this entire ordeal.

The keeper of one too many secrets.

The ruiner of my life.

The Goddess of Magic.

Hecate smiles at me in a way that makes my blood curdle. Jack's horror-stricken face matches mine.

It all makes sense now.

Who the hell are you lying to?

Chapter 33

Jack Fynn is the son of Hecate.

No, no – that can't be true. It doesn't add up. He is—

Was ravishingly handsome and loving.

Jack Fynn killed my sister.

His mother killed my mother.

None of this can be true. Maybe this is an illusion, a nightmare. I'm sure as Hell that I'm imagining this. *Jack was the monster that night*. No. Jack and the monster don't go together in the same sentence.

I whisper '*Sradag*' and char the skin of my arm. It hisses like a serpent as I extinguish the fire by conjuring a small tide of water.

This is real. The people in front of me are real. Whatever intimacy between Jack and I was most definitely not.

My legs give away, disbelieving the sight before my betraying eyes. Jack Fynn, standing, mouth agape, next to his mother, goddamn Hecate. It was Jack all along.

I am a fool.

'I-I…' I fall over the words as I have no idea what to say at this moment. *I'm going to die tonight. Hecate will fulfil her prophecy. Jack will forget me. I will never be with Esther again.*

'I've been waiting for a long time, dear Jessica.' Hecate snickers. Her voice sounds so deep and unnatural, much like *her son's*. I wince as a mixed pain of realisation and remorse hits me like a bullet. *Jack Fynn. Jack Fynn. Jack Fynn.* His name races through my mind quicker than an impulse from the brain. Assuming I even have one.

'You.' I snap. Courage unleashes itself from some hidden chamber in my heart.

'Yes, meeeeee!' Hecate cackles distortedly, as though her own voice is a blend of millions of evil voices, speaking out of turn.

I swear I hear thunder tearing the sky open.

'Rather… regretful, about your mother…' She continues, 'But she knew what was coming at her. She shouldn't have tried to be too… powerful… should've known her limits. She knew the consequences, yet chose to walk the perilous path.'

Hecate runs her abnormally long, ghostly fingers through her dark, snake-like hair, exposing her gloomy pools of eyes. As she brushes the curtain of her locks away, her face becomes clearer. *She has no eyes.* Her skull is hollowed where the eyes should have been.

'Of course, I couldn't let her descendant inherit the powers that she possessed. So Jack did the needful.' She gives Jack a disgusted look. 'Unfortunately… he turned out to be rather useless. Lady Harrington is *alive*. And so are you! That wasn't part of the plan. Guess, he got swayed by the trivial notion of love.' The holes in her skull, not only in her head but also the ones on her fingers, move up and down, as though they're scrutinising me collectively. 'He could do better.' She shrugs.

Instantaneously, a roar from Jack's mouth rips through the dark atmosphere of the crypt. He hurls a brass candelabra at Hecate. But it doesn't hit her. *It goes right through her.* She stands, unperturbed, waving at me aimlessly like a child. Her unnatural cheerfulness right now vexes me.

I don't care if she is the Goddess of Magic.

I'm the daughter of Winnie of the Willows, a witch far more powerful and talented than Hecate ever was or ever will be.

I magick an orb of fire and throw it right at the floating, imaginary heart of her ghost. Surprisingly, she falls back, making a loud 'thump' sound reverberate within the walls of the crypt.

With unwavering strength, I create another one, and another, and then spin my fingers to form a soft breeze, flowing in a spiral, sort of like a tornado.

My patience is like a candle.

Hecate has hurt me and my loved ones for too long.

And now, I will burn her to the ground.

Measuredly, I edge closer towards her, where she lies, almost lifeless, stuck to the wall. *Is she dead?*

A potent tempest pushes me back. It feels as though all air has left my body. I hit my head against the coffin in the centre of the room. A violent shudder of pain shoots through me. I let out a guttural scream. I dare to touch the place where my head met the hard stone, and my hand comes back wet and bloodied. Soon, I find blood trailing down my arm, all the way to my fingertips, dripping like dew drops from leaves in the morning.

Who dares to be mightier than Her will truly meet the end of their path.

Jack inches towards me, but Hecate snaps her fingers, and he screams and convulses right where he stands. Twisting and writhing unusually, he drops to the floor, his eyes closed shut. A part of me feels regret, for just lying here, helpless, wanting to help him, *protect him*, like he would have done for me. But my world is shrouded in confusion right now. I don't know who he is or what his intentions are. I wanted to spend the rest of my life with him, but maybe this is how it's meant to be. I'll never see him standing at an altar, embellished in an immaculate suit, his tousled hair unkempt as always.

At least we're dying together. That's reassuring.

As my head bleeds to the point of unconsciousness, Hecate gives me one last, devilish smirk and ebbs away. I lie, dumbstruck, with my body giving up. This is how I am going to die. Bleed to death in Hecate's crypt. Fulfill what she began.

As my eyes fight unconsciousness by shivering open and shut like the wings of a butterfly, I glimpse golden hair peeking out from the stone of the coffin. I think the casket opened when my head banged against it. There's a woman inside.

This might not be Hecate's crypt after all.

I may not remember my mother much, but I'd recognise her golden tresses anywhere, resembling Esther's.

This is Mother's crypt. That's why my blood opened the bloodlock.

She truly was magical.

'Jessica…' Jack whispers, his body still looking quite soulless. I want to reach forth and touch him, say his name, tell him it'll all end alright.

But I won't fraternise with my sister's killer any longer. It may have been Hecate's plan, but he was a cardinal instrument to it. He agreed. That's as good as betrayal.

My mind swings back and forth, between lethargy and wakefulness, I take in my surroundings one last time. I burn the little of my mother that is visible in my memory. I memorise the features of Jack's perfect face, unmarred by Hecate's cruelty. *He may have been part of Hecate's bloodbath, but he will always be my Jack—No. You can't possibly still love him after what he has done. He's the reason for your mental instability at this point.* No. His mother was.

But still.

There are some feelings that you just can't swallow, no matter how hard you try.

As my senses escape from my grasp, leaving me in a numb, shadowed void, I fall into the abyss of oblivion and evanesce into silence.

Chapter 34

I wake up tied to a tree.

No kidding.

Everything around me seems like a blue haze. Maybe that's because I was knocked out for a while, and it's taking me some time to register my surroundings. The part of the forest beyond me is unfamiliar. Towering pines grow apart from each other, their branches sticking out unusually, much like Hecate's angular limbs. The small of my back scratches against the tree bark behind me. The calloused ropes tying me firmly to the pine pierce my skin, surely leaving permanent marks in the process. I try to move my legs, but my ankles too are bound securely with rigid twine. Did Hecate do this to me? She disappeared after I struck my head. *What happened last night? Morning? What time of day is it? Why is it so unnaturally quiet here? Am I alive?*

I'm alive.

I thought I died there in the crypt, with Jack. *Jack.* My breathing becomes laboured, and tears threaten to spill as my mind chants his name. A sacred word, a prayer.

Why? God, why? Hecate, why? Out of all the people in the world who could have been the son of Hecate, it had to be *Jack Fynn.* Of course, it had to be. Whoever I love is punished in one way or another. Mother. Esther. And now Jack.

Do I have to forgive Jack for his wrongdoings, or does Jack have to forgive me? Which way is it?

'Jess?' Someone calls out distantly. *No. No. No. No. No.*

'Jessica?' The cry comes closer. A man. A boy. A forest-boy. Someone I might even love. *No. No. No. No.*

Let it be Ailis. Let it be Honour. Let it be Hecate. Let it be the Lords who want nothing more than to subjugate me and all the preternatural witches here.

But I can't face him right now. I don't want to face him. After all he has done. How dare he kiss me, knowing that he was behind this all along? How dare he walk me to my cabin, or sign my dance card, or trail his hand along my waist, or run his fingers through my hair, or tell me that it's okay to not be okay when he knew. When he was whatever he was. How dare he?

Jack Fynn can burn in the deepest circle of Hell for all I care.

He walks closer to where I'm tied, a shattered blade in his hand. My heart skips a beat. So after killing my sister, he is going to kill me?

Jack stops in front of me, panting, all his shirt buttons open, exposing his— I turn my head away disdainfully. He's had enough of me. He's not going to get any more.

A single tear rolls down. Another. Then another.

Please, please, please, please, please don't cry in front of him.

The voices inside my head urge me not to submit to the fresh wave of sorrow, but to no avail.

I fill my lungs to the top, turn my head, and lock eyes with him. Let him see me cry. Maybe some basic human sense will enter that tiny brain of his.

'Jessica.' He breathes. His gaze doesn't leave my eyes, bleeding tears.

He steps closer, the blade glinting in the weak sunlight peeking through the murky clouds, watching this whole drama unfold.

Kill me and get this all over with. I have no purpose anyway.

This is how it's meant to be.

Die at the hands of someone I loved.

I scrunch my eyes shut to try and numb the pain, as he *starts cutting the rope*?

What?

Like a skilled craftsman, he slices his knife through the fibrous, brawny twine, till it frays at the ends and eventually severs. He breaks the cords binding my ankles too, gently, so as to not accidentally cut my skin.

Once I'm freed, he takes my hand and pulls me up so that I'm standing. The action is so swift that I almost bash into him.

The Jessica of two days ago would have liked that.

I leave his hand, which has wrapped itself around mine. My legs scream out in anguish as I right myself. How long was I tied to that tree? Days? Why has no one come to find me yet? Except Jack? Why has he come to find me?

'Jessica…' Jack murmurs, so soft it's almost like a peaceful zephyr. His hand reaches out to hold mine, but I slap it away. 'I want nothing to do with you,' I snap, venom rising along with more tears.

'Jess, please.'

'It's Lady Harrington to you.'

'Milady, please let me explain.'

'Explain? Explain the process of how you wanted to kill me but accidentally killed my sister. Is there anything to explain in that? I gather that a simple shot to the head would have done it, but you wanted to be old-fashioned and use a knife.'

His features morph into a look of genuine hurt and desperation. He gets to act like a wounded animal now? After all the pain that was inflicted on me, on my sister, on my entire family?

'I didn't kill your sister,' he utters solemnly. His eyes are trained on the ground. He doesn't fidget, doesn't move, doesn't show the slightest sliver of emotion. He's serious. He didn't kill Esther.

But that doesn't make our situation any better.

'Happy late realisation, SHE'S ALIVE YOU SCOUNDREL.'

'It was all an illusion.' *An illusion*? Well, she was brought back to life. Resurrected. But what if she never died in the first place?

But I don't care. Let him see the most terrible parts of tonight.

'Do you realise how stupid you look while saying that?' I scream. *And utterly handsome... forgot to add that part.* A whisper in my head that I beg to go away, to torment me some other time when all this is over.

'Jess, if you would please listen to me, *I did it on purpose*.'

'You killed my sister on purpose? Wow, didn't expect that from—'

'*Jessica*, I never wanted to abide by my mother's orders. I wanted to defy her. She didn't know…'

'Know what?' I fold my arms across my chest.

'That there were two of you. She thought Winifred had only one daughter, and that she was the only magical one. Hecate sent me out to kill her, *kill you*. But I couldn't. Not after I saw you… I… sort of… got captivated by you.' He pauses for a moment, trying to collect his words.

Captivated by me.

'And I knew I couldn't harm you or anyone you loved. I tracked you and your movements and found out you had a sister, who was, in fact, non-magical. A plan hatched in my mind. I could defy my mother but make it seem as though I'd obeyed her. I created an illusion that Esther was dead and made my monster fight with you so that your powers could be unleashed. Then, Heather would ultimately find out and take you to the Merrycks for elemental training. There, you'd grow to be the witch you were always destined to be. I don't follow my mother, she doesn't deserve to be called one. I know this is a lot to comprehend, but… Jess, you need to know… everything I ever did… was… *for you*.'

'You… you *helped* Esther? It was an *illusion*?'

None of this makes sense. I haven't the faintest idea what he is prattling about.

Illusion?

Just like the carnival? The monster?

Is he seriously telling me that everything is a lie?

'Yes, yes, I helped her. Please understand, I know you might be thinking that I'm spewing lies, but please, look into my heart and know that I'm telling you the truth. I always will. I… I'm sorry. I… I shouldn't have supported my mother in any of this… she can be manipulative sometimes… she threatened me… said she'd strip me of my position here… my life, the life that I'd built over here, as a sole part of the Merrycks. I was selfish… I'm so sorry, Jessica. I should have known that nothing was more imperative than your happiness. You might never be able to forgive me, but just know that I'm not on Hecate's side. Never was and never will be.'

My legs go numb and stiff. I try to open my mouth and say *something*, but saying something feels… feels—wrong. My hands hang by my sides, my fingers drumming a monotonous rhythm on the folds of my dress.

Nausea hits me, like stones thrown at a window on a late, rainy night. My vision becomes obscured, making Jack circle in and out of focus. This can't be happening.

It was Jack who killed my sister but saved both her and me at the same time.

It was Jack who disobeyed the Goddess of Magic, and went against everything she stood for, only to save a girl he hardly knew.

Is this what mental instability feels like?

A gunshot pierces the serenity of the forest. Trepidation slithers like a serpent down my back. Jack grabs me by the arm, and we lumber after safety, behind an oak tree, as a chorus of gunshots follows, like knuckles rapping on a door, demanding to be let in.

Screams. Bodies ripping open. Birds abandoning their perches. The smell of smoke. The gush of water. Sounds of the wood carried by the wind.

And in the distance, surfacing from the depths of the forest is Esther. The second she meets my travelling gaze, she skids towards me, and I clamber through the sticks, stones, and pine cones and collapse into her arms.

I never thought that I would hold her again.

I embrace her ardently, perplexed at her arrival here, yet soothed. Her arms mean home. Her smile means hope.

And then, it happens.

With the union of two estranged sisters, within the wafting wind and the woods, it happens.

From our right, the Merrycks appear, bloodstained, a tide of indignation rolling through the throng of them. I glimpse Heather, Caitlyn, Ailis, Honour, Theodore, Priscilla, and so many others, parading towards Jack, Esther, and me, fire burning in their eyes and coursing through their veins.

From my left, ordinary townsfolk and the entirety of the House of Lords appear.

Lady Leigh.

Lord Duxubury.

Father.

Charles.

Arms raised, ready to fire.

And from behind me, like the destroyers of the world, ghostly white-skinned women wrapped in black emerge from the copses. Silver skulls cling, from red thread to their angular frames. Inky snakes grow from the crowns of their heads, forming a halo around their marred faces. Unseeing. Hollows for eyes. Hecate's followers.

A three-sided battle.

And I am at the heart of it all.

Chapter 35

Gunfire shatters the silence.

Swords dismember flesh.

Balls of fire, gusts of wind, magicked monsters, zoom through the forest, like shooting stars in the sky.

Everything is a blur of red, green, black, and violet.

Blood. Trees. Hecate. Merrycks.

Jack, Esther, and I trudge through the three forces, hand in hand, careful to avoid any contact with Hecate's followers. We need to get to safety, assuming there's any left in this fresh Hell that used to be Heaven.

I almost fall on a body thrown carelessly near rose bushes. Jack uprights me, not leaving my hand.

Thorns prick the delicate skin. A covering of snow, unusual as it is, hides her short stature. Raven-dark hair peeks through the concealment. A faded, scabbed-over scar down the length of her arm.

Honour.

The girl I falsely accused of being Hecate's daughter.

How could she be her anyways? Hecate did this to her.

Honour is dead because of me. Any other casualties are all because of me. I'm the centre of this entire ordeal, this *war*.

I pluck a rose from the nearest bush and lay it respectfully down on Honour's chest. I mutter a small, simple prayer, hoping that God will carry her to a better place.

The forest was her home. The Merrycks were her family.

And I robbed her away of everything she held dear to her heart.

Wrestling against a new surge of emotions, I complete her informal funeral ceremony by thanking her for her companionship and hoping to see her soon.

What funeral?

A blanket of snow is her coffin.

Chapter 36

Night has fallen, encompassing the Abandoned in its ethereal, peaceful darkness. Yet, quite unusually, the birds continue to mellifluously chirp their song, unruffled by the events that took place last night.

Or was it three nights ago? Maybe more?

How many days have passed? I might never know. I was knocked unconscious by a black ribbon-like billow produced by one of Hecate's necromancers and hauled to God knows where by God knows who. It's a wonder I'm still in the Abandoned and not lost on some strange island, for the war was fought throughout the entirety of Haeems, engulfing part of the Vale in its destruction and aftermath.

It's a wonder that I'm not dead.

I tiptoe into the Dining Hall, where an entire infirmary has been set up to care for the wounded and to supply amenities for the rest of us who are left.

Honour died. Priscilla died. Theodore died.

News about Ailis's death is also being revised, for if the truth isn't in our favour, the Merrycks Home might collapse. *Might?*

It already has.

The Lords abandoned the scene of the war immediately after Heather conjured a bomb the size of a manor that wiped out the majority of the townsfolk, the House, and Hecate's practitioners, save for the forest.

A remarkable feat, if you ask me. Destroying the evil human population, but keeping the environment intact.

Well, she is part of the Harringtons, after all.

Esther is here though. She's currently meeting with Caitlyn. Hopefully, they're not engaged in an awkward conversation. Caitlyn absconded abruptly when she uncovered her powers. It left Esther quite heartbroken. But they've reunited now. At least there are some silver linings to this dark, gloomy cloud that looms above us.

Like the majority of the Merrycks, I too suffered a gunshot wound, though it merely grazed my shoulder. Jack carried me to the infirmary just in time, so that I wouldn't bleed to death and would be cured promptly.

Esther is here.

That's reassuring.

I won't be able to live with myself if I lose her again.

I step through the bodies, covered with white cloth stained red, and reach the central dining table, where all the remaining food has been spread out. The stock is meagre, save for broth, overripe tomatoes, and wine. I'll take what I can get.

I leave the cabin and head aimlessly into the woods. Half the cabins were destroyed in the atrocities. Ailis's spacious abode is temporarily being used as a dormitory for the girls. As for the boys, who are few in number, God knows where they are making camp.

Everything is gone. Everything Ailis and her ancestors worked for is gone. Because of Hecate. Because of the Lords. Because of me.

At this point, all I crave is peace and closure.

The three-sided battle, among the Merrycks, Hecate's followers, and the Lords, is over.

Esther is alive.

Jack is on my side.

And maybe, just maybe… I might be going home.

Chapter 37

'Hey, Jess,' says Jack, sitting comfortably on a humongous branch of a willow tree.

My mother's willow.

I find a sense of tranquillity, perhaps reassurance, standing under the willow, Jack and my clandestine meeting spot.

'Oh, Jack.' I cry. He takes me into his arms and rubs circles on my back, calming my nerves.

'I'm sorry for how I acted,' I whimper.

'No, no, no. Jessica, you don't need to apologise one bit—'

'I do.'

'Are you mad? This wasn't your fault. It was all because of Hecate and her pledge for vengeance.'

'But the Lords. They've been subduing the Merrycks for centuries, that makes me—'

'Anything but the enemy. Jessica, you are *not them*. And neither is your sister. Or Silasbury. I know you three are going to work towards the greater good. Even if you're in their position, but you're still resilient. You have to trust me on that.'

'Really?'

'Yes. Really.'

We sit in peaceful silence under the willow tree, our legs outstretched, our fingers intertwined.

I can give myself this.

I can fill my lungs to the very top with whatever fragrant pine-scented air is left, and for once in my life, look to the future with the possibility that everything will turn out well.

I only need to be hopeful.

In desperate need of a leisurely stroll, I persuade Jack to walk with me. He acquiesces easily and remarks that he wants nothing more than to stroll with *his beloved*. My cheeks burn with the tell-tale pink, and he gives me his playful, light-hearted smirk, the one that's only saved for me.

Midway through our walk, he asks, 'What's the funniest thing that a servant has ever done?'

'Are you trying to replicate it?' I reply, the corners of my lips pulling up into a smile. A smile that I haven't felt in so long that it feels like an unnatural movement of my muscles.

'Ouch.' We both laugh.

'Morela, I think that was her name. Comedic, really. I remember whiling away time in the kitchens just for fun, seeing what the cooks were up to. Wanting to join them although I knew I'd either brew up a disaster or burn the kitchens down.' The memories come back to me. A simple girl with a not-so-simple title. But everything was ordinary then, every supernatural occurrence was diminished to ash the second it caught fire. 'Chef instructed her to dress the chicken for lunch. She walked to the pantry, and instead of spices, she pulled out an old rag doll. Literally began dressing the chicken. We all made a good laugh out of it.'

'Y'know, Jess, for a Marquess's daughter, you're quite intimate with the commonplace. Heather, your maid. Caitlyn, a crew hand who evanesced without a notice.' He runs a hand through his hair nervously and bites his lip. I feel him inching closer. 'Me… the forest boy,' he continues. 'You may think you're soulless, but you're everything but that. Jess… you're different. Your heart is... it's magical. *You are magical.*'

Tears spring to my eyes, and I scrunch them shut, trying to unspool the entanglement of his words. He said I'm intimate with him. I want to say *That's everything I've ever wanted to hear*. The words aren't physically forming in my mouth. But if I act like a thankless coward and just nod in reply to his compliments, whatever he said does not stand true at all. He called me *magical*. He's so kind. Jack is the magical one here, not me.

Gathering the remnants of my broken courage, I turn to face him and press my lips to his. His eyes are filled with longing when he kisses me back with the same fierceness. His right arm circles around my waist, pulling me closer, and his left-hand reaches to cup my chin. *Oh, I want this. I want it too much.*

I'm pressed against Jack, the warmth of his delicate touch reverberates inside me. He may be a forest boy with rough, scratched hands, but his beautiful arms are wrapped around me like I'm a dainty little thing. I embrace him further, edging closer, increasing the intensity of this enchanting moment. I never realised he felt this way too. I didn't know our little intimate moment in the carriage meant this much.

He reaches down to plant soft kisses on my neck, making me tilt my head back, then returns to my lips with a ferocity I can never match. My hands find solace in his tousled, curly hair, and I caress his raven locks. Slivers of moonlight reflect off Jack's perfect, pretty face, marking all the angles, the impeccable jawline, and gibbous moon-shaped freckles. His grip around my waist tightens, as does my grip around his neck. I never want to let go.

We pull away together, but he still encompasses me. We let our foreheads touch, his hands search for mine, and they entwine. His lips briefly brush over mine. I'm thankful for this new memory to cherish. I'm grateful Jack is in it.

'I'd pick your thunder, your rain, your shallowest days over anyone's sunshine.'

'Why me? I—what is there about me to love?' I cry softly, pathetically, like a child.

'The greatest lie I have ever heard. Jess, you're the most breathtaking creature I've laid my eyes on. The most resilient person. I fell in love with you the second you gathered the valour to fight my monster that night your sister died. I know no girl or boy or human who would've done that. You're strong. Not broken. Let the voices at the back of your head tell you the opposite. You're a safe harbour in a stormy sea. You've kept me going despite my mother's antics an—and every sin—the single thing that has happened so far.'

His confession sinks into me. His forehead is still pressed against mine, his hands still clutch my trembling fingers like he is holding his world. I want to be his world. I want him to be mine.

'I'm sorry for everything, Jessica. For the beguiling, the illusions, the battle, my mother's mistakes. My own. I tried to stop her, I really did. I hope you'll—'

'For God's sake, shut up.' I kiss him again.

When we pull back, we both chuckle softly. I love him, and he loves me. I hope it is like that forever.

The forest is quiet. No crickets are chirping. No owls hoot in their homes. No zephyrs rush through the trees. A silent, almost intimidating night. But Jack and I are together. He is my moon, showering light on me despite the darkness. He is my lantern, which guides me while I search for myself and my purpose. I'm so happy I didn't stomp out whatever sparked between us because of the suspicions I held against him. His flames have engulfed me whole. And they're not even the dangerous kind that burns down a house. Jack isn't a house on fire, but rather a fireplace, that provides warmth and constancy to that home. The road built over the gravel that hurts my feet. The river that waters the godforsaken flowers grows in my own personal cemetery.

We may not be together in the future. What we're sharing now might be short-lived. But it's genuine. Much more than a stolen kiss in a hallway, a furtive glance across a classroom, or a single night of intimacy that means nothing.

But I love Jack too much to not march along with him into the unknown future. If I go back home, I'll resume my duties as a Lady, or perhaps be hanged for heresy. Esther reassured me that she would figure something out so that I'd be able to reunite with her. But, as for Jack, he will continue living his life in the woods, being a master of magic, only remembering me. I've known him for a short time. I can't bear only *remembering* him forever.

'Will you return to Marilyn with me?' The question slips out of my mouth before I have the chance to contemplate the thoughts zooming in my mind. *I can't ask this from him. He belongs here.*

Jack stays silent for a long time. Time passes agonisingly slowly, making me regret my selfish request. *Oh God, help me.* His hands slip from mine. He inches a few steps away. He fiddles with the string of his threadbare coat. His eyes don't meet mine like they did a few moments back. *No. Please, no.*

'I can't do that. Abandoned Haeems, it's my home. I'm a sole part of the Merrycks... I'm so sorry, Jess, I can't permanently—'

'Forget it. Forget that I asked. It was foolish, stupid anyway. I should be the one to apologise.' *I knew he'd say no. I think I'm doomed like this.*

'We will meet again, at the opportune moment.' Jack hopelessly says. *What's the point? What did that fiery kiss mean? A final goodbye?*

He places one last kiss on my forehead, but it feels heartbreakingly wrong.

I step back, careful not to trip over stones or branches, but what does it matter? I'll fall, Jack will catch me, take me to my cabin, and leave me there. Next morning, I'll be returning to Marilyn, and he'll be left behind. Watching me go. My muscles argue with me on my every move, but I need to do this.

'Goodbye, Jack.' Every cell in my body is fighting with my brain, screaming at me to stay with him till the night fades into dawn. But begging won't do me any good. He's made his decision. I have to respect that and deal with the reality of it, which tears my soul apart.

I start walking to my cabin. If anyone else was lurking in the forest this late at night, they'd hear my heavy footfalls and understand I'm angry. I turn my head back slightly to see if darling Jack is following me, but no. He's gone. He's really gone. He's walked away faster than I got to forget about what we just shared.

An owl hoots in the trees and I shriek. This gets on my nerves. I scream '*Sradag*' and set fire to the branches of the tree where the careless owl was perching. The bird flaps its wings boisterously and rudely flies away. Get the hell out of here. No one will annoy me tonight.

A patch of wildflowers is growing to my left, undisturbed by my indignation. They're basking in the light generously donated by the moon, living in the surety and permanence the woods provide. How lucky they are to have this. Growing side by side for all eternity, till wilting and death separate them. I think about picking a yellow wildflower to leave at Jack's cabin before I go, but the thought pains me too much. He's made his decision. He wants to be left behind. *He doesn't care about your mental stability at this point. Just go. Forget what happened and move on.*

I return to my cabin, sobbing, my head hanging low. The battle fought by the Merrycks against Hecate and the Lords is over. The first three-sided battle in history. And Jack and I were cardinal parts of it. Maybe this is how I can remember him. The boy whose mother had a rivalry against mine. The boy who killed my sister, but saved her and me both. The boy who smiled and laughed and enjoyed life, to hide the agony caused by what Hecate was making him do. The boy who had the bearings to stand up against the Goddess of Magic, to save a little rich girl and her sister, to reunite her with her family. There's no end to how much I could think about and admire him. Hopefully, he'll fade away with time, so I don't go mad wishing he'd stayed with me.

I walk across the room, careful to step warily on the creaking floorboards. Esther and Caitlyn are sleeping, clinging to each other like lost souls. Honour's old bed is empty. I stagger to my bed and sink into it. I don't bother changing into a nightgown. The itchiness of my Merryck's cloak soothes me.

My eyes well with tears and I start to cry. Tears slip down my cheeks. I pick at my nails, and blood begins to flow from the raw skin. *Goodbye, Jack.* I mutter a small, simple prayer.

Chapter 38

I'm going home today.

I don't know how the Lords are letting me step into Marilyn, but they are.

I guess Esther used her 'marchioness powers'.

But I'm going home today. *Leaving Jack behind.*

But I'm going home today.

Only on one condition.

That the Lords sign a bill to introduce welfare schemes for the Merrycks Home for Witches and Magicians. And under that name. No guise of an asylum. The Merrycks will be given the respectable treatment they deserve.

Furthermore, the Lords agreed that they wouldn't force the Merrycks to pay for the repair of Aurelian Manor, for they are hardly making ends meet.

They've suffered the worst.

And I can do this much, for Ailis. News of her death circulated like wildfire. Ailis Millerwood, the determined, frustratingly annoying, but tenacious Head of the Home, died. No one knows the exact date. But it's alright.

I'll make sure her legacy is one worth leaving behind.

Through the warmth, through the cold, through the darkness, and through the light, I kept running till I was there.

I reunited with Esther.

And that's all that matters.

The sound of the wind whispers in my head. *You're going to be with Esther. With the girl you love most in the world.*

I can feel home coming back.

I'm coming home now.

Chapter 39

My legs are swung over the leather armchair of the Manor Library. A murder-mystery novel lies on my lap. Esther gently strokes my hair, massaging my temples, warding off a persistent headache.

A footman appears at the door frame, and Esther consents to him entering. He bows to her, then nods his head in my direction.

'Yes, Martin?' Esther speaks.

'Your Ladyship, a visitor has arrived to meet Her Grace, Lady Jessica Harrington.' *Him.*

'Send him to the sitting room. We'll address him there.'

'Your Ladyship, he insists that Her Grace meets him at the gate.'

A wave of thrill and anticipation makes my hair stand on end. *It's been what? A month?*

Nervously, skittishly, I make my way towards the main entrance. I told Esther to wait inside. I want us to be alone.

And there he is.

Tousled raven hair, crisp white shirt, dark trousers, freckles in the shape of gibbous moons. All that separates us is a wrought-iron gate. The guards won't let me open it without Esther's consent.

And my legs are too sore to climb the stairs all the way up to the Library and ask her. God, where is Heather when you need her to annihilate another iron structure for you?

I find myself running towards him. Practically flying.

'Jack,' I breathe. It's been only a little over a month since I last whispered his name to him, a secret, single syllable, yet meaning so much.

'Lady Jessica,' he grins.

'How many times have I asked you to call me just Jess?' I chuckle, enjoying teasing him. *Goddamnit, I've missed you so much.*

'Just once more, Lady Jessica.' He cocks his head to the side and smirks devilishly.

'What brings you here? I thought you couldn't come to Marilyn.'

'I said I couldn't stay, but I never said that I couldn't come visit. Do you know how arduous it has been, not seeing your beautiful face?'

'But why can't you really stay?' I choke on fresh tears.

'You know why.'

'Because you're a forest boy and I a Lady? You know I don't care, right? After all you've done *for me*.'

'Jess, if anyone finds out that the goddamn son of Hecate is standing right outside Marilyn Manor, *you won't see me again*. Or maybe you will see me at the Gallows.' He laughs.

After pausing to sigh, he continues, 'I guess then, what starts in beautiful rooms and embellished hallways, ends with stolen glances at the threshold of a gate?'

'That's the thing about illicit affairs… clandestine meetings.'

'An affair. Hm.' He smirks.

'Shut up.'

'I didn't say anything.' He raises his hands in defence.

'You did.' I laugh.

'No, I didn't.'

'You're literally speaking right now.'

'Maybe it's all just an illuuuuusion.' He twists his fingers hilariously in front of my face, rolling his eyes, and acting like a circus clown.

'I will never forget you,' Jack says, his gaze trained on mine.

'Neither will I,' I reply, edging closer, curling my fingers around the bar of the wrought-iron gate.

'I'll live and die for moments that we steal, Jess, on begged or borrowed time.'

'And I promise that I will do everything in my power to ensure the wellbeing of the Merrycks.'

'You don't need to do that.'

'Yes, I do.'

'Are we getting married?'

'What?'

'You said I do.'

'And I'll say it again at the altar.'

Memorise this moment. Carve it into your memory.

A happy one, to reflect on when times are rough. A home to return to for when I'm lost.

'Thank you, Jack… for everything…' I say. And I genuinely mean it.

'Farewell, Lady Jessica. Till we meet again.' His fingers curl around mine on the gate. I know in my heart that this isn't a final goodbye.

And I hope that there will never be one.

'Till we meet again.'

Epilogue

The Vale, Frances

The girls braided flowers into crowns.

Chrysanthemums. Rosebay. Saxifrage. Rhododendrons. Daisies. Dandelions.

Lilies that a boy had once gifted to a girl, thinking that she resembled the beautiful blossom. Knowing.

A thicket of trees encircled them, hiding them, from anyone who'd come searching, by the weeping catkins of the willows.

The older, wiser one stroked the dark hairs of the younger, who was still learning her place in the world.

As the younger, magical one wove dandelions into her floral circle, she softly whispered a prayer into the flower crown, a message.

A message that would be carried aloft by the wings of the breeze, to the boy living just a brief carriage ride away. A ride that they could not take. A path they could not walk. But the girl and the boy both knew that by providence, they would meet again. At the opportune moment.

Like the willow tree, the girl and the boy's sacred meeting point, the girl chose a similar one, where she and her sister could retreat when duties became too daunting and society's rules became too rigid. Because here, in their secret spot within the winds and woods.

They could be free.

The End.

ACKNOWLEDGEMENTS

To Mihika Salunkhe, you never abandoned me. Thank you for everything that you have done for me. You are epic (born cool and still cool). Just one more thing: charge your phone, and then you're 100% epic.

To Gargee Vaidya and Zahin Noorani, the sole inspirations behind this book. Thank you for the happiest years of my life. I think I'll end up dedicating my entire life to you.

To Aarav Kharnare, who always persuades me to see the light in life, even when there's darkness all around. (I'm trying.)

To Jessica Varghese, Aaniya Shenoy, and Eestha Tagade. Jessica Harrington wouldn't be alive without the three of you.

(I stole your name Jess :))

To my parents, who kept asking me whether my book was finished, kept motivating me till the end, and kept telling the world that I wished to write for a living. Thank you for all the fantasy novels, my laptop, writing notebooks, and invigorating trips around the world to help me find inspiration.

To my 10-year-old sister, thank you for being annoying enough for me to create annoying characters. I love you the most.

To Ahana Shah, my eternal book-buddy, the girl I will fangirl over Thomas Cresswell, Finn D'arcy, Jack Fynn, Malyen Oretsev, Nikolai Lantsov, and so many, many, many imaginary men with. You've supported me the most throughout this journey. I'm forever indebted to you. #cressworth.

To Aanishka Thacker, the girl I will take a thousand punches with any day. Become a writer. Please. I beg you. Screw some US universities and stay here and do karate. The amount of classes you've missed. (shaking head emoji)

To Avishka Bhor, Shreya Devarajan, Loukika, and Vinita Sunder, (I call you my daughters, but you guys are much smarter than me.) Dancing with you is the most wonderful memory of my life. Thank you for bringing a smile to my face (and giving me 9th-grade gossip :)) every time I see you.

To Samika Agrawal and Swara Inamdar, you were there for me when I couldn't be there for myself. You've seen me at my craziest and have still dealt with me. That's a remarkable feat.

To all the teachers who've continually encouraged me to pick up a pen and jot down my thoughts, who've been with me through every step of the way, not necessarily throughout the journey of this book, but through the journey of my life. Kumar Sir, for being the most patient and understanding person in my life, Miss Nivedhitha, for assuring me I'll get a 100 in Literature, Miss Haeems and Miss Moses for empowering me to write, and Miss Hill, for saying 'I see her in the Student Council one day.' Such a small remark, but what a meaning it carried, what an impact it made on me. I actually was part of the Student Council, and I aim to run for it in 11th too! Thank you so much for everything.

To all the writers whose books I've read, namely Sasha Peyton Smith, Katherine Livesey, Ruskin Bond, Leigh Bardugo, and

Kerri Maniscalco. Thank you, thank you, thank you, thank you, thank you, thank you, thank you for writing.

You save my life continually and you don't even know it.

To my school, to karate, and to piano, for inculcating the precious art of discipline in me. Because of that discipline and determination, I've been able to reach the end. Through the warmth, through the cold, I kept running till I was there. And here I am!

And finally, to the protagonist of this book, Jessica Harrington. The reason I kept writing Sisters of Wind & Wood throughout two years, and never contemplated giving up, was because of you. You and I are very much alike. I've poured out my heart and soul into your character, made my thoughts your thoughts, my emotions your emotions. You've breathed more life into me than I have you. You've helped me more than anyone else has. Thank you, Jessica, for all you've done for me. (I will write your character again, don't worry :))

(a warning to all the readers out there—this is a subtle hint for a sequel; I cannot make promises)

Thank you, everyone, I never thought that this book would be moving from my laptop out into the world.

Everything I am today is because of you.